POOLE'S GOLD

AN ISLAND MYSTERY

MICHAEL DUBEAU

ISBN: 0990758400
ISBN 13: 978-0990758402
Library of Congress Control Number: 2014915699
Pirate Publishing, LLC, Bellevue, Washington

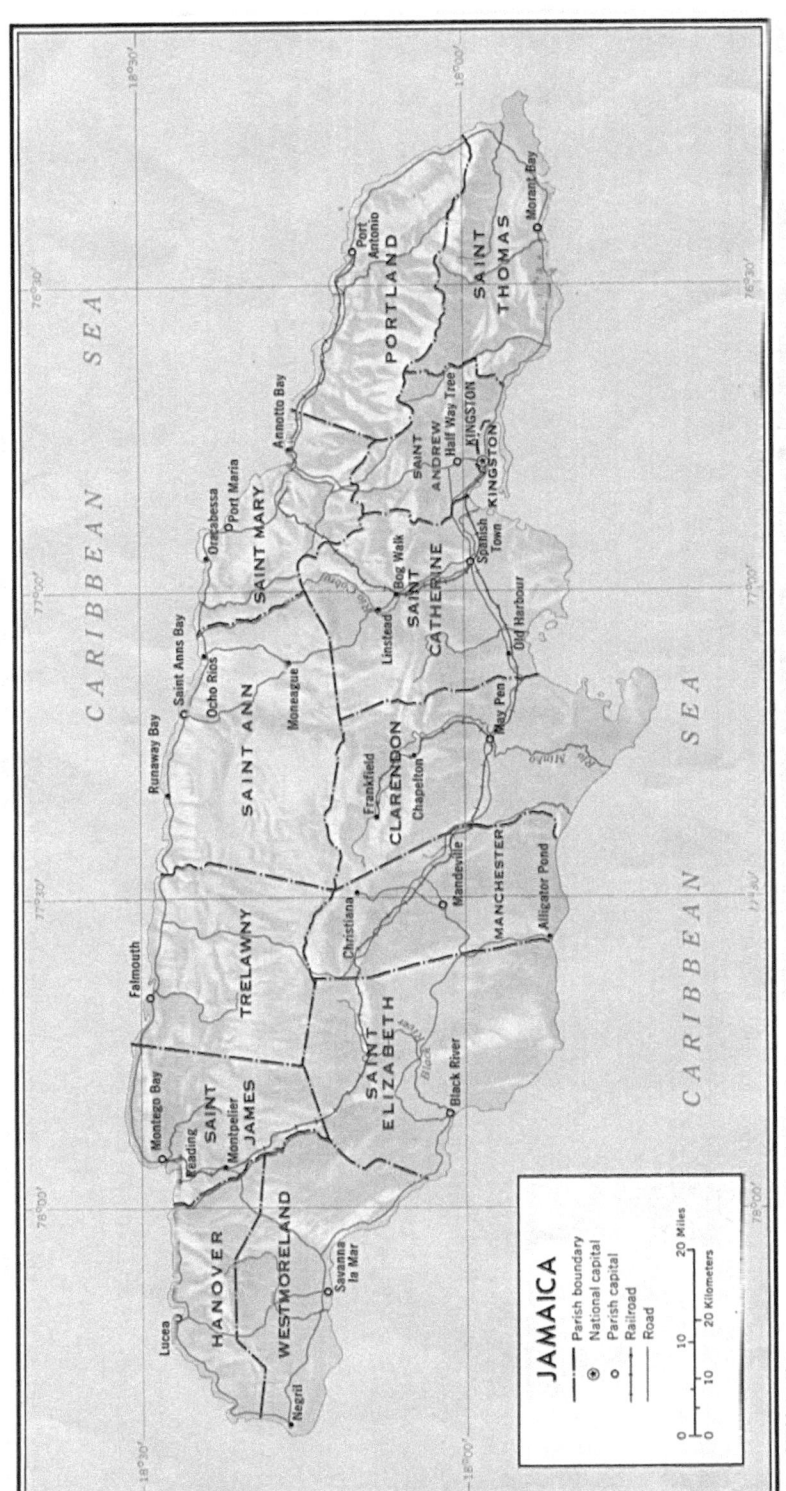

CARIBBEAN SEA

CARIBBEAN SEA

CARIBBEAN SEA

JAMAICA

Parish boundary
National capital
Parish capital
Railroad
Road

20 Miles

20 Kilometers

Morant Bay

SAINT THOMAS

Port Antonio

PORTLAND

Half Way Tree
KINGSTON
KINGSTON

SAINT ANDREW

Annotto Bay

SAINT MARY

Port Maria
Oracabessa

Bog Walk
Spanish Town
Old Harbour

SAINT CATHERINE

Linstead

May Pen

Saint Anns Bay
Ocho Rios
Runaway Bay

Moneague

SAINT ANN

Frankfield
Chapelton

CLARENDON

Falmouth

TRELAWNY

Christiana

Mandeville
Alligator Pond

MANCHESTER

SAINT ELIZABETH

Black River

Montego Bay
Reading
Montpelier

SAINT JAMES

HANOVER

WESTMORELAND

Lucea

Savanna la Mar

Negril

ONE

Poole had just opened the front door when the phone rang. Sweat dripping from his brown hair after a morning run, he grabbed the stained dish towel lying by the kitchen sink and picked up the receiver on the fourth ring.

"John Poole here," he said, noticing the unfamiliar area code on the display.

"Mr. Poole, this is Dr. Martine at the Kingston Public Hospital in Jamaica. It's about your father," a woman's voice stated without inflection.

"My father? Excuse me, Doctor, but I haven't seen or spoken to him in years. What's this all about?"

"He's been beaten severely and has extensive head and internal injuries. He slips in and out of consciousness, but asked for you the last time he was able to communicate."

"How bad is it?" Poole asked.

"It's serious, I'm afraid. There's no way of knowing for sure, but he may not have much time left," she said impassively. "It would be my recommendation that you fly down here at your earliest convenience."

Poole rinsed out a cup that was sitting on the counter, poured himself half a cup of black coffee and took a small sip.

"I'm sorry, Dr. Martine, but I'm just not sure why you need me there. I really don't know the man anymore, and I certainly don't have any legal authority to deal with you or his affairs."

"On the contrary, Mr. Poole. You're listed as next of kin, and a power of attorney was delivered to the hospital last night naming you as his attorney-in-fact. That's how we got your contact information," she said.

Poole stared at the butcher-block counter and wiped up an errant drip of coffee with the sleeve of his gray sweatshirt.

"Mr. Poole?"

"Yes, I'm sorry, Doctor. I guess I can come down, but it will take a few days to make arrangements," Poole said absently.

"Begging your pardon, Mr. Poole, but I'm not sure he has a few days."

Poole sighed and slugged down the rest of his coffee. "You're the doctor, Doctor. I'll see what I can do."

"Oh, one last thing, Mr. Poole. Your father wanted to make sure that I mentioned that he'd found her," she said.

"Found what?"

"I'm sorry, he didn't say. I assumed you knew what he was talking about."

"No clue, Doctor, but thanks for letting me know," he replied as he jotted down her contact information. It was only when he hung up the phone that he realized that the sweat on his skin had dried, and he could taste salt on his lips. He pulled off his sweatshirt and ran it over his hair and face as he headed for a shower.

"That son of a bitch," he said to himself as he stared at his reflection in the bathroom mirror. "Now the great John Morgan Poole Sr. wants to talk with his son."

His father had left for good twenty-five years earlier, when Poole was fourteen. Not that he'd seen much of him before that anyway. "John Morgan," as his mother always called him, had a wanderlust that was never quenched. He claimed to be a direct descendant of Sir Henry Morgan, the infamous privateer of the mid-1600s, and devoured anything having to do with the pirate and his treasures. It was said that much of Henry Morgan's treasure was lost to history, but his father didn't believe it and spent most of his life searching for that gold.

It was on a Caribbean cruise layover in Jamaica where Poole's mother, Rebecca, met her future husband. He was a tall, dark-haired boat captain in his mid-twenties, and she was a California beach girl, five foot seven with long flaxen hair, newly graduated from the University of San Diego. They made a striking couple, and they knew it. It was love at first sight.

She decided to stay with John Morgan and not go back to California, and her parents didn't approve at all. They said she was wasting her college education and had been swept away by a ne'er-do-well. It was a decision that she'd never regretted, even though her parents had turned their backs on her.

John Morgan and Rebecca Poole lived on a thirty-eight foot Hatteras that he and the bank owned, and they worked the diving business together for several years. Sun-drenched bodies, Jamaican rum, making love in the moonlight. On their days off, John Morgan took Rebecca all over the islands chasing the dream of sunken treasure. There was always the thrill of finding a clue in an old letter or a notation on an ancient chart. On occasion, they even found an artifact or piece of eight that kept them going. She always said that those were the happiest days of her life—that is, until her beautiful baby boy was born, and she finally found a treasure of her own.

The Hatteras was fine for the two of them, but it was no place to raise a baby, and they both knew it. Rebecca ended up moving to Seattle, and John Morgan only saw his son on special occasions as he grew up. He continued to run the diving business and sent money each month, but his trips to Seattle became less frequent, and then stopped altogether.

Poole graduated from high school with honors, and his mother's parents attended his graduation. It was the first time he had ever met them in person. John Morgan didn't show up at all. When

Rebecca saw the disappointment in Poole's eyes, she could only say that his father loved him very much and would have come if he could.

It wasn't until her funeral that he saw his father again; at least he thought he had. It was a snowy day in December. The church was crowded with friends offering their condolences, but Poole was too distracted to notice. The woman who had raised him to adulthood had just died of cancer.

She had always been there for him; seeing him through college at the University of Washington, where he starred on the swim team, then through law school and beyond. She always seemed to be able to help pay for tuition and books, even on a secretary's salary. And she was there when he started his own maritime law firm in Seattle. She had cried then, for the first time that Poole could remember. It was only a few months later that Poole realized she hadn't been crying for his success, but for his future loss.

Poole sat in the front pew, and after the eulogy he was asked to say a few words. As he stood before the gathering of black coats and muted scarves, he put down the notes he had prepared, cleared his throat, and said, "My mother raised me to be the man I am today. Throughout my life, my friends would make fun of me and call me a 'momma's boy.' As I stand before you, the only son of Rebecca Poole, I've come to realize that being called a 'momma's boy' was the highest compliment I could ever receive."

His throat became tight, and he couldn't go on; all he could do was look beyond the sea of faces and out toward the church entrance. It was then that he thought he caught a glimpse of a salt-and-pepper beard jutting from a ruddy face. An overcoat and stocking cap hid the man's features, but he thought he recognized the piercing blue eyes of John Morgan Poole Sr. before the visage disappeared into the cold, gray December morning.

TWO

The plane was on its final descent toward Manley International Airport in Kingston. It had been a long flight from Seattle, with a three-hour layover in Atlanta. Poole hated flying, and there wasn't enough alcohol on a jet to make him feel any better about it. In order not to drink too much, he made up a one-drink-per-hour rule, but even with his six-foot-two-inch frame, he was feeling the effects. It was a good thing his drinking rule didn't include the layover.

The sun was streaming in on his window seat as he looked down toward the island paradise below. The translucent blue-green sea along the coastline was breathtaking, and the boats dotting the water, their white sails reflecting the sun, were like stars shining in a turquoise sky.

"I found her" was the message the doctor was asked to relay. Found whom? What? His God-almighty treasure? Jesus, Poole thought. A lifetime of chasing a ghost, and when he finally catches it, he becomes one. Brilliant.

Poole drained the last of his bourbon and stuffed the empty plastic cup in the pouch in front of him. To say the plane "touched down" was generous. The heavy thud made his palms sweat, and the squeal of the brakes made him cinch his seatbelt a bit tighter. As the plane rolled down the tarmac, he could feel the sweltering Jamaican heat seep into the cabin. The blue jeans and white, long-sleeved shirt that he'd worn for the flight had seemed like a good idea in Seattle. It was late March, after all. But it was clear that he was going to have to break out his "island wear" sooner rather than later.

Since it was going to be a short stay, he'd only packed a carry-on for the trip. He waited for everyone else to file out before he stretched out to the aisle and grabbed his duffel from the overhead.

The cute blond flight attendant made a special effort to thank him for flying Delta and mentioned under her breath that she'd be staying at the Holiday Inn near the airport. He looked at her with his blue eyes, touched her arm, and smiled without saying a word. Perhaps the trip wouldn't be a complete waste after all, he thought.

The airport's air-conditioning system was working overtime, but it was losing its battle with the elements, and already Poole felt sticky and constrained in his jeans. After going through customs, he followed the signs marked "Transportation" and started looking for a taxi to take him to the hospital. It was then that he saw a sign with his name on it. An exotic-looking, dark-haired woman in tight, pink shorts and flip-flops held it. Her hair was pulled back in a ponytail, and the white tank top she wore didn't leave much to the imagination.

She saw him and waved. "Mr. Poole!" she yelled, her startlingly white smile illuminating her dark features.

Poole walked over to her. "Yes, I'm John Poole. Excuse me, but how do you know me?"

"From your pictures. Your dad said you would look just like him."

"I'm sorry, my father sent you? I'm afraid I don't understand," Poole said, feeling a trickle of sweat run down his back.

"He's in the hospital. Before he lost consciousness, he asked me to bring you to him," she said.

"But how did you know what flight I would be on?"

"Your office told me, of course. We have the Internet down here too, you know."

"Well, OK then. Please remind me to fire my legal assistant when I get back home," Poole said with a small smile. "I'm afraid you have me at a disadvantage. You know my name, but I don't know yours."

"Maria Robeson. But you can call me Mari; everyone else does," she said.

"Nice to meet you, Mari," Poole replied. "So how in the world do you know my father?"

"I work for him as his diver. Hasn't he mentioned me to you before?"

"There're a lot of things he hasn't mentioned to me," Poole said over the roar of a jet taking off.

"Then we'd better grab your luggage and head to the hospital," she said.

Poole patted his duffel. "We're all set. You lead the way."

Mari grabbed the bag, and they went out to the parking lot. She walked behind a bright yellow Hummer and tossed his bag into the next car over. "Here she is in all her glory," Mari said proudly. "They don't make them like this anymore!"

She was right, Poole thought, as she opened the door of her early sixties Volkswagen Beetle convertible. The sun had baked out most of what used to be the factory, pale-green paint job, and the faded red seats looked like they had slumped a few inches sideways. Poole laughed and hoped his fear of flying didn't transfer over to being a passenger in Mari's Beetle. "Where's a shot of Jack Daniels when you need one?" he said.

Mari looked up, realizing his concern. "Don't worry, Mr. Poole. The brakes are good, and this thing doesn't go over fifty miles per hour," she said. "One more thing. You're in Jamaica now. We only drink rum down here!"

Poole smiled and performed an exaggerated genuflection before he crawled into the passenger seat. "Hospital first, rum later," he said as he put on his sunglasses, and the bug sputtered to life. It turned out that Mari was short for Mario Andretti. She weaved her way through the traffic as if it was the Monaco Grand Prix. But she was right; the brakes were good. And she used them—a lot.

Poole gripped his arm rest tightly as Mari maneuvered the Beetle. "Do you know what happened to my father?" he asked, tilting his head toward Mari but keeping a wary eye on the road ahead.

"He was found unconscious next to his car," she replied, the wind whipping her ponytail. "The police said that he was probably beat up somewhere else and just left for dead in the parking lot."

"Are there any suspects?"

"Not that I know of," she said, glancing his way. "But I wouldn't hold my breath. The police have a full plate with assaults and other violent crimes."

"What about a police report?" Poole asked.

"They told me it was just another robbery gone wrong, and that's what they were going to put in the report." She shrugged. "Welcome to Jamaica, Mr. Poole."

Poole looked over at Mari and pondered her almost casual acceptance of the crime. Welcome to Jamaica, indeed, he thought.

Poole exited the elevator on the third floor of the hospital. He announced himself to an older woman at the nurse's station, who paged the physician on duty. Five minutes later, a short woman in a white lab coat approached him.

"Hello, Mr. Poole, I'm Dr. Martine. We spoke on the phone." Emmy Martine was about five feet tall, on a good day, and in her late forties. Her graying hair was pulled back, which gave her a severe, uninviting look. She was a no-nonsense physician, and it was clear that she'd missed the class on bedside manner in medical school.

She didn't extend her hand to Poole, so he kept his in his pockets.

"For the record, would you mind showing me some identification? I have to follow protocol here to make sure I'm communicating with the proper person."

Poole showed both his passport and driver's license to Dr. Martine.

"If you don't mind, we'll need to make a copy for our files. Everything is kept confidential, you understand."

"Copy away, Doctor."

"Follow me," she said as they walked down a long hallway strewn with carts carrying monitors and various instruments the staff used for poking and prodding. They stopped in front of the last room on the right. "He's stabilized, but still in critical condition. Although it is clear that he's had an active lifestyle, his age is a concern. You should be aware that he falls in and out of consciousness, and he's on pain medication, which most certainly affects his lucidity." She opened the door and waved him in. "He woke up briefly last night. Although I tried to communicate with him, he refused to answer any of my questions. He only asked if you were here yet."

She checked his vital signs and noted them in a chart at the foot of the bed. "I can't tell you when he'll be awake again, if at all. We don't have a rule against family members staying by the bedside, so my advice is to make yourself comfortable. I'm afraid you might have to wait awhile."

After Dr. Martine left, Mari lightly knocked on the door and let herself in. She had out a loose-fitting, light pink blouse over her tank top, but her shorts were as tight as ever. She had a blanket and a pillow under one arm and a cup of coffee in her free hand. "These are for you, Mr. Poole." She placed the coffee on the nightstand and filled the open chair with the bedding.

"Here is my number in case you need anything. You've had a long flight, and I've arranged for your stay. Don't worry; I cleared t with your secretary." She winked. "We're having dinner in an hour. I'll pick you up here—and jeans are fine." She smiled and left, closing the door gently behind her.

It was only then that Poole really looked at the man lying in the hospital bed. His salt-and-pepper beard was now totally white, and a mass of bruises and welts hid his ruddy complexion. His eyelids were swollen-shut and yards of gauze wrapped around his forehead. John Morgan Poole Sr. was beyond recognition.

Poole sat there in the quiet, staring at the man who had abandoned him so many years ago, the man who left his loving wife for a dream of sunken treasure. "Look where it got you, old man. Was it all worth it?" Poole asked as he grabbed his coffee, stood, and walked out of the room.

THREE

Poole paced outside the main entrance of the hospital. He'd forgotten that he didn't have a car or a place he could go, and Mari still had his duffel bag. He couldn't remember the last time he'd been so distracted and irresponsible. At least he'd remembered to retrieve his identification from the nurse's station before he left.

He was going to call Mari's number but held off, needing the extra time to think. The sun had set rapidly, and the evening air had cooled enough to be bearable. He couldn't believe how his father looked. It was a miracle that he was still alive. His father was sixty-eight, but his injuries made him look twenty years older. Who could have done something like that to him? Poole wondered. Was it just some random beating spurred by rum and the need for whatever was in his wallet?

Poole mulled over the possibilities. Certainly, it seemed to be more than just a coincidence that this attack had followed some discovery Poole's father had made, whatever it was. Could it be possible that he'd found something that every other treasure hunter in the area had missed? Hardly. The deeds of the pirate, Henry Morgan, were well chronicled; that much he knew. There were dozens of books on the subject. Some were based on conjecture, to be sure, but there was enough information to figure out that whatever wealth Morgan had hidden away had sunk on one of his ships or was lost when his final resting place in Port Royal had slid into the sea.

The honk of the Beetle's horn broke Poole's train of thought. Mari had pulled up to the curb and waved him over. She'd changed into a flowered sundress and covered her shoulders with a loose-knit cotton shawl. Lips the color of the Caribbean sunset framed her smile, and her dark hair was no longer pulled back in a ponytail. It flowed to her shoulders in a way that was both coiffed and carefree. She looked different—still incredibly attractive, but different. This wasn't the same woman he'd met at the airport.

"Are you going to stand there and stare or are you getting in?" she asked.

Poole smiled, thoughts of his father in the room upstairs dissipating for the moment. "You don't have to ask me twice," he replied. "Once again, I'm at your mercy."

They drove with the top down, and the fresh air soothed Poole as he took in deep, cleansing breaths. Thankfully, Mari was driving at a normal pace as they passed out of the city and entered a world of lush greens and red earth. The sand and surf lazed on their right as the Beetle eased over a ridge and headed down toward the beach and a small marina.

"There's a nice little café down here that I like. Nothing fancy, but the food is good and the beer is cold," she said.

"Good by me. It's been a long day," Poole said as he looked out at the beach and the rocking masts of the sailboats. "One thing's for sure. I'm not in Seattle anymore."

Mari parked the car near the marina entrance, and they walked over to the café. They ascended a short flight of stairs and entered through a brightly colored green door. There was a long counter on the right, and to the left was a covered seating area that opened to a small veranda. Paddle fans turned lazily overhead, accenting the cozy, wood-clad interior. Mari led him to the veranda and a small table overlooking the marina and beyond.

"It looks like you've been here before," Poole said.

"You could say that I grew up here," she said, smiling. "My parents ran this place for twenty years until I left for college."

Poole tilted his head and showed a slight look of surprise.

"Don't be shocked, John. I've done more than wear bathing suits. May I call you John?" she asked.

"Please. Where did you go to school?"

"I ended up getting my masters in marine biology at the University of Miami. I was accepted to Harvard, Duke, Cal Berkeley, and even the University of Washington," she said with a bit of pride. "But I wanted to stay close to home for my parents. Besides, Miami's program is top-notch. Second only to Harvard, I've heard."

"I'm impressed. Brains and a great—" Poole was stopped by the presence of a towering waiter before he could put the rest of his foot in his mouth.

"Good to see you again, Mari!" the broad-shouldered and big-bellied man exclaimed.

"It's been a whole two days, Robert," she laughed. "Don't worry; you don't have to be extra nice to get a tip!"

Robert's laugh was as large as his belly. "What can I get you two?"

"Two Red Stripes to start, hon," Mari replied. "We'll get back to you after I tell my guest what's good here."

"If it's all the same, I'd appreciate it if you told him the snapper was good. The word is we need to push it tonight." He winked and lumbered off.

Poole couldn't help but smile. He liked Robert, and he liked the café. It was just his kind of place. Low key and friendly; no snobs allowed.

The Red Stripes arrived and were as cold as advertised. The condensation trickled down the bottles as Poole and Mari raised them toward each other. The beer was perfect, and Poole couldn't help but drain half his bottle in three swallows. With the exception of why he was there in the first place, Poole thought he could get used to this island.

"If you don't mind me asking," he said to Mari, "with a degree like yours, how in the world did you get back here and working for my father?"

Mari raised her bottle and took another drink. "This is home. I wanted to come back to make a difference. Jamaica isn't just sandy beaches and resorts. There's a lot of poverty and not much education. People around here don't think about preserving the shoreline or the marine life. They're too busy just trying to make ends meet.

"But when my parents' health started failing," she continued, "I put my career on hold and ran this joint for them for a few years. I owed it to them." She finished her beer, and Robert magically appeared with two more Red Stripes.

"I get it, I do. My mother was real sick for a couple of years, and I worked part time in my law practice just to make things better for her. I was lucky I had a law partner who understood," Poole said. "But where does my father come into the picture?"

"To be honest, he just showed up one day out of the blue. He was looking for a place to keep his new boat and started mooring it down there," she said, pointing to the small flotilla. "He's a funny guy, your dad. Usually men come in and try to hit on me, especially the older ones. He didn't at all. He'd just come in and mostly ask questions about my background, things like that. He talked about you a lot too."

Her last statement caught Poole by surprise. "That can't really be," he said. "He hasn't seen or talked to me in years."

Mari smiled. "He chatted about you all of the time. About all of your swimming medals when you were younger, how much of a big-shot lawyer you were now, yada, yada, yada," she said. "You'd think you were special or something."

Poole stared at Mari without saying a word and started on his second beer.

"When my parents died—first my dad from heart failure and then my mom, mostly from a broken heart, I think—your father offered me a job working in his diving business." Mari paused for a moment and looked around the café. "This place was left to me, but I didn't have a good reason to run it anymore. So, my cousin, Robert, offered to run it for me. I was so touched that I gave him half the business for the love he showed and, in exchange, he feeds me every now and then." She shrugged. "Hey, lazy bones!" she yelled to Robert. "We're paying customers over here, you know!"

Robert intentionally took his time sauntering over to their table. "Don't get bossy with me, Miss Mari!" He laughed. "Are you two ready for the snapper now?"

"The snapper would be great," Poole said.

"Now, this brother knows how to treat the hired help! You need to pay more attention, young lady!" Robert bellowed as he disappeared into the kitchen.

Mari screwed up her face and stuck out her tongue at her cousin once the kitchen doors closed. For the first time in a long time, Poole laughed aloud.

"Don't you go siding with him!" She pouted, hitting him on the shoulder.

In no time, Robert returned with their dinners. The snapper was excellent. Poole hadn't realized how hungry he was, and they both devoured their meals in record time, finishing them off with one more Red Stripe. The evening air had cooled to a pleasant seventy-five degrees, and Poole was finally feeling the effects of the long day.

"So my father hired you to be his diver," he stated, taking in the warm, evening breeze. "Did he get you involved with his Morgan-the-pirate nonsense as well?"

Mari nodded. "I worked the business with him by day and, when he let me, I helped him sort through old maps and manuscripts, searching for clues in our down time. I didn't mind at all. In fact, I got into it after a while. Running a restaurant wasn't exactly the most intellectually challenging thing for me. His search gave me a chance to exercise my mind."

Poole gave her a side-long glance, wondering if there was any other "exercising" going on. "Do you know what he was talking about when he said he 'found her'?" Poole asked.

"I'm sorry, I don't," she said, shaking her head. "We spent hours going through his research, and on some of our diving trips we combed well-known wreck sites that he thought were important.

We even found a few pieces of gold that weren't scooped up by some previous dredging operation. But he never let me know of some great find."

"Do you think this assault had something to do with the treasure?"

"I don't have a clue, to be honest. But I suppose it's possible.'

"How was he acting the last few days? Did he seem different at all?"

"Come to think of it, he did seem a little 'close to the vest', if you know what I mean."

"In what way?" Poole asked.

"I don't know. He seemed to have a lot of errands to run, that sort of thing. And he recently turned down a couple of jobs, which was unusual for him. It wouldn't hurt to ask him when he comes back around," she said.

"Well, judging by his current condition, we might be in for a long wait," Poole said, stifling a small yawn.

"I'm sorry, John. You've had a long, long day, and we should get you settled in for the night," Mari said.

"Yeah, that would be great. Is the hotel far from here?" he asked.

"Not far at all," she replied. "You don't get seasick, do you?

"Holy Bejesus," Poole murmured as Mari stopped in front of the gleaming, sixty-foot vessel. The flying bridge was framed by two V-shaped stabilizer bars that towered over the expansive aft deck. Its beam must have been twenty feet across, and the bow stretched majestically toward the exit channel leading out of the small harbor.

A light on the dock illuminated the stern of the boat. A beautiful, reddish-brown teak dive platform stretched along its length. Above it, written in script, was the name of the vessel, *Rebecca*, his mother's name.

"Sorry it's not the Hilton," Mari said. "But the room rate is a little bit better."

Poole threw his duffel bag over his shoulder and followed Mari aboard. She disappeared into the main cabin. In a few seconds, he heard the whir of a generator, and the interior lights came to life. He stepped into the cabin, which was a masterwork of teak and chrome, with a galley toward the bow, a dining table in the middle, and a wrap-around seating area toward the stern. He'd lived in apartments in Seattle that were smaller.

"Well, I wasn't quite expecting this," he said to Mari.

"Your father always says there's no reason to go without creature comforts," she replied. "Make yourself at home. There are two staterooms below, and that seating area over there can be converted into a queen-sized bed. You can have the stateroom on the starboard side down below. I've already made the bed, so it's all set. I'll stay up here."

"Sounds like a plan," Poole responded, although his mind had briefly touched on another plan as he glanced in her direction. "It's definitely time for some shut-eye. Thanks for your help today, Mari."

"No worries," she said. "Wake up when you wake up. I'll have the coffee going when you do."

They said their good-nights, and Poole descended to the stateroom on the starboard side. He kicked off his shoes and stretched out on the bed, thinking about the events of the day as he stared at the ceiling.

"What other surprises do you have in store for me, John Morgan?" he whispered, thinking about the man lying in the hospital bed miles away. And as he drifted off without bothering to remove his clothes, Poole wondered why he even cared.

FOUR

Poole woke up to the sound of small waves lapping against the hull of the boat. Sunlight beamed through the rectangular cabin window above his head. He yawned and rolled over to the side of the bed, checked his watch, which read 9:00 a.m. local time, and swung his legs to the floor.

He grabbed his duffel and stepped into the adjoining head. As he changed out of the jeans and shirt he'd slept in, he noticed that a couple of bikini tops and the sundress Mari had been wearing at the café were hanging by the shower stall.

"Good. You're up!" Mari yelled from the main cabin. "How do you take your coffee?"

"Black, please," Poole replied as he climbed up the small stairway to the main level. Mari greeted him with a steaming cup.

"Follow me," she said, and led him to the aft deck where two folding chairs were waiting. "Anyone ever tell you you're a deep sleeper?"

"Not lately," Poole said, yawning once more. "But how would you know that?" he asked.

"Well, I needed a shower, and that's the one I use," she replied. "I don't think you budged an inch while I was in there."

Poole looked her over. The tight shorts were back. "My loss, definitely," he said, smiling.

Mari pretended not to hear the comment. "There's some fruit and pastries in the galley, if you want. I need to go pick up some supplies for the boat. Besides, I figured you'd need time to check your messages."

"When will you be back?" Poole asked. "I was planning to go to the hospital this morning to check in."

She reached into her pocket and tossed him a set of keys. "Your father's car," she said. "It's the gray Ford parked behind the café. I'm pretty sure you're allowed to take it, if I don't get back fast enough for you," she teased.

Poole thanked her as she jumped to the dock. He watched her walk away for a moment, enjoying the view, and then turned his attention to the fruit and pastries.

It was still early in Seattle, so he didn't bother checking his e-mail. His assistant, Angie, was a master at fielding calls and messages anyway, and he knew that his partner, Tom Patterson, had a handle on the rest. Shrugging, he relaxed on the aft deck and decided to enjoy the fine Jamaican morning.

He heard a small clatter up near the café and spied Robert opening its brightly colored shutters to let in the morning sea breeze. Poole finished his coffee and decided he'd see if Robert was open for breakfast.

Robert was sweeping the veranda deck as Poole neared the café. "Hello there, Mr. Poole!" he called out. "Come on in!"

He motioned for Poole to sit at the counter. He met him on the other side and poured him a cup of coffee without being asked.

"Thank you," Poole said. "You know, I don't think we've been formally introduced." He extended his hand.

"Robert Coy." He nodded with a large smile, enveloping Poole's hand in his huge meat hook. "And you're John Morgan Poole Jr."

"I guess my reputation has preceded me," Poole said as he nodded back. "Did your cousin, Mari, give you the full rundown?"

"Just the broad strokes, Mr. John. But I always seem to find out what I need to know." He winked.

"Can you tell me this?" Poole paused. "Do you know how my father got beat up?"

"Did Mari tell you that I found him? I came in to open up shop two days ago, and there he was in the parking lot, slumped against the driver's side door of his car." Robert shook his head. "It was way bad, Mr. John. After I called the police, it took me a while to find a pulse."

"Jesus," Poole whispered as he stared out toward the parking lot.

"I called Mari right away too," Robert continued. "It could have been a robbery, I guess, but he still had some cash on him. The police said that there wasn't a sign of a struggle at the scene, so your guess is as good as mine. Mari said she didn't hear a thing either. She lives on your father's boat, you know," Robert added.

Poole raised his eyebrows slightly. "Something going on there?" he asked.

Robert tilted his head back and chuckled. "That's a laugh! Working relationship only, my friend."

Poole found it hard to believe.

Robert grabbed a towel and wiped down the counter. "If he ever made a pass at Mari, he knew I'd kick his fanny right after she did! Besides, he always said that he only had room for one woman in his life."

Poole looked up at Robert's clear, soulful eyes, trying to form the question.

"Don't know, Mr. John," Robert answered. "I asked him who that special lady was one time. All he said was 'the one that I'm waiting for.' That was good enough for me. Heck, I guess that describes most single guys." His broad smile matched the morning sun.

"There's some truth to that," Poole agreed, raising his cup to Robert. Just then, his cell phone rang. It was the hospital. "John Poole here," he answered.

"Mr. Poole, this is Dr. Martine. Your father has come down with a slight fever, but he appears to be stirring. Perhaps you should come."

"Thank you, Doctor. I'll get there as soon as I figure out my transportation," he replied and hit the "end" button.

"Your father?" Robert asked.

"Yep. It looks like I should get over there. The only problem is I don't know how I can get to the hospital from here." Poole stopped. "Oh, wait. I've got some keys here. Mari said that my father's car was around back."

"Then this is your lucky day, Mr. John," Robert said, laughing. "As long as you're an old-school kind of guy."

Robert took Poole through the kitchen and out to an old shed in the back. He opened the two swinging doors wide, the rusty hinges squealing in protest, and revealed a 1968 Ford Mustang GT. The top had been cut off to create a makeshift convertible, and the doors were welded shut. It was dark gray with a white racing stripe running along the passenger's side of the hood and trunk. A couple of oversized fog lights were welded onto the front bumper for good measure.

"Well, well! I guess I must be an old-school kind of guy, Robert." Poole whistled as he walked around the Jamaicanized classic. "I just have two questions for you. How do I get to the hospital, and what's the speed limit?"

Robert's directions were spot on. Poole turned off the throaty engine of the Mustang and climbed over the welded, driver's side door in the parking lot of the Kingston Public Hospital. Walking toward the main entrance, he slowed slightly, having the distinct impression that he was being watched. "Too much coffee, Mr. John," he whispered as he walked through the automatic doors.

He stepped off the elevator and met Dr. Martine at the nurse's station. "His fever has increased, and he's still under heavy sedation," she said as they walked toward his father's room. "You're allowed to stay here if you like, but I need to be notified if there is any change in his condition."

The blanket and pillow were still in the chair next to the window where Mari had left them. The blinds were open, but the west-facing window wouldn't be letting in direct sunlight for hours. If it was possible, his father looked worse. The dark red bruises had turned a deep purple overnight, and the bandages on his forehead were damp with the sweat of his fever. A dark, yellow ooze seeped from the corners of his swollen eyelids.

Poole sat in the chair next to the bed and stared at the scene. The steady drip of the IV bags matched the beat of the heart monitor. His father's breathing was slow and steady, but shallow. His head moved briefly, but then settled back to its original position.

Poole bowed his head and sighed. He disliked the man, but what kind of guy was he to sit there and think that his father deserved what had happened to him? No one did, he thought, as a wave of guilt washed over him for his selfishness. His mother had once told him that when he was ever in doubt about something, he should take the high road. Poole knew that was what he should do now, but years of well-cultivated anger stood in the way.

He picked up a magazine titled *Diving in Jamaica* from the nightstand and made himself comfortable. The front cover showed a sea turtle gliding in crystal-blue water over a multicolored coral reef, and the caption read, "The Real Treasures of the Caribbean."

Poole read the magazine from front to back and then examined a center pullout that showed a map of the island. Kingston was nestled on the southeast shore and Montego Bay was on the northwest. The Blue Mountains bisected the island—although "mountain" was a relative term when it came to Caribbean islands. Poole laughed. "These folks don't know what mountains are. They'd soil their britches if Mount Rainier landed on this place."

"Moun' Rainier," a weak voice rasped from the bed.

Poole stiffened and looked up at his father. He moved his chair closer to the bed and leaned forward.

"Moun' Rainier...Moun' Rainier," his father whispered as he slowly came to.

Poole had no idea what to do. He thought about calling Dr. Martine or one of the nurses, but he sat frozen. He just concentrated on the bruised face and the crusted lips that were open ever so slightly.

"John. John, that you?" his father croaked.

"Yes," Poole replied, too stunned to say anything else.

"Good. Tha's good. All good," his father mumbled. The sweat on his forehead glistened though the room was cool. His head inched back and forth in slow motion as if he was looking for something. "Can' see. Where?" he asked with extreme effort.

"Over here," Poole said a bit louder, gently grabbing his father's right arm.

His father raised his index finger in reply. For a second, Poole thought he saw the glimpse of an upturned lip underneath the swollen mess of his father's face.

"List'n. List'n, don' talk. List'n," his father slurred. Poole didn't move; his senses were on edge.

"I foun' her," his father rasped. "You nee' to know. How. Where." He went silent for a full minute, his breathing labored, before he continued. "Duh...bar. Keys hold the se...cret. Key to first love..."

Poole's father lay motionless for several minutes. The monitor over the bed beeped at a faster clip, but there was no indication that he would utter another word.

Poole repeated his father's words over and over to memorize the ramblings. I found her. Duhbar. Keys hold the secret. First love.

Just then, a nurse entered the room to check on the patient. She smiled briefly and went about her business as though she was a mechanic changing the oil on an old Buick. First, she replaced his bandages and dabbed his forehead, and then she used a soft cloth to wipe the spittle from the corners of his mouth. Finally, she cleaned the yellow ooze from his swollen eyes.

She shook her head slightly and looked over at Poole. "His temperature is over 101 degrees now. We're going to be increasing his fluids shortly, and I'll be calling in the doctor. You have about five more minutes," she said.

"Thank you, sister," Poole replied, meaning it.

The nurse nodded and placed a gentle hand on his shoulder. "You're a good son," she said and then she left the room.

The nurse's last words rolled around in Poole's head. Locks can certainly be deceiving, he thought.

He stared at his father. In spite of all the changing, dabbing, and wiping, he didn't look any better. Poole stood and paced in the small room to stretch his legs. He figured that Mari would be calling or coming by soon, so he looked out the window toward the parking lot below for any sign of her Beetle. It was another beautiful day, and the sun's reflection glinted off the sea of windshields in the lot. He couldn't see the pale-green convertible, so he looked for his father's Mustang to pass the time. He got his bearings and followed a row of cars until he spotted the classic. At the same time, two dark men in sandals, cargo shorts, and short-sleeved island shirts stopped in front of the car.

At first, Poole thought they had stopped to admire the old muscle car, but they lingered a bit longer than normal. The taller one snooped around the interior as if he was looking for a loose bag or anything valuable. The shorter one tried to open the trunk, but it appeared that his father had welded that shut too.

Just then, Mari drove down the row of cars and slammed on her brakes in front of the Mustang. She slid up and sat on the back of her driver's seat and started waving her hands, honking the horn, and yelling at the two. They ran off without looking back.

"That girl's got some big *cajones*," Poole whispered, liking what he saw.

Mari parked in the next row over and started toward the hospital entrance. She stopped to look back at the Mustang, but she must have been confident enough to leave the car unattended because she turned back toward the hospital and walked out of his view.

"Sor...ry," the voice rasped, jolting Poole. He whirled around to see his father's head tilted toward him. His eyes were open to tiny slits, and it seemed as if he was looking straight at Poole.

"So sor...ry," Poole's father whispered. "No faul', all good now," he continued to ramble, his words coming faster.

"Lis'n. Follow woman. Mos' beautiful. Mari help. Keys hold the key." His father stopped and chuckled as if he had just told a joke. "Donna's heart. In her hands." He stopped, breathing heavily. The sweat started to pour off his forehead.

Mari entered the room and stopped immediately, standing still in the corner.

"Duh...bar. Need Duh...bar," his father said, becoming more agitated. "Only love, key to my Donna's heart."

"Morgan. End...start. Woman...girl...woman...girl..." he said, trailing off.

Mari walked over to the bed and was about to say something to his father, but Poole stopped her with a finger to his lips. "Let him speak. He told me to listen. It's important. Listen, Mari," Poole whispered, squeezing her arm gently.

It was quiet for another minute, and then his father continued in short breaths. "Birthday a good thing to remember. I remember... you were there...you remember. Love you...your mother..."

The heart monitor started beeping faster, and Poole's father was clearly laboring. Poole whispered in Mari's ear, "I think we need to get Dr. Martine. Can you find her?" Mari looked at Poole with tears welling in her eyes. She nodded and left without saying a word.

Poole felt that his father wanted—no—needed a response from him, but didn't know what to think or say. He was conflicted by years of disdain for the man lying before him. Hate keeps you looking back when you need to look forward, his mother had always reminded him.

Poole sat down again in the bedside chair and held his father's hand as firmly as he dared. He lifted himself to his father's ear, but hesitated. No words came.

Just then, Dr. Martine walked in briskly, followed by the nurse who had just been in. Poole looked up and saw Mari standing in the hallway. Her arms were crossed and she was frowning. Dr. Martine quickly checked the vitals and barked an order to the nurse. "His temp is spiking. Get Dr. Collins up here." The nurse disappeared, leaving Mari in her wake.

Dr. Martine slowly walked around to Poole's side of the bed and, in what seemed to be an out-of-character gesture, gently took his hand from his father's. "You'll have to leave now, Mr. Poole." Her tone was calm and caring.

Poole looked up at the doctor, and then stood. He clenched his jaw and didn't say a word as he rounded the bed and headed toward the door. For a brief moment he stopped, glancing at Mari as he did. He sighed as he wrestled with his thoughts, and then took a deep breath. Hate is a powerful thing, he thought as he walked past Mari. In spite of the urge, he didn't look back and headed down the hall.

FIVE

Poole and Mari sat in the hospital cafeteria waiting for word from Dr. Martine. Poole was lost in thought, and Mari sensed that it was best to keep conversation to a minimum. It was lunchtime, and the cafeteria was noisy with the clatter of plastic trays and silverware. Without asking, Mari entered the queue and came back with a Cuban sandwich for them to share.

Poole looked up and gave her a small smile of thanks. At first, he picked at the sandwich, taking small pinches of bread and ham. But after a couple of nibbles he grabbed his half and took a large, satisfying bite. "If this is hospital food, I can't wait to try one of these at a good place," Poole said.

Mari was relieved that Poole was coming around. "Stick with me, John," she said, finishing her part of the sandwich. "I have a cousin who has a shop that makes the best on the island."

"Are all your cousins in the food business?" Poole asked, half kidding.

"No, you smart aleck," Mari replied. "I have cousins who are nurses, cops, fishermen—even lawyers."

"And they have a cousin who's a marine biologist," Poole added. Mari bowed her head slightly at the compliment. "How many cousins do you have here anyway?"

"Probably more than I know," she said, laughing. "This is an island, after all. If you stay here long enough, you end up knowing a lot of folks—or marrying them!"

Her smile was contagious, and Poole couldn't help but join her. "Thanks," he said. "I needed the pick-me-up. I have to admit, though, that I sort of feel guilty letting out a laugh in a place like this."

"I get it, John. You've been on a whirlwind downer since you've been here. As your doctor, I'm ordering you to laugh without guilt every now and again."

Poole laughed again, enjoying Mari's company, though he couldn't help but wonder about her connection with his father.

He was about to get them a couple of sodas when Dr. Martine entered the cafeteria. Poole stood and walked over to meet her. "How is he, Doctor?" Poole asked.

She sighed and pulled at her name tag. "He's weak, and the fever is getting stronger. We're hydrating him as best we can, but it appears that he's lapsed back into a coma."

"A coma? How can that be? Not that long ago, he was jabbering like a mad man."

"It's hard to explain, Mr. Poole. Quite frankly, I was surprised that he regained consciousness at all once the fever started spiking. It seems like he was hell-bent on speaking with you."

Poole paused. "OK. What happens next?"

"We wait," Dr. Martine answered. "There's no reason for you to hang around here, though. Get out and get some fresh air. I'll call your cell if there is any change at all."

Poole looked at the tile floor and nodded. "Thanks, Doctor," he said, but when he looked up, she was already heading toward the cafeteria doors.

Mari walked up to Poole's side as he stared after the doctor. "Let's get the hell out of here," she said. "We can get a Coke someplace else. Besides, I need to get my head around what your father was rambling about."

Poole nodded. "That's half a good idea, Mari," he said, grabbing her hand. "The Coke sounds great, but weren't you saying something about Jamaican rum the other day?"

The half sandwich wasn't enough for Poole, so Mari decided they needed to find a full-blown jerk chicken lunch. Poole's Mustang followed Mari's Beetle out of the city to a small roadside restaurant. It was more of a shack, really, with electric-blue, green, and red exterior walls and a corrugated metal roof. A few picnic tables surrounded the place, signaling to passersby that it was actually a restaurant.

"Moncrief's has been here since I was a little girl," Mari said after Poole met her in the red-dirt parking area.

"Which cousin runs this place?" Poole asked.

"No cousins here, just good food. Family devotion only goes so far when it comes to good jerk. Now take a seat, and let the maestro do her thing."

Poole settled in at one of the empty tables. Before he knew it, Mari appeared with two paper plates loaded with fragrant chicken, a side of fried plantains, and coleslaw. "One more trip," she said. She soon came back with two large, plastic cups of Coke.

Poole immediately took a sip. "Jesus!" he said, coughing. "This isn't how they serve it at home!"

"You asked for the rum," Mari said innocently. "Don't worry. I'll make sure you get home safe."

"I'm sorry, but this place doesn't look like a cocktail lounge to me!" Poole exclaimed.

She tossed her hair out of her face. "I told you, I know a lot of people. All I did was ask my 'brudda' for a hookup. Now enough of the chitchat; let's dig in!"

Poole had never tasted anything like it. The jerk spices enveloped the chicken in a blanket of smoked goodness. He nibbled at the side dishes, but devoured the main course. And the soothing rum and Coke started to relax him from the stress of the morning.

"Thank you, Mari," he said, touching her hand. "This was a great idea."

She looked briefly at their touching hands. "I'll be right back," she said as she gathered the empty plates. She then went over to her Beetle, pulled her backpack from the backseat and brought it to their table.

"We need to take down some notes. Maybe what your dad was saying might be a clue as to who beat him up," she said as she dug a pad and pencil from the backpack. "OK, you first."

Poole paused and took another sip of his drink. "Let's see. He said something about a love, a first love, I think, or something like that."

Mari wrote it down and looked back at Poole.

"He also said something about keys and another thing I didn't understand. He kept saying 'Duhbar.'" Poole paused, looking at the teal garbage can next to Moncrief's takeout counter. "Oh, and 'follow the woman,' whatever that means."

"OK," Mari said as she scribbled on her notepad. "Yeah, he kept saying first love or only love. That I do remember. And he mentioned Morgan. I assume he meant Morgan, the pirate. Hmmm," she stopped, thinking.

"There was also something else. 'End,' I think," he said, pausing for a moment. "No, it was 'end' then 'start.' End, start...What the hell does that mean?"

"Sorry, I'm just the stenographer here," Mari said with a shrug.

"There was something else though. Think John!"

"My Donna's heart!" Mari exclaimed. "My Donna's heart, it's in her hands!"

"That's right. Good!" He nodded. "So what's on your list so far?"

"A bunch of nonsense, if you ask me," Mari muttered and then read the list to Poole. "First love, Duhbar, keys, Morgan, follow the woman, end/start, my Donna's heart, and it's in her hands."

"Clear as mud," Poole said, taking an extra big gulp from his drink. "Is any of his research on the boat, Mari?"

"Tons. Charts, books, correspondence. Several boxes worth," she replied. "We can go back to the *Rebecca* and check that stuff out if you want."

"Sure. But I think I'd like to talk to the police first. Where do we go for that?"

"Annotto Bay. They were the closest JCF station."

"JCF?"

"Jamaica Constabulary Force. I spoke with a Sergeant Crawford. He's the one who was at the scene," Mari replied.

"Sergeant Crawford it is, then," Poole stated. "I'll follow you."

"Are you OK to drive?" Mari teased.

"Very funny. Let's go before I'm tempted to order another Coke."

Mari laughed and they headed back to the cars. She peeled out of the driveway, spewing reddish dust behind her. Poole shook his head as he eased out onto the road in the Mustang. "Sorry, Old Paint," Poole said as he patted the dash. "I'll take you for a gallop some other time."

Poole followed Mari's Beetle as they took the A-3 to the north side of the island. The small town of Annotto Bay was a few miles east of the marina, and the police station was on the main road. Mari met him on the porch of the small, clean building, and they entered together.

Mari took the lead and asked the petite, female officer at the front desk if Sergeant Crawford was available. She disappeared for a moment and returned with a tall, muscular Jamaican dressed in a crisp, white short-sleeve shirt, and dark-blue trousers sporting red stripes down each seam.

"Sergeant Crawford. I'm Mari Robeson. We spoke the other day when John Morgan Poole was found in our marina parking lot."

"Yes, Ms. Robeson, I remember. How can I help you?"

"This is Mr. Poole's son, John Poole Jr."

Poole stuck out his hand and Sergeant Crawford gave it a strong shake. "Please, let's go to my office," Crawford said as he led the way down a narrow corridor.

Crawford's office was small, but immaculate. The desk was remarkably clean. Only a telephone, a picture of a beautiful woman with two young children, and a yellow pad were on its surface. The credenza behind his chair held dozens of file folders, neatly stacked in stand-up file racks. Crawford sat and motioned for Poole and Mari to sit in the chairs on the opposite side of his desk.

"It's a shame about your father, Mr. Poole. We get far too many cases like his on this island."

"I appreciate your time, Sergeant. I just wanted to ask a couple of questions, if you don't mind." Poole responded.

"That's why I'm here. Please, what can I tell you?"

"I understand that you're calling this a robbery and assault?"

"Yes, I believe that's correct. Just a moment, please." He turned to the credenza and fished out a manila folder. "Here it is, yes. He was found in the marina parking lot by a Robert Coy. Severely beaten, but there were no apparent signs of struggle."

Poole held up his hand. "I spoke with Robert Coy and he said that my father still had his wallet on him."

Crawford nodded. "That's certainly unusual, Mr. Poole. But in my experience, robbery is the usual motive, especially when the victim is a wealthy white male."

"But if they didn't want his money, what else could it be?"

"That's a very good question, and one I can't answer at this time. We'll continue to investigate, of course. But, as you can see, our station is small and our workload is quite large," Crawford replied, pointing to the files behind him.

Poole shook his head. "So at this point, you have no suspects and no prospects to speak of."

"Unfortunately, that's correct. You may not be aware of this, Mr. Poole, but Jamaica has one of the highest crime rates in the world. There have been over one hundred murders on the island since the beginning of January, and in the last two months there have been three murders in our little town alone. One victim was no more than ten years old."

Poole was staggered by the numbers. "I had no idea, Sergeant."

"Unless you live here, you wouldn't. Our office of tourism is doing their best to paint a much different picture of Jamaica."

"Is there anything I can do at this point?"

"See after your father. We'll do what we can from here."

"Thank you Sergeant. Please, let me know if you come up with anything."

Crawford pushed his yellow pad over to Poole and asked for his contact information. "I'll be in touch if we have something for you, Mr. Poole. In the meantime, it wouldn't hurt to be cautious in your travels."

"Why is that?"

"It's just a thought, mind you. But if they didn't take your father's money, perhaps they were looking to take something else of value. If they got what they were after, then that's probably the end of the story. If not, then they may come back."

Poole pursed his lips and nodded. "Thanks for the advice, Sergeant. Very comforting."

"I'm sorry, just doing my job. All the same, keep an eye out for anything unusual."

Poole stood and extended his hand. "We will. Thanks again for your time."

They exited the station and stood next to the cars. "You were right, Mari. I guess beating up an old white guy doesn't have the same priority as the murder of a ten-year-old."

Mari shook her head and shrugged. "Like I said, welcome to Jamaica."

Six

Poole parked next to Mari's Beetle at the marina. It was low tide, so the ramp to the floating docks was at a slight incline. He shuffled down the ramp to keep his balance and made his way over to his father's boat. In the daytime, the boat seemed even larger, and its gleaming white hull was a sharp contrast to the translucent blue-green of the water around it. Poole couldn't help but wonder how much the damned thing had cost. It wasn't quite big enough to be called a yacht, but it wasn't a dinghy either. In Seattle, these were million-dollar boats. He couldn't imagine that they cost much less in Jamaica.

Mari was already on the aft deck. She had taken off her blouse in favor of one of her bikini tops and was surrounded by old cardboard boxes. "Permission to come aboard, Captain," Poole said with a small salute.

Mari smiled and saluted back. "Permission granted, Mr. Poole. What took you so long?"

"I thought I'd take my time and look for anything *unusual*," he said, as he climbed aboard. "What have you got there?"

"These are the boxes your dad shared with me. They were in the stern storage locker."

"Is this all of them?" Poole asked as he sat next to Mari.

"Yeah, at least the ones I know about," she replied. "He has some theories about various wreckage locations. But he's also really into genealogical records and learning as much as he can about Henry Morgan."

"He always brags about being a direct descendant of Morgan," Mari continued. "I think part of his search had to do with proving that connection. Probably as much as finding treasure."

33

"I don't get it," Poole said. "Maybe I'm missing something here. Morgan was a licensed privateer, right?"

"Yes, that's right. England had given him letters of marque, which was sort of a license back then, to go out and fight the Spanish for control of the waters. He wasn't a pirate like the rum bottles suggest at all. I'm pretty sure he was allowed to keep a substantial share of whatever he plundered, and the rest went back to England. It was a great relationship, really. He fought against their enemy, and they both made money in the process. Win-win all the way," Mari replied.

Poole went further. "So pirates would have had to hide or spend their booty because they took it illegally. But Morgan wouldn't have needed to do that. What he took was legal and aboveboard, so there was no need to hide anything, right?"

"Right. But it really bothered your dad that there was always the consistent rumor that Morgan had left a treasure somewhere," Mari replied. "His main ship, the *Oxford*, was lost in an explosion before an attack on Cartagena, and it was believed that it had held much of Morgan's wealth. But when the wreck was found, nothing was discovered. They also came up empty a couple of years ago when they discovered his next flagship, the *Satisfaction*, near Panama."

"So he looked for wrecks of Morgan's ships and found nothing. Or more accurately, other treasure hunters searched and came up empty," Poole said.

"Correct. Your dad figured it was probably a dead end, but he couldn't discount the possibility that Morgan had lost a ship that nobody knew about or somehow had a reason to hide some of his wealth. One thing was for sure, though: Morgan was a smart guy. Your dad said that he wasn't much of a sailor, but he was an excellent tactician and never lost a battle."

"One thing I don't get is why people thought that Morgan had more wealth than he was letting on," Poole said.

"I think most of it had to do with his last will and testament. He gave most of his estate to his godsons, who were his nephews, but they really didn't get that much. He had his 1,200-acre plantation near Port Maria, and some slaves that went with it, but not much money. It didn't seem like a lot for a guy who was considered one of the wealthiest men in Jamaica at the time."

"Wait a second," Poole said, stopping Mari's history lesson. "You said that he had a will, and everything went to his nephews?"

"Yes, that's right. He didn't have children of his own. In fact, I think he married his first cousin, if I'm not mistaken."

"Then how in the heck did my father ever figure that he was a direct descendant of Henry Morgan if he never had children?"

Mari looked stumped. "You've got me there. That doesn't make sense at all. Maybe that's why your father was so into those genealogical records."

"Could be," Poole replied. "Either way, maybe these boxes can tell us something."

They picked through the boxes on the aft deck, but the sun finally forced Poole into the cabin. His skin was used to the gray skies of Seattle, not the fierce Caribbean sun. Once inside, he called the hospital for an update, but his father's condition remained unchanged.

"I'm not used to being in limbo like this," Poole admitted to Mari.

"We can go back to the hospital if you want. Just say the word," she responded.

"And sit there instead of here? No thanks. I'd rather do something to take my mind off the wait. If you don't mind, let's keep going. At least this feels productive."

Mari laid out her notes on the dining table, and they again tried to find a link between the cryptic ramblings of Poole's father and the scraps of paper they were sifting through.

"OK, one more time, Mari," Poole persisted.

"First love, Duhbar, keys, Morgan, follow the woman, end/start, my Donna's heart, and it's in her hands," Mari recited.

"Well, I think the reference to Morgan is self-explanatory," Poole said.

"OK," Mari said. "How about first love?"

"Not a clue," Poole said truthfully. "Morgan's first love could have been his cousin or, I suppose, the sea. Although if he was such a bad sailor, that might be doubtful. My father could have also been talking about my mom, I guess. Too many options right now. Keep going."

"Duhbar."

"That one doesn't make sense at all. Is it a place? I've never heard the term before. Let me do an Internet search tonight on my tablet to see if something comes up."

"The next one is 'keys,'" Mari said.

"The 'keys are the key' could be a number of things. It could be a physical key or keys, a key to a map or chart, or even the Florida Keys, I guess," Poole said. "What's next?"

"OK, the next ones are 'end/start' and 'follow the woman,'" Mari said, resting on her elbows. She was clearly getting tired.

"Hang with me for a bit more, Mari. 'Follow the woman' can't be about Morgan's wife. I remember reading in here somewhere that she ended up going back to England. You'd think that if she took a treasure with her, there'd be a record of it somewhere. Morgan was the pirate; she wasn't."

"So that leaves 'end/start,'" Mari said, continuing Poole's train of thought. "You either start something or end something. I don't get it."

"Well, let's just concentrate on one at a time. What was something that Morgan started?"

Mari looked at her notes. "Well, he showed up in the West Indies in 1655. His first command was in 1662. He was married then and was building his holdings."

"I'm guessing that he wasn't around long enough then to build significant wealth, and probably didn't have the experience yet, with England or his men, to take a cut under the table," Poole surmised. "What about the 'end'?"

"The 'end' offers a couple of options," Mari said. "He died n 1688 and was buried in Port Royal, which later fell into the sea during an earthquake in 1692." She paused, reviewing her notes. "Let's see, the 'end' could also be in 1672 when he lost his commission and was forced to go back to England. But he returned to Jamaica a couple of years later as Sir Henry Morgan, and I think he was even governor for a while."

"Were there any other 'ends' or 'lasts' or anything like that?" Poole asked, getting somewhat frustrated.

"Well, he did have a last battle—a raid, actually. It was the sack of Panama City. It's pretty well documented. It happened in 1671, right before he was sent back to England," Mari said.

"Stop there," Poole said, raising his hand. "That might be promising. I'm going to do some online searching on that raid. Maybe there's a connection." Poole was somewhat encouraged. At least he and Mari had one thing to show for their efforts that afternoon.

He could see that Mari was tired, not only from the research but also from the morning at the hospital. Poole was starting to feel the effects as well.

"Let's take a break," Poole suggested. "I might even take a little catnap, if it's OK with you."

"You read my mind, John," Mari said, stifling a small yawn. "But this time, I get the bed!"

"Aye, aye, Captain," Poole responded. As soon as she went below he took in a deep breath and stretched his arms over his head. He then gazed at the stacks of documents on the dining table one more time before he closed his eyes and dreamed of Panama.

SEVEN

January 1671

Diego Rodriguez stood guard on the bow of the merchant ship, *Valencia*, for the last time in Panama. They were leaving on the morning tide to return to his home in Santiago. He was on edge because he had heard that Morgan's men were approaching. There had been reports for days that at least a thousand English were hacking their way west from the jungles, coming across land to Panama City.

"One more night," he whispered under his breath. One more night and he would be heading south, back to his family and his fiancée, Isabel. He longed for the day when he could lie by her side. He could still remember the scent of her raven hair as they said their good-byes, while her father glowered behind her.

He was eighteen and she, sixteen, when he boarded the ship to Panama City. Two years was the agreement. His father was poor, and they were of a different class than Isabel's family. But his father was acquainted with a ship captain who agreed to take Diego on to learn the merchant trade. The captain could tell that Diego was bright and mentioned on more than one occasion that Diego would have a ship of his own before he knew it.

Diego worked hard and managed to save what little money he made. He learned how to hold his own against the more seasoned crew members and earned their respect. In two years, Diego learned how to navigate by the stars and could interpret the charts. When the ship's navigator died of malaria, the captain promoted Diego. He thought that might cause resentment among the crew, but the men approved of the selection, as if they were proud fathers in their own right.

On two occasions, he had met Don Guzman, the governor of Panama City. He was humbled to be included in these meetings and kept his distance as his captain discussed trade issues w th the governor. There was talk about trade increasing with the prospect of peace between England and Spain and that more ships would have to be built or commandeered. During the last meeting, Don Guzman even glanced over to Diego briefly, nodded his head, and turned back to the conversation. Diego couldn't believe the acknowledgment.

"Eyes sharp, Diego!" his captain said, clapping him on the shoulder. "I can tell you're dreaming of that pretty girl of yours! You'll be with her soon enough!"

"Sorry, sir!" Diego responded, straightening his tunic.

His captain smiled. "You're a good man, Diego. Your father will be proud of you. You've done everything that he had hoped for and, quite frankly, more than I expected."

Diego bowed his head slightly but soaked in the praise from the man he respected so much.

"You've done well and you've saved your money, and I have not been unaware of how much the men respect you. In a few short years, I could see you running your own ship if that's what you want," the captain said, looking intently into Diego's eyes.

Diego was stunned. It was more than he could ever dream. A captain's wages would secure his future with Isabel. He could raise a family and not worry about filling the dinner table. Even Isabel's father couldn't complain about his prospects then!

"I am humbled, sir," Diego replied. "You have given me more than I ever could have imagined. I will always be in your debt."

"Good!" his captain said, laughing. "I want you to remember this night when I come looking for a job from you one day!" The captain slapped Diego on the shoulder one more time and walked back to his quarters at the stern of the vessel. He turned back anc yelled, "Eyes sharp, Diego! Eyes sharp!" before he entered his cabin and closed the door behind him.

Diego was reeling with excitement. The usual tedium of the watch was replaced by thoughts of his future with Isabel, and the time flew by. He could tell by the position of the stars that daylight would come within the hour. Soon his replacement would arrive, and he could get some needed sleep before they set sail with the tide. He peered out toward the city, and all was quiet except for the clatter of the bakers, who were already preparing for their morning customers, and the scuffling of a few drunks, who were just then heading for their beds.

Diego thought he heard the rustle of a few men down below as they readied for their shift. Finally, he thought, the morning is almost upon us, and my triumphant return will begin. Again, he thought of Isabel. Her full lips and almond-shaped eyes were mesmerizing to him, even though it had been two years since he had last seen her. In four weeks he would be with her, holding her close, feeling the warmth of her breasts as they pressed against his chest, kissing her tender lips. He briefly closed his eyes as the thought of her aroused him.

He had to will himself to open his eyes again and force the sleep away. He took a deep breath and looked up at the stars once more.

It came fast, before he understood what was happening. A gritty palm covered his mouth, and he felt a pinch in his side. Immediately, he felt a warm trickle spread down his trousers as the pain started to swell. Then his head was yanked back as something scraped across his neck. He fell to the deck on his back, eyes wide with fear. He tried to yell, but only a sickening gurgle came. He looked up to see the tooth-less grin of a filthy English face. The man winked and was gone, leaving the bright evening stars in his wake. Diego couldn't move. He simply stared toward the heavens until the stars slowly faded from his view.

Morgan stood on a rise overlooking a vast field leading up to Panama City. It had rained heavily for three days before the skies cleared during the night. He and his men were tired and hungry. It had taken almost ten days to traverse the isthmus, floating along the Chagres River and then hacking their way through the dense jungle. The Spaniards had burned almost everything of value—especially food—as they continued to fall back while Morgan and his men advanced. At one point, Morgan's men had been reduced to boiling leather to make soup. It was a good day when they were able to shoot the buzzards that were feeding on the corpses of the dead.

Morgan had started with over two thousand men. He left five hundred to protect their ships and another three hundred or so to watch over the cannons and other equipment that they couldn't carry through the jungle. Jungle sickness and starvation claimed dozens. The wounded, many by the arrows of natives allied with the Spaniards, were left behind to fend for themselves.

Standing on the rise, Morgan was left with about a thousand men. During the night, he dispatched a band of his pirates to scuttle the few ships left in the harbor to make sure the Spaniards' escape route was cut off. He also directed a hundred men to take to the jungle on the east side of the field.

Morgan's troops were outnumbered, but he had enlisted the services of the finest buccaneers for the raid. The French, two hundred strong, were excellent marksmen, and his English countrymen were ruthless and gave no quarter. They were all there for one thing. The politics of the day and the war between England and Spain meant nothing to them—or to Morgan, for that matter. Untold treasure from the richest city in the new world was waiting for them on the other side of the field.

The Spanish troops numbered over two thousand, and they assembled in the traditional manner to defend their city. In addition to the infantry, there was a small unit of cavalry. The horses were beautiful, and the armor strapped over their heads and long noses reminded Morgan of the mounts of the conquistadors. They might pose a challenge, he thought.

The Spanish governor, Don Guzman, was atop the largest stallion, a black horse at least sixteen hands high. Its nostrils flared, and puffs of steam escaped from them in a steady rhythm.

Morgan looked at the expanse before him and decided there was no need to delay. His men would only get more tired and hungry the longer they waited on the rise. He ordered the French to lead the contingent, fifty abreast. The English followed with their guns, swords, and axes.

The Spanish also advanced, with Guzman and his cadre of horsemen leading the way. The horses were skittish as they struggled to gain footholds on the muddy ground, but they continued to advance across the field until the two forces were two hundred yards apart.

The French loaded their muskets, which were accurate to only about one hundred yards. The Spanish kept advancing while the first line of French waited patiently, aiming their muskets with practiced hands. Morgan, still on the rise, lifted his left arm slowly as the Spanish advanced to within range. He then dropped it quickly. The leader of the French gave the command to fire, and his troops let loose the first volley.

The Spanish charged as the French continued to fire, the first and second lines alternating as one line shot and the other reloaded. The devastation was immediate. The Spaniards started dropping in waves. The horses, spooked by the flashes and sounds of the muskets, reared on the muddy field, many throwing their riders or losing their footing entirely. As the Spanish infantry continued to advance, the English rushed the field with their swords and axes and started to push them back.

As the sun crested over the jungle canopy, Morgan calmly raised his right hand. When he dropped it, his men, who had been waiting in hiding, charged the field. They let off a series of shots from their flintlocks and attacked the flank of the Spaniards. Left exposed, the Spanish ranks deteriorated, and the majority fled toward the city. Morgan's men followed eagerly behind. The city was theirs before nightfall.

Morgan thought that the Spaniards would have put up a better fight. By his count, they lost over six hundred men and left many more wounded on the battlefield. The rest were taken prisoner. Only twenty of his men were killed and an equal number wounded. Not a bad day's work, he thought, as he walked through the burning streets of Panama City. "Let the boys have fun tonight," he said, smiling. "And then let us see what the richest city in the new world has to offer."

EIGHT

A tap on his shoulder interrupted Poole's catnap. Mari stood above him with a cup of tea in her hand. "Here, sleepyhead. You're going to waste a beautiful day if you sit there and snore!"

Poole ran his hand over his face and took the cup. "How long have I been out?" he asked.

"Don't worry; only about an hour. I just thought it would screw up your sleep pattern if I let you go much longer," she said. "Besides, I wanted someone to talk to before I started checking out this Panama thing."

"I'm happy to oblige," Poole said, smiling. "Give me a second to clear the cobwebs, and then we'll figure out what's what."

It was close to five o'clock, and the Jamaican sun was starting its descent. The heat of the day was less stifling, and a breeze freshened the cabin. Poole went out to the aft deck and took a sip of the tea. He was surprised by the sweetness, but then took several more gulps, relishing the flavor. Mari joined him with a cup of her own.

"So Robert was telling me that you actually live aboard?" Poole asked.

"Yes, that's right. It was a generous offer. I had mentioned to your father that I needed to start saving for retirement and thought it might be best if I found a job in the States," Mari recounted. "He immediately offered up the free rent and doubled my salary. I was shocked. He also told me that he would help with my financial planning. He said that he had done OK with his money and that chasing around in a nine-to-five job wasn't the only way to get ahead in the world," she said. "He had a point. I always wondered how he could afford this beast, so I took him at his word. I loved the lifestyle and

44

the island weather. Home is home, after all. So I accepted the offer and have been putting away money ever since."

"So what happens now? I mean, if he doesn't get better?" he asked, the battered face of his father still fresh in Poole's mind.

"Frankly, I haven't thought that far ahead. I figure I'll take it one day at a time."

"That's all either one of us can do," Poole said, appreciating her answer.

The sun started to set, and the sky began to turn a spectacular shade of orange. They both stood in silence while they sipped the last of their sweetened tea. A gust from the ocean tossed Poole's hair and he closed his eyes to smell the salt air. Mari touched his arm and motioned him inside. She disappeared to start the generator and came back to turn on the cabin lights.

"Do you want to go back to the hospital tonight?" Mari asked.

"I spoke with Dr. Martine a couple of hours ago and she said that she would call me when he woke up. I doubt my being there is going to make that happen any faster."

"Then let's just hang out here for the time being. I'm tired anyway. I don't know how you lawyers can look at paperwork all day without getting exhausted."

Poole laughed. "What makes you think we don't? I'll be the first to admit I don't race to my office each morning. Maybe my father had it right with this lifestyle, although I have a serious problem with the way he went about it."

"I understand. I know you haven't thought real highly of him, but maybe he's trying to make amends with all this stuff," she said, pointing to the papers on the dining table.

"Did he tell you that I tried to reach out to him a couple of times?" Poole asked. "I wrote letters and even called his number in the phone book, back when they had phone books, but never got an answer. That's a pretty tough thing to do to a kid."

"It doesn't figure. I haven't known your dad all that long, but he's never come across as that kind of guy."

"Yeah, well maybe I'll ask him when he comes to. It's the least I deserve," Poole said, turning his attention back to the dining table. "OK, where were we?"

Mari set her cup down in the sink and sat on the other side of the table. She reviewed her notes. "Panama," she replied.

"That's right," he said as he pulled out his tablet. After a few keystrokes, dozens of sites popped up on the screen. It surprised Poole to find so much material on the subject. He picked the most promising sites and perused the account of the battle.

"This is pretty interesting," Poole related. "It turns out that this was Morgan's last major raid, so it could fit the 'end' my father mentioned. From the accounts, Morgan and his men traversed over the Isthmus of Panama and approached Panama City from the east."

Poole continued. "At the time, Panama City was considered the wealthiest settlement in the Americas, maybe even the world. In fact, here's a notation where Morgan was surprised at how large the city was. After the city was sacked, there are reports that hundreds of thousands of pieces of eight were recovered along with a treasure-trove of jewels."

"But I thought I'd read that the take wasn't that great, and the raid was considered a general failure by the buccaneers," Mari countered.

"Well, there certainly seems to be a gap in the story," Poole replied. "Some say that the Spanish emptied the city of most of its wealth before Morgan arrived, which is plausible since it appears that they were well aware that he and his men were approaching. But I suppose there's another explanation as well."

"What's that?" Mari asked.

"Morgan lied," Poole said simply.

"Lied? Lied about what?"

"Maybe he took more than he said. Maybe he was working on a little retirement plan of his own. We've got to dig deeper to see if there's any truth to that."

"I'm sure that will be a piece of cake after three hundred and fifty years," Mari said sarcastically.

"There must be something. Maybe it has to do with the 'start' my father rambled about," Poole suggested.

"You keep reading. I asked Robert to put a couple of snacks together for us. I'll pop up there and grab them. We've got cold drinks in the fridge, if you want something." Mari hopped off the boat and headed to the café.

Poole opened up some more sites that discussed the raid on Panama City. He skipped over much of Morgan's trek leading up to the actual taking of the city and concentrated on what happened after. Not surprisingly, the accounts were sketchy, at best. Supposedly, Morgan and his men returned to their ships at the end of February or early March. There was some unrest among the crew because the take was not as large as they thought it would be, especially after the struggle they went through.

One account caught Poole's attention. The author explained that when they made it back to the Caribbean, Morgan was told that the war between England and Spain had ended. Shortly thereafter, Morgan and some of his men stole away in the middle of the night on his fastest ship, leaving the majority of his men behind.

"Interesting," Poole said as he stared at the screen. "This was truly going to be the end for Morgan. Nothing left to plunder. Maybe my retirement idea has some legs."

Mari returned with a plastic takeout bag. "Just some munchies," she said, opening the bag.

"Fine by me. I'm still full from our lunch," Poole replied.

"Find anything out while I was out hunting and gathering?"

"A little," Poole answered. "I'm getting the impression that Morgan did hold out on his crew. In fact, there are a couple of stories confirming that when Morgan reached the Caribbean, he bugged out in the middle of the night, leaving most of his men behind."

"So it's possible that he hid some treasure without England knowing about it—that is, if he could manage to unload it on his own. But how in the world would his crew not know about it? They had to lug crates of the stuff back from Panama City, after all," Mari said.

"My thoughts too, Mari," Poole nodded. "There has to be something else that ties this all together."

Mari disappeared down below. "Just going to put on something more comfortable," she called back to Poole.

Poole raised his eyebrows a bit since she was already wearing a pretty comfortable bikini top. "Hey, Mari," he called down to her. "Does my father happen to have anything else around here on Morgan?"

"Maybe in his stateroom. Let me check."

A couple of minutes later, Mari reappeared in a loose, pink tank and thin, gray sweatpants that had the faded word PINK stenciled on the seat. "Voila!" she said holding a tattered hardback book. The cover read simply *Henry Morgan, Life and Times*. "This was in a bookcase against the wall."

"Great!" Poole exclaimed, trying hard to concentrate on the book. Mari tossed it to Poole and then went to the fridge and grabbed a couple of Red Stripes.

Poole leafed briefly through the pages and looked up at Mari. "Have you seen this book before?" he asked.

"First time," she responded. "In fact, that was the first time I dared go into his stateroom. He laid down some strict rules when I started living aboard. The first was that his room was off limits, which was fine by me since I didn't want things to get weird, if you know what I mean."

"Were there any other books on Morgan down there?"

"Nope. That was it."

"You should check this out. There are notations all over the place. Highlighted passages, notes scribbled in the margins, you name it."

Mari slid in next to Poole and looked at the book with him. "Is there a section on Panama?" she asked.

"Pass me that Red Stripe first," he answered with a crooked smile, "and we can find out together."

Poole continued to leaf through the book until he came to a dog-eared page that marked the chapter on the raid on Panama.

Poole quickly scanned each page, searching for any kind of key word or phrase. He paid particular attention to his father's notes in the margins and the underlined passages.

"OK, now we're into the time after Morgan took the city and they were searching the homes and surrounding area for things of value," Poole said.

"Look at that paragraph," Mari said, pointing. "It talks about a man they found in an abandoned villa. It says that he was holding a golden key when he was taken by Morgan's men."

"Good eye," Poole responded. "Remember, my father did mention something about a key. Maybe this key is the 'start.' Let's keep going."

Poole turned a couple more pages and stopped, staring at a highlighted paragraph and a notation in the margin. "Listen to this, Mari," Poole said. He took a long pull on the Red Stripe, paused for a second, and then continued. "It says that Morgan's men collected as much treasure as they could find. They also took several prisoners to be held for ransom or taken back to Jamaica as slaves. This paragraph talks about 'a woman of unsurpassed beauty.' According to this book, Morgan was captivated by her and made arrangements for her to stay in his quarters."

Poole rapidly tapped his index finger on the galley table as he read. "Supposedly, Morgan was as ruthless as his men when it came to the women they captured. But this passage says that Morgan treated her with the utmost respect and courtesy. The author is even suggesting that Morgan tried to woo her."

"But how does that tie in to the clues we have?" Mari asked.

"All we have to do is read my father's notation in the margin."

"What's it say?" Mari asked.

"It says, 'Follow the woman' with a big old exclamation point at the end!" Poole said, opening his mouth and raising his eyebrows in mock amazement.

"Follow the woman? No way!" Mari said, shaking her head.

"Clear as day. I wonder if this was the 'start' my father was talking about?" Poole asked.

"My vote is yes. It makes a lot of sense, if you put it all together. Morgan was nearing the end of his pirating days and at the same time he meets a woman who, by all accounts, he's fallen in love with. That's a 'start' in my book."

"I can't disagree with you, but it also seems like we might be grasping at straws a bit to make my father's clues fit a random theory we've come up with. It's a surefire way to head down a dead end," Poole cautioned.

"Said by a guy who clearly doesn't have a romantic bone in his body," Mari said, shaking her head. "Think about this. Morgan was married to his first cousin *and* they didn't have children. I bet you their sex life was as dusty and lifeless as those old wigs they used to wear back then. Now he comes across a beautiful Spanish woman and he starts to woo her? That guy was in loovvvee!"

"Maybe it was just lust?" Poole questioned.

"Not with Morgan. He could have taken her and any other woman he wanted as a spoil of war. This one was different. We need to follow the woman!" she said emphatically.

"OK then," Poole said, raising his hands in surrender. "All we need to do is go to the Panama City directory from 1671 and look for the listing that says 'most beautiful woman.'"

"Oh, ye of little faith," Mari retorted, picking up their empty bottles. "Keep reading. I'm going to the fridge for reinforcements."

Poole and Mari reread the chapter on Panama and scanned the rest of the book from front to back. There was no other note or marking that led them any closer to the name of the mysterious woman. The book later mentioned that Morgan took her with him, along with other slaves and Spaniards held for ransom.

"This is weird," Poole said. "So he brings this woman all the way across the Isthmus of Panama. Then there's a passage that says he let her go."

"No way!" Mari said.

"Yeah, it says that she had told some friars where they could find money to pay for her ransom. When Morgan found out that the friars used the money to free some other prisoners, he felt sorry for her and released her," Poole read.

"Bull!" Mari practically yelled. "That doesn't smell right to me If you're into a woman that much, you don't just let her go."

His brow furrowed, and Poole pondered Mari's last sentence silently for a few seconds. "Well, it can happen. Just ask my father," he said as he took a pull from the Red Stripe.

"I'm sorry, John. I didn't mean it that way."

"That's OK. I know you didn't. I guess it just struck me that this whole search thing is just one big fantasy. Here I'm getting swept up in all of this, just like him. But that's not why I'm down here. Jesus, I still don't know why I even bothered to come. All I know is there's a real world out there that my father chose to ignore. It's called reality. Reality is where he left my mother. Reality is where you and I live now."

Poole shoved the book aside. "I'm done with this. I'm going to the hospital in the morning and tell him what I think. He needs to hear it, and I don't give a damn what condition he's in."

The ring of his cell phone interrupted Poole's rant. He knew the local number but hesitated a moment before answering.

"John Poole here."

"Mr. Poole? This is Dr. Martine." She paused, her voice tired. "Your father went into cardiac arrest about an hour ago. I'm sorry In spite of our efforts, he didn't make it."

Poole sat silent, stunned. He stared across the marina at a white-hulled sloop rocking gently with the evening breeze and could hear the laughter of a small group having a late dinner at the café. A lone sea gull, napping on one of the dock's lampposts, caught his eye as it ruffled its feathers slightly and then settled back on its perch.

"Mr. Poole, are you all right?" Dr. Martine asked.

"Uh, yes, sorry," he replied. "What happens next?"

"Come down in the morning. There will be some paperwork to fill out. I'll be here at eight."

"OK, thank you." Poole ended the call.

Mari interrupted Poole's train of thought. "Who was that?" she asked, concerned.

Poole drained the last of his beer and carefully placed the bottle down on the table. He looked over to her questioning face and replied, "That, Mari, was reality calling."

NINE

A morning service was held on the following Sunday. It had rained steadily overnight, but the storm finally blew through in the early hours. Steam caused by the evaporation of the moisture cast an eerie pall over the small, outdoor gathering. Mari had picked a chapel near Port Maria that she knew Poole's father liked. The Catholic priest said a simple eulogy while Poole sat in a white folding chair next to Mari. Robert; his wife, Marthy; and a few of their family members attended as well, more out of respect for Mari than for his father, Poole thought.

Poole made it clear that he did not want to say any words of his own, and the priest, Father Michael, respected his wishes. A small box was presented to Poole at the conclusion of the affair. It contained the remains of John Morgan Poole Sr.

Mari told Poole that his father had said that he wanted to be buried at sea, if possible. He always mentioned it when his favorite Jimmy Buffet tune, "A Pirate Looks at Forty," came on the radio. They agreed to take the boat out later that day to spread his ashes.

Poole thanked Robert and the other attendees as they each left and went back to their regular Sunday routines. He then turned to Mari and gave her a long, heartfelt hug. She buried her face in his shoulder, and he could feel the dampness of her shedding tears.

She pulled slightly away but stayed in his arms. "He was a good man, John," she said, staring intently into his eyes. "I hope you come to know that in time."

Poole nodded without saying a word. When they ended their embrace, he walked over to Father Michael and thanked him for his kind words.

"How did you know my father?" Poole asked.

Father Michael smiled sadly. "He started coming to our church a couple of years ago. He was quite a character, that one."

"In what way?"

"Oh, for one, he would always tell me that he wasn't the church-going type and that he wanted to see how the other half lived," Father Michael said with a chuckle.

"He also asked about the church and its history. He was fascinated with it, really. After a while, he became my friend as well as a friend to the church. We would sit for hours discussing the history of the island and how Catholic churches survived under English rule; things like that. He even stayed in our cottage in the back when our conversations ran late into the night. You know, with the passage of time I think he truly started believing in the power of God."

"Why do you say that, Father?" Poole asked.

"I just remember one particular time when he said that things have a way of coming full circle. That there must be a higher power that watches over us all and gives us a path to follow," he answered.

"Did you know what he was taking about?" Poole persisted.

"Not specifically, no. But I do know one thing. He was right," Father Michael answered, placing his hand on Poole's shoulder. "Peace be with you, my son."

Poole retrieved Mari and they made their way back to the marina. Mari drove, but this time only a little over the speed limit. It was noon when they pulled into the parking lot. Poole gently grabbed the small box from the backseat of the Beetle and they boarded the *Rebecca*.

"Do you know how to take this thing out?" Mari asked.

"The biggest powerboat I've skippered was a twenty-four-foot runabout," Poole said truthfully. "You better take her out. I'll man the lines."

Mari idled the large craft out of the marina and into the channel. Poole secured all of the lines and pulled up the elongated blue
bumpers that were hanging from the port side of the boat that were
used to protect it from chafing against the dock. Mari opened the
throttle a bit when they reached a safe distance from the harbor.
The change of speed almost made Poole lose his balance, but he
recovered before Mari could see his misstep.

She was controlling the vessel from the flying bridge, so Poole
climbed the ladder to join her. The boat's Bimini top was up to
deflect the rays of the midday sun. That, along with the fresh sea
breeze created by their speed, made for a pleasant voyage.

"I thought we'd go over to Cabarita Island, one of his favorite
spots," Mari said.

"That's fine," Poole replied. "You knew him better than I did."

In forty-five minutes, they reached their destination. Mari idled
the main engines and took the boat out of gear, letting it drift with
the current. The purr from the exhaust was a stark contrast from the
roar of the twin diesels at speed, and the tranquility enveloped them
both.

"What's so special about this place?" Poole asked as they drifted
along the north shore of the small island. "It doesn't seem that exotic
compared to some of the other islands we passed."

"I think it had to do with Morgan, really," Mari replied. "If you
look over at that bluff above the harbor, that's where Morgan owned
a sugar plantation. His holdings extended down to the harbor and
included this island."

"It doesn't seem very inviting. Maybe my father thought this was
where Morgan's secret treasure was buried."

"Maybe. We actually did do some diving around here, but the
currents can be pretty tricky. He even took the dinghy to shore a
couple of times but there wasn't anything except brush and bugs,
according to him," Mari related.

They idled around to the south side of the island, which faced
Port Maria. Simple, multicolored buildings lined the harbor. The

white masts of sailboats bobbed with the incoming tide, and the heat distorted their shapes as they danced on the waves.

The water on the south side of Cabarita Island was calm, sheltered from the swells coming in from the north. The crystalline-blue water was so clear that it seemed like the bottom was just a few feet below the surface, but the fathometer registered ten meters in depth. A solitary ray glided by, its long spike tail waving lazily in its wake. The gulls flying overhead created a halo over the crown of the small island.

Poole was mesmerized by the scene. He now understood the attraction this place had for his father. The island seemed frozen in time, untouched since the days of Morgan. It rose like a sentry in the bay, sheltering the harbor from the weather, protecting it from intruders.

"You're right, Mari," Poole said. "I think this place will do." He went into the cabin and returned with the small box. Mari, still on the flying bridge, checked the depth sounder and the current, and then shut down the engines.

"You go ahead, John," she called down. "I'll stay up here and watch."

Poole nodded in reply. He walked over to the downwind side of the aft deck and held the box to his chest. He stood motionless for close to a minute, his mind whirling. He had just come to the realization that he was now alone, the last survivor of his small, fractured nuclear family. The feelings welling up were foreign to him. As he extended his arms, lifted the lid, and gently freed its contents, Poole was overwhelmed with a sadness that he hadn't felt since he was a young boy.

The breeze took his father toward Port Maria, and the ashes disappeared from view somewhere between the sky and the sea. He let the small box slip from his hands and watched it slowly sink to the seafloor below.

Turning toward the stern, away from the flying bridge, short, hesitant breaths overcame him. And for the briefest of moments, John Morgan Poole Jr. cried.

TEN

They made the trip back to the marina in silence. Poole rejoined Mari on the flying bridge and sat next to her on the bench seat as she navigated the boat. Their legs touched briefly as the boat was tossed by a small swell, and Mari grabbed his knee in reflex. She left her hand there as the boat righted itself, and Poole gently put his hand over hers. She made no effort to pull away, and they made their way back to the marina oblivious of the world around them.

When they reached the marina, Mari expertly guided the boat to its berth. Poole jumped off the aft deck and secured the stern line to the dock, then did the same with the bow line and spring line. Mari idled the engines for a moment before shutting them down for good. She then hopped off the boat to double-check the lines. Poole appreciated her thoroughness and was impressed by her seamanship. She looked up briefly at him, expecting a snide comment, but Poole just smiled.

"Quite a morning and afternoon, so far," Mari said absently.

"Another day in paradise," Poole replied with a sigh.

"Have you heard anything from Crawford?"

"Nothing. The only thing he said was they would change the file to a manslaughter investigation, and he would get back to me if there was something new to report."

"Something tells me we won't be hearing from him any time soon."

"I wish you were wrong, Mari, but I think my father's file will be collecting dust in no time."

"Isn't there anything that can be done?" she asked.

"Maybe. Maybe not. Either way, I'm probably on my own."

"*We're* probably on *our* own, you mean."

Poole smiled. "OK, I stand corrected. But for now, I think *we* need a break. How does a drive up the coast sound? I'd like to find a nice place for an early dinner."

"You read my mind. I just need to clean up a bit. Give me a few minutes."

Poole sat on the aft deck looking up at the café parking lot. Robert was back at work, and a small but lively crowd had filled the veranda. An old green Range Rover pulled up near the marina entrance as Poole got up to get a Red Stripe. He came back and sat in his folding chair as a short, overweight man in his late fifties got out of the Range Rover and walked out toward the docks. He carried a briefcase in one hand, and a small package was tucked under his arm. The man stumbled on the ramp to the main dock but then regained his composure and walked right up to the stern of the boat.

"Pardon me. Is your name John Poole?" the man asked.

Poole sized up the man, from his rumpled slacks to his vintage island shirt. His thin, gray, disheveled hair danced in the breeze. "Yes, that's me," Poole responded. "How can I help you?"

"I'm your father's lawyer. I am truly sorry to hear about his passing," he said. "I had instructions to contact you upon his death, and your office indicated that you would be here during your stay on the island," he said in an accent that suggested he was originally from Great Britain. "May I come aboard?"

"Yes, I'm sorry, please do," Poole responded.

The lawyer clumsily climbed over the gunnels, careful not to drop his case or the package. He sat down in the folding chair opposite Poole and pulled out a handkerchief to wipe the perspiration from his red face. He opened the briefcase and pulled out an official-looking cardboard portfolio, which he handed to Poole. "This is your father's last will and testament," he stated. "Of course, I expect you to peruse it on your own, but the long and short of it is that he's left everything to you."

Poole stared down at the packet and didn't reply.

"I've also been instructed to deliver this package to you upon his death."

Poole took the package and was too stunned to say anything other than "thank you."

"Lastly, your father asked that I deliver this letter, which is personally addressed to you." he said, handing a white envelope to Poole.

"There are some other boxes and belongings of his at my office that he asked that I hold for safekeeping. I can deliver them to you here, or you can pick them up at my office, whichever is more convenient for you," he continued.

Again, Poole's only words were "thank you."

Mari stepped out from the cabin in another one of her stunning sundresses. Poole and the lawyer stood up in unison. "Mari, this is my father's lawyer. He's brought some of his things for me."

Mari walked out to the deck and extended her hand. "Please excuse my friend. He's still getting used to properly introducing people. My name is Maria Robeson. And you are?"

He offered his card in return and smiled awkwardly. "Dunbar. Warren Dunbar, at your service."

Mari and Poole looked at each other and didn't say a word.

ELEVEN

They had agreed to meet Warren Dunbar at his office at ten o'clock the following morning to collect the remainder of his father's materials. After Dunbar took his leave, Poole and Mari started their long drive up the coast to the other side of the island. Mari said there was a beautiful spot overlooking Montego Bay that would be a good place to recharge. They took the Mustang, and Poole insisted on driving. He decided not to tell Mari that the real reason was that he wanted to get there in one piece.

Although Poole wasn't thrilled by the idea, Mari brought the items Dunbar had given him and was checking out the package while giving Poole directions.

"Well, it looks like we now know what 'Duhbar' meant," she said looking over at Poole.

"Yeah, that came as a little bit of a shock. It was nice of him to come and meet us at the boat, though. It saved us the time and effort of trying to figure that one out."

"Aren't you dying to open any of the stuff he gave you?" Mari asked, shaking the package and then putting it to her ear.

"Trying to hear the ocean?" Poole teased. "Or is there something ticking?"

"Neither, smart guy. I just thought you might be a little curious is all."

"To be honest, I am," he confessed. "But I'm also a little drained and hungry. I thought we could just drive for a while and you could be my personal tour guide, if you're OK with that."

"My pleasure, Mr. Poole. On your right, you'll see the beautiful Caribbean Sea. In the distance, you can just make out the lovely island of Cuba. I hear they make excellent cigars over there. On your left, you have red dirt and green grass. That'll be twenty-five US dollars, please!" Mari said, laughing.

"OK, OK!" Poole relerted, holding up his right hand in surrender. "I'll make you a deal. Let's enjoy the ride, and we'll take a look at some of that stuff over a nice Cuba Libre."

"You drive a hard barçain, Mr. Poole. It's a deal. You go ahead and do your thing, and I'll enjoy the scenery," she answered, resting her gaze on the blue-eyed man behind the wheel.

Poole was finally relaxing and leaving the events of the morning behind. It had been a good hour behind the wheel of the Mustang. Something about the old-school sound of the engine and the wind whipping through his hair made him feel one with the road. Much to Mari's dismay, Poole took his time and went the speed limit most of the way.

Mari pointed to a stately, whitewashed picket fence that opened to a circular driveway. "Take a right in here," she said. "I think you'll like the views."

A smartly dressed valet gave Poole a numbered card while Mari grabbed the package and other items and stuffed them into her satchel. Poole helped Mari over the passenger-side door. The attendant hopped over the driver's side-door in one motion and then idled the Mustang over to a parking lot across the road as Poole and Mari entered the colonial-style restaurant.

"You weren't kidding," Poole exclaimed. "This view is spectacular!"

They walked through the restaurant to an open deck outside that overlooked the water at least three hundred feet below. The crescent-shaped bay was an iridescent turquoise surrounded by lush, green hills. A massive ocean liner, moored at an immense pier, dwarfed the sailboats and other watercraft dotting the bay. The sun had burned away all remnants of the storm, and the air smelled of the fresh bougainvilleas that surrounded the restaurant.

A young Jamaican man sporting short, well-kept dreadlocks presented himself after they sat at a table near the railing. He wore black shorts and a crisp, white, cotton shirt. His name tag said "F. Williams."

"Good afternoon! Welcome to the Cliffs. My name is Fredrickson, and I will be your server."

"Thank you, Fredrickson," Poole replied. "What a great place you have here. Would it be possible for us to get two Cuba Libres?"

"It would be my pleasure, sir," he said, after opening their linen napkins and leaving two menus on the table. "Can I interest you in an appetizer as well?"

Mari answered. "For now, just keep the cocktails coming. We'll flag you down when we're ready."

With that, Fredrickson was gone.

"Sorry to jump in, but this place can get a little too polite for my taste. Besides, I'm ready to open this thing up!" she said, shaking the package.

"No worries. But can you at least wait for our provisions to arrive? You're as bad as a kid on Christmas!" Poole laughed.

A few minutes later, Fredrickson delivered two highball glasses filled with the dark cola-and-rum drink. Poole took a small sip, testing the alcohol content, before he slugged it down. "Thank you, Fredrickson," he said. "By the way, I was wondering about your name. It's unique. How did you come by it?"

"Thank you, sir. Um, I guess it's not all that complicated. My father's name is Fredrick. When I was born, they named me Fredrickson. Get it?"

Poole smiled. "I do now. Very interesting."

"I know, sir. I should come up with a better answer. Like I'm related to a famous pirate or something?" He laughed.

"That could work," Poole said wryly. "Right, Mari?" They both grinned as Fredrickson sailed to another table.

As Poole took another sip of his drink, Mari slid the package in front of him.

"OK, OK. You do the honors. I'm a little preoccupied with this little package over here," he said as he twirled the swizzle stick in his cocktail.

Mari wasted no time in not-so-carefully ripping open the brown-paper wrapping. Inside were dozens of old, water-spotted letters, all postmarked from Seattle. "What the heck? Some of these go back at least thirty years," Mari exclaimed.

Poole put down his drink and grabbed one of the letters. The flap was carefully folded inside the envelope to keep its contents secure. It was addressed to John Morgan Poole, Port Antonio, Jamaica. His heart skipped a beat as he recognized his mother's flowing script. He turned the letter over in his hands a couple of times and then lifted it to his nose, hoping to smell the scent of his mother's perfume, but instead he found the musty remnants of age.

"Are these what I think they are?" Mari asked, looking down at the package filled with dozens of other letters. "What's the date on that one?"

"The postmark says December 21, 1988. I would have been fourteen then."

"These are private, John. I can put them away for now," Mari said.

Poole looked at her and shook his head. "That's OK. I want you here. In fact, I'd appreciate it if you'd read it," he said, handing the envelope to Mari.

Mari was going to protest, but decided against it once she looked in his eyes. Poole picked up his drink and savored the sweetness of the rum as he stared off toward the bay below. Mari took out the yellowed paper. She hesitated for a moment, noting Poole's gaze, and then began to read:

12/21/88

Dearest John Morgan,

The passing of the minutes seems longer each day that we are apart. I know the decision we made will be the best for John Jr., one I know that you and I will never regret, but it pains my heart to think that the man I love is so far away.

I received your last letter two days ago. I know it's silly, but I've kept it under my pillow as a way to feel you next to me. I long for the days when we were young and the pull of my parents was not as strong. I guess things changed, didn't they?

Your beautiful son is growing up so fast! Every day he looks a little more like you. He's so smart. He gets nothing but high marks in school. And you should see him in the pool! He's almost as fast as me turning laps. You'd be so proud...

Mother and father are living up to their end of the bargain, and I want you to know that although our decision was a sacrifice for our current happiness, we'll be together soon enough. Yes, soon enough.

I know it's hardest this time of year, being the holidays and all. This will be the first Christmas we haven't all been together, and the first of many more. But the tree is full of presents, and I will make sure that John Jr. gets enough love from me for the both of us.

I don't need to ask, as your letters always find me, but please keep writing, my love. I do miss you so.

Rebecca

Mari folded the letter again and placed it carefully in its envelope. She didn't say a word as she looked over at Poole. His furrowed brow and confused look said it all.

"I'm sorry, Mari, this doesn't make sense at all. My mom told me that she hadn't heard from my father since I was fourteen, and that their lives had drifted apart. She said that she wanted a life on the mainland and he didn't want to leave the Jamaican weather and his diving business," Poole said.

"What I just read didn't sound like a person who had drifted apart from her husband, John," she replied. "In fact, it sounded like…well, you know what it sounded like."

"I know. And I can't believe it. Do you think that they kept in contact all of those years?"

"Looking at a l these letters, I'd say yes," Mari said as she dug through the package, searching for the most recent postmark dates. After about a minute, she pulled out another envelope. "Here's one from a little over five years ago." She handed the envelope to Poole.

"The postmark date is October 14, 2008. That was six weeks before she died." Poole's voice trailed away.

Mari reached over and touched his hand. "It's OK. You reed to do this."

Poole cleared his throat and slowly unfolded the letter. He looked at the shaky handwriting and started reading aloud:

10/14/08

Dearest John Morgan,

It looks like we've been cheated in spite of all our plans. I've tried my best to fight, but the doctors say that there's nothing left that they can do. I understand and have reached a level of peace with it. Although i miss you so much, I'm glad that you haven't been here to see my looks stolen from me. I know a woman of fifty-six shouldn't worry about things like that, but I did so want to be that young woman you remembered when we were finally able to share our lives together again.

John has been everything that we've dreamed. So strong and handsome; he's an image of his father. I am comforted by the knowledge that it won't be long before you will be back in his life. I only hope that he will understand and be able to forgive us.

I've come to question some of the things we've done, but hindsight is twenty-twenty, as they say.

Your letters still remain a joy to me. My only regret is that soon they will stop. For your sake, I hope that you find love again in your life, John Morgan. I truly do.

You are, and always will be, my first and only love.

Rebecca

Poole looked over at Mari as she was wiping the tears away from her eyes. Although he too was emotional, Poole was too stunned to say another word or shed another tear. He shoved the letter and the envelope back into the package and pushed it toward Mari. "Please keep these for now, would you? I'm thinking I just need to clear my head for a while," Poole said with a weak smile.

"Oh, John. You've had one hell of a day. Make that one hell of a week," Mari said, trying to comfort him. "Every time you turn around, there seems to be something else slapping you in the face."

"Slapping might be kind, actually. I will say that this trip is turning out to be a little bit different than I had originally planned," Poole replied.

"Did you have any idea that your mother and father were communicating all those years?"

"None," he said truthfully.

"The other thing I'm trying to figure out is why in the world they even decided to split apart in the first place. It's clear they didn't really want to."

"I was thinking the same thing, Mari," Poole agreed. "Both letters mention some sort of decision. And they also mention my mother's parents as being players in all of it."

"Are your grandparents still alive, or are they gone too?" she asked.

"They passed away a couple of years after my mom did. I didn't know them well at all, really. They came to visit a couple of times, but that was it. After she died, I started receiving small checks from a trust fund that I guess was originally earmarked for her. Nothing to write home about, but it did cover food and gas."

"Did you ever ask anything more about that?"

"No. I wasn't involved in the administration of her estate, and I really didn't want anything to do with it or any inheritance. I figured it was just blood money anyway. I would rather have had my mother back," Poole said.

Mari nodded, thinking of her own father and mother. She understood.

She looked at the package and then realized that she had more of Dunbar's items in her satchel. "Gawd, I'm afraid to even ask what this letter from your father says," Mari said seriously.

"I was sort of thinking the same thing," Poole said. "If you don't mind, I think I'll hold off on that for now. Instead, I think there's something else we need to do."

"What's that?"

Poole waved to Fredrickson. "Order another drink."

TWELVE

Dunbar's law office was in the heart of the market district of Port Maria. The card Dunbar had given to Mari did little good, as she and Poole were unable to find any address numbers to follow. After asking a few locals, they found their way to a small storefront wedged between the stand of a fruit vendor and the clothing racks of a garment maker. The faded blue paint on the small, uninviting door was scarred and blistered. The sign on the window read simply, "W. Dunbar, Esq."

They entered warily at the stroke of ten. The small waiting room contained three worn chairs and a small teak table with faded water stains left by unattended cups and glasses. The outside light filtered in through the dirty front window, making the place feel like it was straight out of a forties movie. Boxes were stacked against the wall to the right of the entrance, and a series of filing cabinets stood guard opposite the window.

A small bell fixed to the top of the door announced their arrival, and immediately Warren Dunbar emerged from a solitary office in the back. "Welcome! Good to see you again, Mr. Poole and Ms. Robeson," he said, offering his hand. "My office is a little messy right now, so please forgive me. Why don't you have a seat here?"

Dunbar motioned to the chairs. Poole and Mari sat opposite Dunbar and waited for him to start the meeting. The sooner the better, as far as Poole was concerned. He had slept like a rock the night before, and the rest had been rejuvenating. His head felt clearer than at any time since he'd stepped foot in Jamaica. But Dunbar's drab office was clouding his mind again, and he couldn't wait to get out of there.

"To start, I want to again extend my condolences to you. I came to know your father based on a mutual interest that we had. In my mind, we were as much friends as counselor and client. Have you had a chance to read your father's will?" Dunbar asked.

"Yes, thank you," Poole replied. "I assume there is a formal administration process that needs to be followed?"

"Yes, there is, but it's not nearly as complicated as in the States. The will needs to be filed with the local magistrate. He issues a certificate of authority, and then you will have the ability to sell or transfer your father's property as you see fit," Dunbar explained.

"Good. I'll need some help with that," Poole replied. "His will specifically listed his boat and a bank account, but that was it. Did he leave some kind of inventory with you?"

"Not an inventory, no; just the items he asked me to hold for him. I'll be right back," Dunbar said as he rose and disappeared into his office.

Poole glanced over at Mari, who was clearly underwhelmed by the environment. She had edged to the front of her seat for a quick getaway.

"Here we go!" Dunbar huffed, as he balanced two boxes and a metal briefcase in front of him.

Poole stood and helped Dunbar. "What's in these?" Poole asked.

"I don't know for sure, but I would guess it's his research," Dunbar replied, as he pulled out a handkerchief to dab his forehead.

"Excuse me. What kind of research?"

"Morgan, of course," he said, as if Poole's question was surprising. "We shared a lot of ideas on the subject. That's how I met your father in the first place."

"How was that?" Poole asked.

"Well, it was quite by accident one day at the Kingston library. We were both perusing accounts of Henry Morgan's campaigns against the Spanish while he was a commissioned privateer for England. After several meetings and hours of speculation, we both became convinced that a large portion of Morgan's wealth was never disclosed or found. Fascinating stuff, really," Dunbar explained.

"So you worked together to find this treasure?" Poole queried.

"I wouldn't go that far. It was more of an academic exercise for me. Your father was the one that was gung ho about actually finding it. It also helped that he was an expert diver and could follow up on his theories. As you can see, I'm not much of a man of action anymore," Dunbar said, shrugging in resignation.

"There's nothing wrong with that, Mr. Dunbar. Being a man of action may very well be the reason why my father is dead," Poole said solemnly.

"Nasty stuff, indeed, Mr. Poole. I can't even imagine," Dunbar said, shaking his head. "Take your time and let me know when you want me to prepare that paperwork we discussed."

Everyone stood. Poole gave the briefcase to Mari, and he easily lifted the two boxes to his waist. "Thank you, Mr. Dunbar. I'm looking forward to working with you. We'll be in touch."

"Please, call me Warren," he said.

"Wait, Mr. Dunbar...I'm sorry, Warren," Mari interjected holding up the briefcase and pointing at the combination lock. "Do you know what the combination code is?"

"I'm sorry, I don't. I assumed that it would be open, but perhaps the code can be found in the boxes," he offered, again wiping his handkerchief over his face.

"We'll figure it out, Mr. Dunbar. Thanks again," Poole said as Mari reached behind him to open the door.

They said their good-byes, and Poole and Mari returned to the now bustling market. Dunbar looked after them until they disappeared into the throng of tourists and local shoppers.

Poole and Mari weaved their way through the streets, ignoring the calls of the merchants, until they reached the Mustang. Once they'd placed the boxes and briefcase in the backseat, they climbed over the welded doors, looked at each other, and shook their heads in unison.

"Unusual little guy," Mari reflected.

"Not the most organized, either. Pretty stark contrast between him and my father," Poole added. "At least they worked together, so maybe he can shed some light on some of those clues down the road."

"All you need is more boxes to open, John," Mari said, staring at the backseat.

"That's OK, Mari. I think it's time to open up everything and find out what I'm supposed to find out."

Safely back on the *Rebecca*, Poole set up shop on the aft deck. He was finally becoming acclimated to the beating Jamaican sun, and his skin was turning a golden brown. He wore a black V-neck T-shirt and khaki-colored cargo shorts as he sat in the folding chair. His bare feet were propped on one of the boxes they had just retrieved from Dunbar's office.

Mari emerged from the main cabin wearing a bright, coral-colored bikini top and a white wraparound skirt. "Can I get you anything, John?" she asked.

Poole looked up and smiled. It amazed him how many different looks Mari had, and it struck him how stunning she was, both physically and mentally. "Thanks, but not right yet," he said. "I have to make a couple of phone calls first."

He then picked up his cell phone and dialed his office in Seattle.

"John, is that you?" the familiar voice of his assistant, Angie, asked mockingly. "I figured you decided to leave me for another woman!"

"Hi Angie, I miss you too," Poole responded, meaning it. He and Angie had been tied at the hip for the past five years, and she was as much his family as anyone was.

"How's it going down there? Did everything work out at the service?" she pressed.

"Everything's fine. But it looks like the administration of the estate might take some more time," Poole replied. "How are we doing up there?'

"Your case load is fine. I've taken care of the small matters, and your clients are all happy. Tom has taken on all the bigger stuff, and he's as happy as a clam. That guy loves to work," Angie responded.

"Well, he's also going to be collecting all those fees too!" Poole said, laughing. "I'll need you to transfer me over to him in a second, though. It looks like I might be here longer than expected."

"How long are you thinking, John?" she asked.

"I haven't really figured it out entirely, but I'm thinking at least a month. Do you think I'll have a practice left if I'm gone that long? More importantly, can you live without me that long?"

"The practice will be fine. As for me, I guess I'll just have to pay more attention to my real husband while you're gone." Angie laughed.

Poole laughed along with her. Angie always called him her second husband. The truth of the matter was that they had become great friends, and she was the only thing that made work bearable for him.

"Tom just got off his phone. I'd better transfer you over before he grabs another line. I'll talk to you soon!" Angie said. Then Poole heard a click, and she was gone.

After a couple of seconds, the chipper voice of Tom Patterson came on the line. "John Boy! How's it going down there?" he asked.

"Hi, Tom. Good to hear your voice," Poole answered. "It looks like I may be taking a bit more time down here than I anticipated."

"No problem. That's what partners are for. How much time do you need?"

"Can you do without me for another month or so? The administration might take a while, and there are some personal things of my father's I need to sort out."

"Take as much time as you need. My caseload has been down a bit, so I've got the extra time to step in. We're managing fine without you," Tom said.

"As long as you're not managing too well without me, buddy!" Poole said, laughing.

"Don't worry about that. I'm not that much of a workaholic," Tom answered. "But Angie's going to be a little bummed that you're gone for that long. She was planning this big birthday deal for your fortieth," Patterson revealed.

"Yeah, I know. The worst-kept secret around," Poole said, smiling. Poole never really enjoyed his birthday as much as his friends enjoyed theirs, since it was on April 15. "I'll try to be back if I can, but if not, Uncle Sam and I will celebrate on our own!" They shared a laugh.

"I'll let you go, Tom. I know you're busy. If you need anything, I'll be right here on this yacht thinking of you."

"Love you too, John. You bastard! We'll talk soon," Tom replied. Laughing aloud, he hung up the phone.

Mari sat down opposite Poole and brought her note pad with her. "So you're staying a bit longer with us, Mr. Poole?" she pried.

Poole pushed his sunglasses down his nose, revealing smiling eyes. "Well, I can't go back now If I'm going to do this, I might as well do it right. I guess I do have to ask you something, though. I know you've got a life of your own, and you don't have to play nursemaid to me. And obviously, the diving business doesn't exist anymore. So why stay?"

"Remember, I've managed to save some money so I don't need to go anywhere or do anything else for a while. And the way I see it, I owe it to your father. He looked after me," she said in a serious tone. "But there are two other reasons," she added.

"What are those?"

"One is that I still live here—at least for the time being—so I'd better do something to earn my keep!" she laughed.

"And the other?" Pool asked.

"I kind of like you," Mari said, giving Poole a small smile before she looked down to her note pad.

Poole and Mari turned their attention back to the boxes and brief-case. Along with the other documents and letters they already had, the task seemed daunting.

"Let's go back to the beginning. It's been almost a week since we went through some of this stuff. I don't know about you, but I'm a little hazy on where we left it," Poole admitted.

"Let's start with my notes on what your father said that morning in the hospital," Mari offered.

"Good."

"Let's see," she said, looking at the yellow pad. "First love, Duhbar, keys, Morgan, follow the woman, end/start, my Donna's heart, and it's in her hands."

"That's right. We now know the good counselor, Dunbar, and I think we've got a good hunch who the woman was that my father said to follow."

"There's also first love," Mari chimed in. "Those were the words your mother used in one of her letters."

"That's one possibility, Mari. But somehow, I can't help but think it also had to do with that Spanish woman," Poole said. "What's left again?"

"Keys, my Donna's heart, and it's in her hands."

"Geez, something's telling me we're missing something. Think, John!" Poole said, showing his frustration.

"Let's look through these boxes. Maybe something will surface," Mari suggested.

They each took a box. The island breeze was gentle, so they decided to stay out on the deck. After peeling off the clear plastic tape that sealed the boxes, they started digging. Poole's box contained copies of old charts from the 1600s and correspondence between Morgan and the governor of Port Royal, Thomas Modyford. At the bottom, he found a thin file labeled "Maria Robeson."

"Hey, I found your employment file!" Poole exclaimed, waving it. "Now I've got the goods on you!"

"Oh, give me that, John!" Mari responded.

"Not quite yet. I need to know if you really have that college degree or you fibbed to get the job!" Poole teased Mari. "Let's see.

College, check. Jamaican heritage, check. Hey, you've got a birth-day coming up! Yours is a week after mine."

"At least you'll always be older than me, John," Mari replied.

Poole raised his eyebrows at her birth date. There's no way you're in your thirties, Mari!"

"Good breeding," she said, patting the underside of her chin. "When's your birthday?"

"April 15, tax day."

"At least that will be easy to remember," Mari said. "Remind me to embarrass you with my horrible rendition of 'Happy Birthday'."

"What was that?" Poole said, sitting up.

"Are you deaf, or do you want me to sing it now?"

"No! You said 'Happy Birthday.' Don't you remember? My father said that at the hospital. Let me think for a second." Poole looked toward the horizon, trying to remember exactly. "He said, 'Birthday is a good thing to remember. Um, I remember, you were there...you remember.' That was it!"

Mari quickly wrote it down in her notes. "That sounds right, John. But what does it mean?"

"Well, if you string it together it kind of sounds like he was talk-ing about my birthday, doesn't it?" Poole guessed.

"Could be," Mari agreed. "He said you were there, you remem-ber. I don't know if there's any other explanation. But what's that got to do with anything?"

Poole was silent for a second. "I have an idea. It's a little too simple, but I guess it's worth a shot."

"What is it?" Mari asked.

"Can you pass that briefcase over to me?" Poole asked. Mari reached over and handed the metal case to Poole. He held it in his lap and looked at the three-digit combinations on each side of the latches. "Here goes nothing. Oh-four, one-five, seven-four."

Poole fixed his gaze on Mari and pulled the slides toward the outside of the case. The latches popped open with a click. Poole and Mari looked at each other, holding their breath, as Poole gave her a smug look.

"Are you going to sit there and feel proud of yourself or are you going to open the damn thing?" Mari cried.

Poole slowly raised the lid and looked inside. Mari couldn't stand his confused look any longer. "So, what the heck is in there?"

Poole turned the briefcase around. Inside was a solitary key with a tag that said First Caribbean Bank Kingston.

"Well, now we know what he meant by that 'key is the key' thing. He even sort of laughed about it. I'm getting the strange feeling that this is going to turn into some kind of scavenger hunt."

"Well, it looks like it belongs to a safe deposit box. When should we go check it out?" Mari asked.

"You know, I think we should just see what you have over there first," Poole said, pointing to her box of documents. "We'll get to it soon enough."

Mari didn't press. "It looks like this one just has a bunch of old birth records or something like that. We're talking very old ledgers, by the looks of them."

"Let me take a peek," Poole said, looking at the contents.

"What do you think?"

"You know, these could be copies of old church records. My guess is that he was searching for some kind of direct link to Henry Morgan, or perhaps even a clue as to the identity of the mysterious Spanish woman."

"But why church records?"

"The church probably kept the best records back in those times. My vote is to take a little trip to visit Father Michael. There might be more to his conversations with my father than he let on."

THIRTEEN

January 1671

Morgan sat near the altar of the Catholic church in the center of Panama City. While he made plans for defending the city from any reprisals from the Spanish, his men would periodically come in with sacks of valuables. One of his lieutenants cataloged the take and put the gold, silver, and jewels into separate piles.

The Spanish had tried desperately to hide their treasures, but Morgan's men ferreted out most of the hiding places. They scoured surrounding woods, dredged cisterns, and even waded the shoreline.

His men also had returned to a better state of health, having eaten well for the last several days. The Spanish had an abundance of grain, and beef cattle were plentiful. As their health returned, so did their voraciousness for drink and women. His men deserved the spoils of war if a raid was successful, and this time was no exception.

Morgan only had one rule. All of the women were to be presented to him personally for inspection. He alone would determine whether a woman would be held for ransom, taken as a slave, or released to his men.

One of his lieutenants entered the church and requested an audience. Morgan looked up from the rough sketch he had made of the city's perimeter. "Yes, Mr. Allenby? What is it?"

"We've rounded up several of the residents hiding in the jungle to the east. Per your orders, I have an inspection ready for you when convenient," his lieutenant reported.

Tiring of his preparations, Morgan needed the distraction. "Show them in, Mr. Allenby," he ordered.

A queue of about twenty women was led into the sanctuary. They ranged from girls just reaching their womanhood to elderly women in their late forties. They were each presented to Morgan, who leaned casually on the edge of the altar. Most entered with their heads bent, staring at the floor. Allenby grabbed their chins so that Morgan could see their faces. Morgan waved his hand casually, indicating their ultimate disposition, as the queue moved past him.

The last woman strode confidently before Morgan. She did not need Allenby's assistance, and she stared directly at her captor. Morgan was taken aback by this woman's defiance. But it was the flash in her dark eyes, the elegance of her nose, and the set of her chin that made him stop and study her. Her beauty was exquisite. He had never seen a woman her equal.

"Do you know who I am?" he asked the raven-haired beauty.

"You are a godless pirate and you have captured my city," she replied, her English remarkably refined.

"Yes, I have captured your city, and you are here at my pleasure." Morgan rose from his perch and approached the woman. "Forgive me, Senora. I forget my manners. My name is Henry Morgan. And you are?"

"Your captive and slave," she replied, staring back.

"Perhaps and perhaps not. We godless pirates can be quite fair in our dealings with our enemies. It really depends on how much they want to make the best of an unfortunate situation."

"That does not change anything, sir. What I want or don't want is unimportant. You will do what you will do," she said, continuing to meet his gaze.

"Well then, so be it," Morgan said. "Mr. Allenby, you are to take this 'slave' to the villa I have taken for quarters. Place her in custody there with Mr. Kirkland. I will decide what to do with her later."

Morgan stared intently at the woman as she was led away. Her posture was perfect, her bearing seemed almost regal, and her manner a well-practiced reaction to the advances of men. Morgan smiled. That is why she's not intimidated or afraid, he thought. She's never had to be.

Morgan went back to the city's defenses. Several other women were presented for review throughout the day, but he took no special notice of them. His mind was elsewhere. His mind was on the beautiful woman who would be waiting for him at his quarters later that evening.

FOURTEEN

The deep voice of Robert Coy greeted Poole as he entered the café. "Mr. John! Take a seat, my friend, and have a cup of coffee."

"Thank you, Robert," Poole said, sitting down at the counter. Mari was still sleeping when he left the boat—a first. They had sifted through the remaining contents of the boxes and done their best to find a clue or pattern in the birth records his father had put together. It was late when they finally retired. Poole stayed in the main cabin, while Mari again took her stateroom below.

"Do you guys actually serve breakfast around here, or do you just talk about it?" Poole teased Robert.

"We talk and we do," Robert replied, smiling and pointing a finger at Poole. "The only thing we don't do is read minds. So if you want something, it would help if you let me know!"

They both laughed.

"Eggs and bacon—or ham or sausage or whatever meat grows on your lovely island, Robert; I don't care," Poole offered.

"Close enough. I'll take care of the rest," Robert said, walking to the kitchen.

Poole sipped on his cup of coffee and pulled the letter from his back pocket. It was plain white, and "John Poole Jr." was printed in simple block letters on its face. Although the flap was glued shut by the traditional lick method, a separate red wax seal also protected the contents of the envelope.

He toyed with his cup of coffee, trying to decide when and how to deal with the letter. He tried to catch a glimpse of the contents by holding it up to the light, and then closely examined the scrollwork of the capital P imbedded in the red wax.

"What have you got there, Mr. John?" Robert asked, as he returned from the kitchen to refill Poole's coffee cup.

"It's a letter from my father. It even has this fancy seal on it. It seems pretty important and, I guess, pretty daunting too. I've been putting it off, and I'm not even sure I want to know what's in it," Poole admitted.

"Only one way to find out what's inside, my friend," Robert said. "My mother used to tell me something that I still follow to this day. 'If you don't ask, you don't dance.'"

Poole smiled. "Well, that's one way to put it," he said as Robert went back to the kitchen for his breakfast. Poole picked up the letter again and placed the seal between his thumb and index finger. "So what do you think, darlin'? Shall we?" he asked as he broke the seal in two.

> *My Dear John:*
>
> *If you are reading this letter then I am gone and you have fulfilled my fervent wish that you come to Jamaica. I can only imagine the conflicts you have felt in doing this. I do not blame you for erasing me from your life based on what you believe I have done to you and your mother. You deserve an explanation, however late it might be.*
>
> *I had hoped to sit with you as father and son, and pray for forgiveness and understanding. The events of my past—and the decisions your mother and I made—cannot be magically undone, but I hope you will eventually know that the best of intentions were the motivation behind them.*
>
> *Your mother and I met in the summer of 1971. She had just graduated from college. Her parents'*

graduation gift was a Caribbean cruise with two of her friends. I met her when her ship laid over at Montego Bay. I can honestly tell you that I fell in love with her at first sight, and we both soon realized that there was a connection between us that could not be ignored. The layover was for two days, but she decided to leave her friends and stay on the island with me.

Rebecca's parents were upset and outraged, and I suppose even feared for her safety, since they didn't know who I was or anything. They even called the local police to investigate. It was a mess. Rebecca refused to leave the island, choosing to stay with me on my little dive boat. We were young and in love, and I guess it was also the times that made her rebel and made me stand with her.

Her parents lived in San Diego. They had some money and threatened to disinherit her and anything else they could think of. Obviously, they hated me for coming into her life and, in their eyes, stealing her away to a penniless life they didn't understand. Rebecca didn't care. She kept telling me that love didn't have a monetary value, and if you were lucky enough to find it, you shouldn't let anyone take it away from you.

When her parents came to realize there was nothing they could do legally, they washed their hands of her. I pleaded with her to reconsider and mend that fence, since my parents abandoned me when I was young and left me to grow up in foster care. But she was just as stubborn as her parents, and the rift between them became a chasm.

So our life together began. We worked my small diving business, and we managed to make a modest living. We really didn't need more than that. We lived *and worked on the boat, and each day our love grew deeper.*

In spite of the difficulties with her parents, your mother knew that I still had to resolve the issues I had with mine. She encouraged me to find out who they were and to know my own history. So we both set out on a journey of exploration. That led to the realization that perhaps my roots went as far back as Sir Henry Morgan! We were both captivated by the prospect of that link. Your mother was even more excited about it than I was. So we started researching all things relating to Morgan, since we lived right where he had sailed so many years before.

You should know that my given name was John Michael Poole. At your mother's insistence, I had it legally changed to John Morgan Poole. It was a lark at the time, but it was a fun secret that we shared. Somewhere, I still have an eye patch she bought me to commemorate the event.

The most priceless moment by far, however, was when we were blessed to have you come into our lives. I remember every detail of that day. The nurses were astounded at the ease of the birth, and how alert and inquisitive you were within hours of being born. Your mother and I couldn't have been happier. And I finally felt like I had a family, a true family for once in my life.

In spite of the love your mother and I had for you and each other, we soon came to realize that we needed to provide a better home for you. My small boat was no place to raise a baby. And our diving business was enough to make ends meet for just me and your mother, but not nearly enough to raise a family on. At that time, there were no other jobs to be had. The economy was suffering, and our options were limited.

One day, your mother came back from a doctor's appointment with you and said that you needed special medical treatment for a blood disorder. It scared us both to death—not only for you, but also for how we could even manage it financially. Later that night, she went out to get some groceries. When she came back, she told me that she had a possible solution.

She said that she had called her parents. I remember that she was crying as she related how difficult it was. Her parents said that they would help, not for her—and certainly not for me—but for their only grandchild. However, that help didn't come without a price. They would step in as long as your mother left me and Jamaica. They would provide for her and you financially as long as I wasn't in the picture.

I can't tell you how difficult that night on the boat was. Love dictated our every decision—our love for you. For once in my life, I had the family that I had dreamed of, only to be left with the decision to break it apart. I was devastated, but knew it was the right thing to do for your sake. So the next morning, your mother called her parents and agreed to their terms.

It disgusts me now, to think that I had consented to see you only occasionally. But you were sick, and I would have agreed to anything at that point. It was touch and go for a while as your condition worsened. But over time you got stronger, and the disorder simply disappeared. The doctors had no explanation, but I truly believe that our love for you had something to do with it.

You need to know that your grandparents set up a trust fund for you and your mother. I don't know the exact details, other than that if the conditions were not met, the financial help would stop. We reluctantly *agreed to those terms. Our only motivation was your health and safety.*

I was allowed to fly up for your birthdays, and we could spend Christmas holidays together. But you and your mother were never allowed to visit me in Jamaica. We found a way to communicate through a friend of hers so as not to violate the terms of the trust. She would send me pictures of you playing ball or swimming. Those pictures made me so happy, and so sad at the same time for not being there with you, guiding you.

You should also know that it wasn't my decision to stop flying up to Seattle. You can blame the Immigration Department for that. They wouldn't allow my continued visits to the country without a work visa or sponsorship. That meant I had to stay on a permanent basis or not at all. That happened when you were around fourteen. Your mother and I were devastated.

Our plan was to become a family again after the terms of the trust were satisfied. In the meantime, my only thought was to try to provide for you and your mother in my own way. She encouraged me to continue to find my roots. So I immersed myself in Henry Morgan. I thought that if I could somehow find a cache of gold or something, I could buy our way out of the trust, and we could be reunited sooner.

But I hadn't counted on your mother's cancer. God had a different plan. It took me a couple of years before my focus returned. I was angry and blamed myself for allowing all of it to happen. I had lost the only woman I ever loved, and without your mother to explain and encourage you, there didn't seem to be any hope for getting you back in my life.

Perhaps in death I can at least give you some answers that I could not give you in life, not only with this letter, but with the work that I've done to find my roots—and yours. You deserve it.

I know that I am very close to the end of that journey. I fear that others want to know what I have learned, so I have left a path for only you to follow. I ask, for your sake, that you follow this path to its end. I truly believe that only then will you be able to find contentment in your own life.

I know this letter will be difficult for you, just as difficult as our decision was to split up our family those many years ago. But you've grown to be the man that we had hoped. That alone was worth it.

Dad

Poole hadn't noticed the plate of ham and eggs that had grown cold while he read his father's letter. After seeing Poole's intent expression, Robert knew better than to interrupt him.

Poole placed the open letter on the counter and looked up at Robert, who was leaning against the wall, trying not to pry. He came over, collected the plate, and filled up a new cup of coffee.

"It looks like you didn't care for the ham," Robert said as he walked back to the kitchen. "Let me see how our thick slab bacon moves you."

Poole took a sip of the steaming coffee and looked out to the marina. He could see Mari walking up the dock to find him. He gazed at the backdrop of the green-blue of the water, and a calm he had never felt before settled over him.

Mari walked into the café and sat next to him. She saw the open letter and looked at him with questioning eyes.

"It's a confessional of sorts," Poole said. "Now I know the whole truth and nothing but the truth."

"What are you going to do now, John?" she asked.

He smiled and realized just then that he had come to a decision. "I'm going to follow the woman."

"That's the first smart thing you've said since you've been here," she said, giving him a light tap on the shoulder with the back of her hand. "But we've gone through those records, and I'm not sure if we've got enough to go on right now."

"On the contrary, we've got a key and the name of a bank," Poole replied. "At least that's a start. Let's go see if the good folks at First Caribbean will let us make a withdrawal."

FIFTEEN

Against his better judgment, Poole flipped the car keys to Mari. According to the tag on the safe deposit key, their next stop was the main branch of the First Caribbean Bank in Kingston. It was a thirty-minute drive that Poole figured Mari could negotiate in about twenty. A bank of clouds had rolled in, obscuring the piercing sun, and Poole relished the break. His Seattle roots ran deep.

Mari revved the throaty engine of the Mustang, and they were off. True to form, Mari took the Mustang through its paces on the straight stretches of the highway but throttled back for the curves. Poole knew she did that for his benefit, and he could see a smile come to her face when she did.

In spite of their speed, a 1980s Mercedes kept pace. A blanket of red dust hid the car's black paint, and a trail of smoke belied its diesel engine. A short Jamaican man was driving and a taller Jamaican was in the passenger seat. A lone figure sat in the back, closely eyeing the gray Mustang as it sped to Kingston.

The bank manager was a pleasant-looking Latin woman in her forties. Her smile was engaging and her pearl earrings complemented her cream-colored dress. Poole introduced himself, and he and Mari sat in padded wicker chairs at the woman's desk.

"Good to meet you, Mr. Poole. My name is Kathleen Melendez. How may I be of assistance?" she asked as she gave Poole her business card.

"I'm not quite sure," Poole admitted. "My father just passed away. No official paperwork has been filed yet, but I was given this key, which I assume belongs to a safe deposit box here."

"Yes, let me see that." She looked at the number on the key. "One moment, please." She walked to a computer on the other side of the lobby and punched in a couple of keystrokes. A minute later, she returned.

"Do you have any identification with you, Mr. Poole?" she asked politely. After Poole showed her his driver's license and passport, she handed the key back to him. "This is one of our deposit-box keys, and it's for this branch. We have several on the island, you know, so you were fortunate to come here first. There won't be any need for additional paperwork at this point, as you're already named as an owner on the account," she continued. "Please follow me."

They all stood, proceeded to a separate area of the main lobby, and entered a large walk-in vault. "You may use one of these tables, if you like." She continued to an adjoining room in which rectangular enclosures covered one wall. "Let's see, Number 256 should be right here," she said, pointing to a door in the corner of the room. "I'll leave you here for now. When you're finished, please dial my extension on this wall phone and I will come and get you."

The door gently closed behind her as she left.

Poole took the key and stood in front of Number 256. He inserted the key and turned. The box slid fluidly out of its housing, and Poole carried it over to the table where Mari was waiting and sat down next to her.

"What do you think?" Poole asked, feeling the anticipation in his stomach.

"No time like the present, John."

Without waiting for Poole, Mari lifted the top of the box. Inside was a folded sheet of paper, an old leather-bound book, a small leather bag with a drawstring pulled tight at the top, and a key to another safe deposit box at First Caribbean.

Both were somewhat disappointed when they looked at the meager contents. "His letter did say that he left a path for me to follow. This must be the start," Poole said.

The number on the key said A-95. He put it in his pocket and reached over to the leather bag while Mari carefully took out the book. After he loosened the tie, he turned it over and gently emptied its contents on the table. The bag was fairly new, but the contents were not. Before them were a handful of old Spanish gold coins and a single emerald, about five carats in size.

Poole let out a low whistle. "I wonder where he got this stuff?" he asked.

"I'd guess he found it over the years. When I dove for him, we found potsherds and an occasional gold nugget or piece of eight, but nothing like this," she offered.

"Well, it looks like he might have found a bit more when you weren't around. This isn't enough to get rich on, but it does have some value," Poole said as he pulled out his phone. "I'm going to take a couple of pictures of this stuff. Mari, can you place the eraser of your pencil in the shot to give it scale?"

After he took some shots, Poole put the coins and jewel back in the pouch and placed it back in the deposit box. They then turned their attention to the small book.

Mari touched it gingerly. "This thing is old. I'm not sure I should even pick it up with my bare hands. I've seen movies where old stuff like this turns to dust if you don't know what you're doing."

Poole gently slid the book from Mari and raised the front cover.

"What language is that?" Mari asked, not recognizing the text.

"Latin, or at least a local form of it. Maybe something did rub off after all those years in law school." Poole shrugged. "But recognizing the language is as far as I can go. Reading it is another story."

"Maybe this will help," she said as she unfolded the sheet of yellow paper. They both read the block letters created by his father's hand. It said Ms. Hattie Dixon, 26-24 Adelaide Street, Spanish Town.

"Unless I miss my guess, I bet Ms. Hattie Dixon knows how to read this book," Poole stated. "What do you say, Mari. Feel like going to Spanish Town?"

She nodded as they carefully placed the book in her satchel. "No problem, as long as I still get to drive."

M s. Hattie Dixon opened the door before Poole and Mari had traversed the pathway from the curb to her porch. Poole stopped in his tracks while she sized him up. "You must be the boy. May your handsome daddy rest in peace," she said, shaking her head. "Come in."

Poole and Mari were offered chairs in the sitting room of the small but comfortable house. Right after they entered, they heard the intermittent patter of raindrops on the metal roof. Their host opened a window to let the cooling air freshen the room.

Hattie Dixon was a large, dark-skinned woman in her late seventies. Her hair was graying, but the color betrayed her age only a little, as her skin didn't have a wrinkle on it. "Your daddy said that there was a chance that I would be visited again by a younger version of himself," she started. "He also said that if that was the case, he'd be dead. Am I right?"

Poole nodded. "Yes, ma'am. I'm his son, John Poole Jr. My father passed away about a week ago."

She shook her head as she made the sign of the cross. "Call me Ms. Hattie, son. Your daddy said that he might be getting into a tight spot. I suppose it had something to do with that book he found."

"I'm not sure, Ms. Hattie, but it might." Poole said honestly. "Is it correct that you were able to read it?"

"That's right, I could. I learned Latin in Catholic school as a little girl. Been around books all my life. I was the librarian here in Spanish Town for forty years until they made me retire. Hell, I'm still better than what they got over there now!" she sniffed.

"How long ago did my father come visit you, Ms. Hattie?" Poole asked, trying to keep her focused.

"About a year ago, give or take," she answered. "I read the book from front to back, and he took notes. It wasn't easy since it was written so long ago and there were some local idioms that I had to interpret. It took us a couple of sessions, but we got it all sorted out."

"Was there anything in particular that my father was trying to find with your help?" Poole asked.

"I'm sorry, darling. My memory isn't quite as good as it used to be," she replied.

Mari gently pulled the book from her satchel. "Ms. Hattie, would it help if you took a look at it again? Of course, we'll pay you for our intrusion."

"Why, thank you, child. A woman's got to eat," Ms. Hattie said as she took the book. After several minutes of silence, she closed the book and gave it back to Mari.

"Now I recall. This was an account of a young boy on one of Morgan's ships that sailed from Panama back to Jamaica. I remember that it said he was around ten years old, which was not uncommon in those days." She stood and put the palm of her hand up, signaling them to stay put. "Please forgive me; I've been a terrible host. I'll be right back with some tea."

A minute later, she returned with a tray of ice-cold, sweetened tea. They all took sips of the nectar, and she continued. "That's better. Now where was I?"

"The trip from Panama," Poole helped.

"That's right, Panama. Well, this young boy was one of the few people aboard. There was a skeleton crew and a handful of passengers. The boy's account suggested that there was a sizable amount of gold and jewels on board. The name of the vessel was never mentioned, as they were all sworn to secrecy on pain of death. But he did mention something that was of great interest to your daddy, Mr. Poole," Ms. Hattie said. "Please let me see that book one more time."

Mari again handed her the book. She carefully leafed through the pages for several more minutes until she stopped about halfway through. "There it is! The boy said that he befriended a woman passenger on board. She was being held under lock and key in the captain's quarters. He was charged with bringing food to her and making sure she received what she wanted or needed."

She continued, "It says here that she was the most beautiful woman he had ever seen, and he had asked her one time if she was a queen or princess. He said her reply was simple. She said that her name was Teresa Montoya Castillo and that she would be the mistress of the house."

Poole took a long sip of the sweet tea and looked at Mari, nodding his head. "Does he say what happened to the cargo that the ship was carrying, Ms. Hattie?"

She looked through the book again, scanning the pages toward the end, read the final page, and closed the book. "It only says that the hold was unloaded in Port Maria, where Morgan owned some land. After it was stowed, the crew never came back for their share. And it mentioned that Morgan somehow got angry with the boy and threatened his life, but the woman interceded. She said that she needed someone to attend to her needs while in Jamaica, so his life was spared."

"Does it mention the boy's name, Ms. Hattie?" Poole asked.

"Yes, of course. It says his name was William Dunn," she answered.

"Thank you so much for your time, Ms. Hattie," Poole said as he stood. Mari walked over to her and shook her hand, giving her several bills as she did.

"Thank you, children. An old woman appreciates it very much!" she said with a well-worn smile. "Any time you need anything, please let me know."

They said their good-byes and jogged to the car, dodging the raindrops. "Time to head back for now," Poole said. "I don't think this bad boy has a retractable roof!"

Mari hopped in behind the wheel and headed off on the slick pavement.

The Mercedes was parked a block down the street. Its wipers swiped away the raindrops every few seconds as they sized up the small house on Adelaide.

"Shall we go in?" the tall man in the front seat asked.

"No. Keep following the Mustang. We can always come back to Spanish Town another day."

SIXTEEN

The rain started coming down harder as they drove toward the north side of the island. For once, Mari took her time.

"The roads can be pretty slick if you don't watch it. You never know if there's a crazy driver around the bend," she said.

Poole felt certain they were safe, since he was riding with the crazy driver. He put Mari's satchel under the passenger seat to keep it dry. "At least we now know the name of the woman, Teresa Montoya Castillo. Even her name sounds beautiful."

"And we also know that the one account we read earlier about Morgan releasing her in Panama was bogus," Mari exclaimed.

"How about the cargo of that ship?" Poole added. "It sure sounds like it made it to Jamaica. It's also interesting that the book said that the skeleton crew never came back for their share. I bet they turned into actual skeletons themselves once they made shore. Morgan was no fool."

"I'm shocked that he let the young boy live," Mari stated. "That woman must have had some pull over him."

"Like Ms. Hattie said, he was only ten, and Morgan probably didn't think he posed much of a threat. Besides, he had no idea where the cargo was stashed. It sounds like he was just trying to please the beautiful Senora Castillo."

"But if the boy didn't know where the cargo was stashed, are we nearing a dead end?"

"Maybe or maybe not. We've got the name of Ms. Castillo, and my father said, 'Follow the woman.' Oh, and we've got this," Poole said, pulling a key from his pocket. "I totally forgot about the other safe deposit box. Maybe we can call the bank and see where this goes. If it's for a local branch, we can drop in on our way back to the marina."

The clouds got darker and the raindrops, larger, as they made their way to the north shore of the island. Besides the rain, they were getting soaked by the spray the Mustang lifted up. Mari checked the rearview mirror and then looked back to the road ahead. "That's weird."

"What's that?" Poole asked with his head tucked behind the windshield.

"Don't turn around, but I swear that car back there was behind us when we went into Kingston this morning. Probably a coincidence." She shrugged.

"I'm beginning to think nothing is a coincidence around here, Mari. Why don't you step on it a little bit and see what happens."

Mari increased her speed by ten miles per hour. Poole glanced into the passenger-side mirror and saw that the Mercedes kept pace.

"Let's forget about any side trips right now. First, give me the number for the café. I want to see if Robert might have a couple of friends who could come and meet us when we get to the marina, just in case," Poole said.

Mari gave him the number, and Robert said he was more than happy to help.

"Second," Poole continued. "We're damned stupid to be traveling around with this book. We need to find a secure place to hide it until we get a chance to put it back in the safe deposit box."

They continued at a steady speed on the A3 heading north. Mari thought briefly about evasive maneuvers. "At least we'd know for sure they're following us," she said.

But Poole talked her out of it. "My father said that others wanted to know what he had learned, so I'm going to take him at his word," Poole replied. "Robert will have a little party waiting for us, so we should be OK. Hell, Robert alone should be enough to scare a bad guy away!"

The rain had turned into a full-blown downpour by the time they got back to the marina. Robert was on the veranda keeping an eye out with a couple of his friends. Mari stopped the Mustang short of the parking lot, and she and Poole stared at the side mirrors. In less than a minute, the Merceces drove past at regular speed and disappeared around the next bend.

Mari looked over at Poole, and they took a collective breath. She pulled the Mustang up behind the café, and Robert met them there. "Hey, Cousin, thanks for meeting us! Can you open the door to the garage for me?" she asked, her hair dripping wet.

Poole grabbed Mari's satchel and jumped over the passenger-side door. He kept it tucked under him as he ran to the kitchen door of the café. Mari followed as soon as the garage doors swung shut and Robert locked them.

Robert took Poole and Mari to a back room and threw them a couple of towels from the kitchen. "Thank you, Robert," Poole said. "Maybe we're being paranoid, but I didn't have a good feeling about that car."

"Don't worry, Mr. John, we've got your back," Robert said looking over to his friends. "These are my poker buddies. They live next door—and they don't like cheaters."

Poole went over to Robert's friends, Gordon and Wesley, who were friendly and quite approachable, in spite of the shotguns propped against their chairs. "Remind me not to play poker with you guys," Poole said appreciatively as he shook their hands.

Robert came over and laid a hand on Poole's shoulder. "I called the missus, and it'll be CK for me to stay here for the night just to keep an eye on things."

"Thank you, Robert," Poole said, grabbing his shoulder in return.

"Now I suggest you and Mari go down to the boat and get cleaned up," Robert said as he looked at his watch. "Dinner is at six, and poker starts at eight!"

Robert pointed a finger at his friends. "It's OK to play, Mr. John. Just as long as you let us win!" His laugh filled the whole room.

Poole and Mari ran down to the boat in the rain. Robert had put Poole's book in a plastic takeout bag to protect it, and it was the only thing dry as they opened the main cabin door.

"You take a shower first," Poole said to Mari. "I'll dry off up here and find a place for this book."

Mari descended to the lower staterooms as Poole pondered their next move. He didn't have a clue of what to do, so he grabbed a towel and started drying off. John Morgan was smart to put this stuff in a secure place, he thought, looking at the book. He hunted around but didn't see any place in the main cabin that would do, so he went below and entered his father's stateroom to look for a place that might work.

It occurred to him that although he had been aboard the *Rebecca* for over a week, it was the first time he set foot in the room. It was a carbon copy of Mari's stateroom with the exception of the bookcase. Shaving cream and cologne sat on the counter in the adjoining head, instead of perfumes and bikini tops.

He sat on the bed and looked around the room. He didn't see any hiding places. He could hear Mari's shower running, and a quick shiver ran through him. It was time to get out of his wet clothes. He looked through his father's closet, sized up some pants and a polo shirt, and decided to take a shower there. He took the ancient book with him and placed it on the counter under a towel.

He needed the warm water cascading over his head and shoulders to ease the tension of the last hour. He picked up the body wash, tilted his head, and chuckled. He used the same brand. The apple doesn't fall far from the tree, he thought.

He jumped out of the shower after only a few minutes, knowing that water was a precious commodity on a boat. After drying off and dressing in a set of his father's clothes, he grabbed the plastic bag and headed up to the main cabin. Mari was already there with a concerned look on her face.

"Oh, John," she said. "What do you think this is all about?"

"I'm not sure, Mari. The only thing I know is that I don't want to get you in the crosshairs of something that doesn't really involve you.

Maybe that car was nothing but a bit of paranoia on our part. But somehow, I don't think so. My gut is telling me that there's somebody out there that wants or needs some information that my father dug up."

Poole went on. "Right now there are only a couple of things we really can do. First, we need to find a place for this book," he said, holding up the white takeout bag. "And second, we can't be driving the Mustang around anymore. If someone is following us around, that car couldn't be any easier to spot."

"When I was in the shower, I thought about a temporary place to keep that book. At least until we take it back to the bank tomorrow," Mari said.

"Where's that?"

Mari grabbed the bag off the dining table and opened the refrigerator door. "It's a takeout bag from the café, right? This seems like a logical place to put leftovers," she announced.

"Good as any." Poole said, admiring her logic. She stuffed the bag on the lower shelf behind a plastic tub of potato salad and a bottle of wine.

"That'll do for now," she said. Since the fridge was open, she brought back an ice-cold bottle of vodka. "Normally, I'd grab a couple of Red Stripes, but right now I think I need something a shade stronger."

Poole grabbed a couple of small glasses from the cupboard and took the bottle. He poured two stiff drinks and handed one to Mari. "You're an incredible woman, Mari," he said, meaning it. He raised his glass, and she walked over to him for the toast.

"I'm seeing this thing through with you, John. It's important to me as well," she said.

They touched glasses, and each took a long sip of the hot, white liquid. Mari didn't move after the toast and the warmth of the vodka filled Poole's senses. He looked into her eyes and felt drawn to her. He touched her shoulder lightly and gently pulled her to him. His lips lingered, almost touching hers, until she reached out to meet him, and they kissed.

SEVENTEEN

March 1671

After several weeks in Panama City, Morgan and his men left with the spoils of their raid. They commandeered oxen and mules from the city to help carry the crates and sacks of treasure as far as they could through the jungle. When they reached the Chagres, his men ordered the slaves to transfer the take onto the flat-bottom boats they had left during their advance. They slaughtered some of the beasts for food and released others into the wild. They'd served their purpose.

Morgan's men bound the hands of the male slaves and tied leather straps tightly around their ankles, leaving just enough slack to allow them to take short, halting strides as they marched. They bound only the hands of the women, as they were too weak to run. One woman was kept separate from the others. Her hands were bound, but loosely. Morgan oversaw every aspect of the returning contingent, but kept a close eye on the woman throughout the journey.

When they reached the mouth of the Chagres, their original five ships were waiting in the harbor along with a sixth, unknown to Morgan. They made camp on the beach to rest and, while Morgan was arranging for the sacks and crates to be loaded, the captain of the guard, who had just landed on an incoming longboat, met him.

"Excuse me, sir. So good to see you! It had been so long that we thought something bad might have happened," he said.

"It'll take more than a few Spaniards for that, Mr. Kemp! However, I don't want to tarry too long on these shores. There's no telling when the Spanish will retaliate, and it seems they have allies in the natives here, as well," Morgan replied.

Kemp hesitated for a moment. "Begging your pardon, sir, but I don't think there will be much worry about reprisals. The *Contessa* arrived two days ago with news," he said, pointing to the sixth vessel. "There has been an accord with Spain for the last few months, even before we landed on these shores. There is talk that the Crown is saying that our raid was unknown to it and unauthorized. The commander of the *Contessa* is requesting an audience in the morning."

Morgan's brow furrowed. He had seen the underbelly of politics and knew nothing good would come of this new development. "Very well then, Mr. Kemp. Please advise the commander that I will be pleased to meet him on shore in the morning."

Morgan continued his preparations. There was much to do before the morning came. He dismissed his purser once the final tally was determined. Then he chose ten of his best men to load selected crates onto the *West Wind*, his fastest ship. He kept one sack in his tent for safekeeping, knowing that none of his men would question him or care enter his quarters.

As dusk approached, Morgan inspected his men and the preparations they were making. He spotted his aide, Kirkland, overseeing the slaves and approached him. "Mr. Kirkland, are you ready to leave this godforsaken place?" Morgan asked, clapping him on the back.

"Aye, aye, sir! Ready as a groom on his wedding night," Kirkland replied.

"Very good. Tell me, how are our captives doing?"

Kirkland leaned closer to Morgan and asked under his breath, "Do you mean Senora Castillo?"

Morgan paused, and then seemed to come to a decision. "Yes, Mr. Kirkland. I'm sure she's had an arduous journey. Please bring her to my tent at your convenience."

Kirkland gave Morgan a quick salute and scurried to comply with his request. Morgan then stopped by the cook's campsite and grabbed some fresh fruit and dried meat to take with him.

Mr. Dunn, a young aide who had stayed back with the shore party, lit the lantern inside Morgan's tent. Morgan then settled back on a small cot delivered from his flagship, *Satisfaction*. Politics, he thought. He knew that greater men than he had incurred the wrath of the Crown so it could avoid embarrassment.

In spite of his success, he knew there would be repercussions. What they would be was uncertain, however. A demotion, he could live with. Or perhaps he would be sent back to England to explain his actions directly to the vice admiral for the West Indies. There was also the real possibility of arrest, or death if his rivals had a say in the matter. Whatever the outcome, he knew this most likely would be his last excursion.

As Morgan was considering the options at hand, the flap of his tent opened and Kirkland ushered in Senora Castillo. "Will that be all, sir?" he asked.

"That will be all for now. Thank you, Mr. Kirkland."

Senora Castillo stood near the entrance of the tent. Morgan rose and offered a seat on the cot. "Please don't be alarmed, Senora. I intend you no further harm and, in spite of what you may be thinking, I ask only that you be my dinner guest this evening."

Morgan offered some of the fruit and dried meat to her. Initially, she stood erect and unmoving, but soon she wavered and grabbed one of the mangoes set out on a small wooden platform.

"Please have a seat. Don't eat too quickly or you'll upset your stomach. Take your time. While you dine, I would like to discuss a matter of importance," Morgan said.

"I have observed you throughout our journey to the Caribbean," he continued as she ate. "You have set a fine example for your people. Although you have had the opportunity for special treatment, you have declined it. I find that an admirable trait—especially in your condition."

Castillo glanced at Morgan with an alarmed look. She sat upright and stopped eating the mango.

"Senora Castillo, while I have taken advantage of my position as a privateer over the years, there were times when I regretted my actions.

This is one of those times. It is apparent that you are showing the first signs of being with child." Morgan stopped and took a drink of wine from the bottle on the platform. "My child, if my calculations are correct."

She lowered her eyes. Her silence confirmed what Morgan had surmised.

"It seems that we are both in a bit of a predicament. I have just learned that an accord has been reached between my country and yours. Should I let you go, I would be forcing you to return to a life of shame. The Catholic Church would require you to give birth to a child not from your marriage, and your husband would disown you out of pride, in spite of your beauty. I can tell by your reaction that I am not far from the truth.

"This fate is not something that you deserve, nor one that you need resign yourself to. So I offer a solution. One, perhaps, that will provide you with a life that will become less painful as the years go by." Morgan paused for a moment and then went on. "I ask that you continue willingly with me to my home in Jamaica. You will be afforded all of the comforts that a man of my wealth and stature can provide. You will have your own house and servants to provide for you. And I will make sure that your child, our child, comes into this world safely."

Senora Castillo broke her silence. "And what does the pirate Morgan wish in return?" she asked.

"That you look beyond the circumstances of our child's conception and you raise it with love and care. That you allow me to visit and do my part to be a father, a privilege that has eluded me so far in my life."

Senora Castillo considered Morgan's proposal. Everything he said was true. Her church left her no options. God forbade the abortion of her child. And taking her own life would condemn her to the eternal fires of hell. She would be ostracized by her church and her husband if she went back, most likely to live a life of poverty in a village far from her home. If she went with Morgan, at least her child would have a chance.

"Is this a 'parlay' in your vernacular, Captain?" she asked.

"Yes, Senora, I suppose it is. I know that my word may mean nothing to you, but I believe both of our circumstances have changed. I fully intend to keep up my end of the bargain."

"Then, under those conditions, I accept," she said.

Morgan smiled. "Excellent. You should know that we will be leaving before the dawn tomorrow. I have made arrangements for a longboat to take us to our ship. You will be spending the night here. I will sleep on the sand, and you shall have the sleeping cot. I ask for your discretion as we depart in the morning. There will be nothing for us to take except what food we have in the tent and that bag in the corner," Morgan said, pointing to the canvas sack he took special care to separate from the others.

"I only ask one more thing of you, and I know it may take many years," Morgan said.

"What is that, Captain?"

Morgan peered intently into her eyes before quickly turning away. "Your forgiveness."

Eighteen

For the first time, Poole slept in his father's stateroom. It felt odd. Lying in his father's bed unleashed a myriad of emotions. Just a few days ago, the man did not even exist in Poole's consciousness. He had never been in his life, and Poole had accepted the fact that his father didn't care about him, in spite of what his mother said. Now the truth had been laid out before him, and the world he knew was completely shaken.

Earlier, Poole and Mari had eaten dinner at the café and joined Robert, Gordon, and Wesley for a game of poker. But Poole had been too distracted to play with any heart. He kept thinking of the kiss he'd shared with Mari. They'd both held their breath afterward as they looked at each other, surprised by the sensation.

When they left the café and walked back to the boat, there was a slight awkwardness between them. They chatted about the money they'd lost to Robert and the things they had to do the following day. When they entered the main cabin, the tension was palpable. It was late, and they each had a few Red Stripes in them. Mari stopped talking and looked briefly at Poole. In that moment, he saw the little girl in her, shy and reserved.

"It's been a long day," she said.

"Yeah," Poole replied. "All the way around."

"Uh," she paused, uncertain of the next words. "I guess it's time for bed."

Poole didn't know exactly how to respond. He was considering the implications of saying the wrong thing. "Yes, I guess you're right," was all that came to mind.

Mari gave him a half smile and descended to her stateroom. Poole stayed in the main cabin to shut down the generator and lock up. He breathed a sigh of relief when he opened the refrigerator and found the takeout bag where they had left it. He pulled it out and took it down to his father's stateroom after turning off the main cabin lights.

He could hear Mari scuffling around in the next cabin as he washed his face and got ready for bed. Damn, he said to himself. Are you a wise man or a fool? He really didn't know the answer.

Poole looked at the small book one more time before he placed it on the shelf behind his head. He closed his eyes and tried to assess the events of the day and concentrate on what they had to do in the morning. But his thoughts kept drifting back to Mari and the taste of her soft, tender lips.

Poole woke up before Mari did for the second day in a row. He was getting acclimated to the time change and looked forward to watching the sun rise. He decided against his usual morning coffee. He opted for some leftover sweetened tea and walked out on the aft deck to breathe in the morning air.

He brought up the small Latin book to look at with fresh eyes, but it was beyond him. Then he pulled out his phone and looked at the photos they'd taken of the gold coins and emerald, trying to discern if there was anything significant about them. He looked through the various shots several times, but nothing came to mind. He put the phone back in his pocket as the sun's first rays peeked over the horizon. He closed his eyes briefly and soaked in the warmth. There would be no rain today, he thought.

He could hear Mari stirring below. His thoughts went back to her and last night. They had reacted like a couple of school kids, shy and uncertain. But somehow, Poole knew that it was OK.

"Good morning!" Mari chirped. "It's going to be a beautiful day!"

"You missed a great sunrise, Mari," Poole responded, wanting to share it with her.

"I'll keep my fingers crossed that it will happen again tomorrow," she said, smiling. "Hey, where's the coffee?"

"I'm sorry. Thought I'd go caffeine-free this morning." Poole shrugged.

"Too late. There's more caffeine in that tea you're drinking than in my coffee. I'm still making a pot if you want some," she said as she walked back to the galley.

Poole followed her. Once the coffee was brewing, Poole walked up behind her. "About last night," he started, but Mari put a finger to his lips.

"Shhh. Last night was last night, today is today, and tomorrow is tomorrow. We have a job to do right now. When that's done, I fully expect to talk about that kiss some more," she said.

Poole smiled and was more impressed than ever. "Then I vote we get to work," Poole teased.

"My thoughts exactly," she said, smiling. "Now pour out that tea; my coffee's ready."

They tried to plan their day but realized it depended in great part on what they found in the next safe deposit box. So they waited for the First Caribbean Bank to open and contacted Kathleen Melendez.

"Hello, Ms. Melendez? This is John Poole from yesterday."

"Oh, yes Mr. Poole. How can I help you now?" she asked.

"It turns out that I have another safe deposit box, but the key number starts with an A. Is that key for your main branch?" Poole asked.

"No, that actually belongs to our branch in Port Antonio. All of our keys are coded that way. A is for Port Antonio, S is for our Spanish Town branch, et cetera," she replied.

"Great. That answers my question perfectly. Thank you so much for your time," Poole said.

"Always my pleasure, Mr. Poole. You have a wonderful day," she said and hung up.

Poole looked up at Mari. "Do you mind if we use your car for a while? I don't think it's a good idea to take the Mustang out anymore."

"No problem. Where are we going?"

"Not that far. Port Antonio is our next stop," Poole said.

"That's my bank too," she said. "My pal, Cindy, will help us out."

"Cousin?" Poole asked.

"Not unless I'm part Chinese. Her name is Cindy Hu."

"Please don't tell me her middle name is Lou," Poole responded with a smirk.

"OK, I won't," she said, as she jingled her keys. Poole grabbed the book and quickly followed her to the parking lot.

As it turned out, Cindy Hu didn't have a middle name. Poole couldn't help but feel a little disappointed—until he met the woman. She was statuesque and looked like she'd seen more than one runway in her younger years. Her exotic eyes and high cheekbones still could have graced any magazine cover.

"Mari, how are you, honey," she said, greeting her friend.

"Hi, Cin. This is John Poole. He's John Morgan's son," Mari explained. They shook hands, and Poole was surprised that she was only a few inches shorter than him.

"Good to meet you, Cindy. It turns out that I, I mean my father, has a safe deposit box here. I've got the key. Would it be possible to go check it out?" Poole asked.

"Sure. I just have to double-check account ownership and verify your identification, John. Please give me a second. I'll be right back," she said as Poole gave her his documentation. In less than a minute, she returned with another key of her own.

"This way. We're a small branch, so the room is a bit crowded. There's a fold-down worktable that you can rest the box on. Come out to get me when you're done, and I'll help lock things up for you." With that, Poole watched Cindy gracefully walk back to her desk.

"Ahem! A-95 is over here John," Mari said. "Cindy can wait."

"Uh, sorry. I was just sort of expecting a shorter, plumper version or something," Poole said sheepishly.

"Mr. Stereotype! Do you have any predispositions of me?" she asked.

"I've learned better than that with you, Mari," Poole smiled. "Shall we get to work?"

Pretending to pout, Mari took the key out of Poole's hand and unlocked the housing for the box while Poole pulled down the fold-out table. They wasted little time opening the box and took a step back to survey the contents. This one held another small, leather pouch tied with a drawstring, what looked like an old letter sealed in clear plastic, and another key.

"Looks like we've got at least one more branch to check out," Mari said.

Poole picked up the leather pouch and emptied its contents on the table. This time, a couple dozen gold coins tumbled out along with one ruby. Again, the gem looked to weigh at least five carats.

"OK, let's take a picture of this. They have value, but I'm getting the sense there might be a pattern to all of this," Poole said.

After taking several pictures with Poole's phone, they turned their attention to the sealed letter. "At least it's in English," Mari said with relief.

"It looks to be correspondence between Morgan and someone else. The name is smudged, so I can't tell. It's talking about the

Panama expedition," Poole related. "Listen to this," he said, reading a passage midway down the page.

> I brought back two extraordinary treasures from the Pacific. One is the most exquisite ruby that I've ever seen. I don't believe it is indigenous to the area because of the craftsmanship. I have heard of rubies mined in the Far East, so perhaps one of the Spanish trade ships brought it to Panama. It is also possible that it is from a lost native culture north of Panama. I have heard references to the Nata and the Mayans, and we have "collected" gold artifacts of these cultures from Spanish ships in the past. In any event, the cut of this gem is unlike any other. It fills the palm of my hand and is in the shape of a heart. It takes one's breath away and must be of great value. I have elected to keep this as part of my private collection and look forward to sharing this find with you.
>
> The other treasure is a woman. I can almost hear your laugh upon reading this missive, but she is different, I can assure you. My dear Mary Elizabeth has been a dutiful wife but loathes the climate here and blames me for not leaving for England sooner. Of course, she will have her wish soon enough! No, this woman is different and I confess that she has stolen my heart. She makes this gem of mine a mere bauble. One day, God willing, I will have the opportunity to show off both of these treasures to you. Until that day, I know I can rely on your discretion, as always.
>
> H. Morgan

"What do you think of that?" Poole asked.

"Well, it's pretty clear he's talking about Teresa Castillo. But this is the first time that there has been any reference to a heart-shaped gem," Mari said.

"Right. A ruby in the shape of a heart. Could this be 'my Donna's heart' that my father had mentioned?"

"What else could it be, John?"

"It certainly makes sense. But where is this path going? Why in the world didn't he just have all of this stuff in one safe deposit box instead of making us traipse all over the island?"

"He had to have a reason," Mari responded. "Maybe he was afraid someone could have somehow broken into one box, but not all of them."

"I guess I'll buy that," Poole conceded. "What's the number on that key, Mari?"

"M-120. Montego Bay?"

"Sounds about right. I'll ask Cindy to verify that before we leave," Poole said.

"Just as long as that's all you ask her," Mari replied, looking at him with mischievous eyes.

Nineteen

Poole thought that if Mari wasn't a marine biologist scuba diver, she'd be a perfect consultant for Conde Nast. She knew all the good spots in Jamaica, and the place they dropped into for an early lunch was to die for. In Seattle, he was used to Starbucks and every kind of salmon preparation known to man. Here too, it was all about the preparation. The difference was that Seattle diners were into the presentation. Jamaicans didn't care about looks as long as the food was good and the company better.

Mari managed to get the Beetle back to the marina in one piece. In spite of his initial trepidations, Poole was actually getting used to her driving. It was like riding a roller coaster over and over again, Poole thought; after a while, you just get used to the thrills.

Once again, they set up shop on the *Rebecca*. It was just after noon, and another glorious Jamaican sun was beating down on them. Mari pulled out all of the boxes, but she and Poole didn't dig into them right away.

"I don't know what we're looking for," Poole said. "And I'm still struggling with the 'why' part."

"I can tell you why, if you want," Mari replied.

Poole looked up at her, somewhat surprised. "I'm all ears," he said.

"You know, you can be pretty dense sometimes," Mari continued. "The 'why' is that you need to know."

"Know what?"

"Everything. You need to know your roots. You need to know your father's story. You need to know why you came down here for a man you never knew. Shall I keep going?"

"I hate to stop you while you're on a roll," Poole said.

"Lastly, this whole thing intrigues the hell out of you. Maybe if you find something, it's somehow going to justify the decisions that your mother and father made. Hell, I don't know. But one thing I do know is that it's not about the treasure. It's about finding you!"

Poole stared at Mari but didn't say a word. He knew that there was truth in her words. He knew he needed to keep going, and it wasn't about the money. It was about making a connection with his father by making a connection with Morgan. He knew his father couldn't rest in peace, and he knew he couldn't find peace, until he did.

"You're right, Mari. You're absolutely right. I want to figure this out just because it needs to be figured out. I don't care about actually finding a pot at the end of the rainbow. I think I just need to know that it exists."

"Well it's about time! Now that you've figured that out, what's the next step?" Mari asked.

"Let's keep having some fun. Screw the boxes. Let's go to Montego Bay," Poole answered.

"Great, I'll get my keys."

"I've got a better idea Why drive when we've got this fabulous boat? I say we enjoy this beautiful sunshine and take our time. The bank's still going to be there no matter what time we cruise in," Poole said.

"Aye, aye, Captain! You take the wheel, and I'll man the lines. This is your boat now anyway. It's about time you learned how to drive it."

"Well, it will be my boat as soon as I visit Mr. Dunbar again," Poole said. "Let's make a point of doing that later this week. In the meantime, let's check the beer cooler to make sure we have enough provisions for the trip!"

The cruise up the coast was just what Poole and Mari needed. The sun sparkled off the calm waters, and it made the lush, green landscape, the white sand, and the turquoise shoreline of the island even more vivid. They headed west by northwest about a half-mile offshore. The island was on their portside, and they gave themselves enough distance to avoid the shoals.

Mari joined Poole on the flying bridge and showed him a chart of the area as they sat under the Bimini top. They cruised at around twenty knots and soon passed Cabarita Island, where Poole had spread his father's ashes. Beyond, the brightly colored buildings of Port Maria provided a shimmering backdrop, belying its narrow streets and jumbled layout.

They continued at their leisurely pace while Mari pointed out landmarks, and related stories she had heard about them. "These waters teemed with pirates back in the day, and it is said that there are still coves with unfound treasure. I suppose that might be true, but you'd think that with modern technology, whatever there was to be found has been found."

"I suppose you're right, Mari. We're not the first ones to this rodeo," Poole agreed.

"There's a different kind of pirate these days," Mari continued. "I've read plenty of reports about pleasure boaters being robbed on the open seas. That's why we're staying within shouting distance of the shore."

"Really? I've heard about that around Somalia, I guess, but nothing this close to home," Poole said, raising his eyebrows.

"You'd be surprised. Remember, there're a whole lot of places outside of the resorts that aren't the safest. You're lucky you've got a local like me to guide you around. You might be a bit of a target otherwise."

"But what happens out here if you do see a suspicious boat approaching?" Poole asked.

"Your father was prepared. There are a couple of rifles and a handgun in the wheelhouse. He also managed to pick up an AK-47," she said. "You can never be too careful."

As they continued up the coastline, Poole couldn't help looking closely at every boat that came into view. He was far from the safe life he had built for himself in Seattle, but for the first time, he felt as if he was really starting to live.

Their journey took a little under four hours, and the sun was starting to wane. They decided to anchor in the bay for the night and find a spot on the main dock to tie up to in the morning. Montego Bay was a picture postcard, and Poole could see why it was so popular with the tourists. He remembered what it looked like from their perch at the Cliffs. Up close, it was even more idyllic.

Boats peppered the bay, which was still alive with activity even as the sky began to darken. On the aft deck, Poole and Mari relaxed with cold beer. Poole could hear the rhythm of steel drums and the laughter of partygoers as they shuttled to and from the cruise ships. The energy was a stark contrast from the sleepy marina to which he had become accustomed.

"I think I might like this place," he said to Mari.

"What's not to like? Beautiful scenery, beautiful beaches, beautiful people. Here and Necril are my favorite spots on the island. I know it's pretty touristy, but I love being around happy people," she replied.

They raised their beers and toasted the scene. "Am I a happy person?" Poole teased.

"You could be," she said. "You just have to get into the Rasta, mon! Den every ting cris!"

They both laughed. "OK you got me! I know what Rasta is. But what's 'crease' mean?" Poole asked.

"Not crease, c-r-i-s, cris! It means cool, mon. Cool!" Mari answered.

"OK. So, since you're about to get up, would you mind getting me another cris beer?" he asked with an innocent look on his face.

"You're hopeless, Poole!" Mari said, as her smile lit up the gathering dusk. "And I'm not going anywhere. Get your damned cris beer yourself!"

Poole and Mari continued their banter on the aft deck long after sunset. The boat swung lazily with the light breeze and the tide, and the hours drifted by.

A solitary figure with a sweating Red Stripe of his own sat at an outdoor bar looking at their boat. He could barely make out their silhouettes on the aft deck of the *Rebecca* in spite of the illumination from the main cabin lights. He lit a cigarette, inhaled deeply, and wondered what their next move would be.

TWENTY

April 1671

The *West Wind* lived up to her name as she raced from Panama to Port Maria. The crew, shorthanded as it was, handled the vessel with aplomb, and Morgan made sure that extra rum was rationed to every man. Senora Castillo was compliant and remained in Morgan's cabin for most of the voyage, attended to by young Mr. Dunn. They both kept up the pretense that she was under lock and key so as not to arouse suspicion, although the crew would never question Morgan in that regard.

They arrived in Port Maria at nightfall, so they put to anchor and waited for first light to go ashore. Morgan had prepared meticulously for the day ahead and thought, if God was willing, his plans would be successful.

At dawn, he gathered the entire crew, save Mr. Dunn, to load the longboats with the gold and jewels that Morgan selected from the trove they found in Panama. Five longboats in all set off for Port Maria, two men in each boat. It was a long day's work hauling the sacks to the hiding place Morgan had selected. The crew was glad to break sweat for a task like that, since they knew that their take would be worth a small fortune for each of them.

They rested at midday, and the cook fed them more fruit and dried meat, along with fresh water from a spring near the hiding spot. After several more trips, the job was finished, and the sun was low in the sky. Morgan personally thanked each man and handed out jugs of rum. He ordered the cook to prepare a fish stew for the crew's dinner, and he personally added a special fish paste he had procured from Panama to enhance the flavor.

They all sat around the cook's fire, agreeing that the smell was unsurpassed, and complimented the cook for his efforts. One young sailor, no more than sixteen years old, raised his jug to Morgan and thanked him for selecting them for the duty. Morgan smiled and took a small sip in acknowledgment. The cook ladled the stew into wooden bowls, and the men ate with gusto.

"But sir," the young sailor stated. "You've not eaten at all."

"The meal was for you fine fellows," Morgan replied. "I did nothing but watch you bend your backs. You deserve a meal like this."

"Thank you, Captain. There's no other man of your equal. I hope—"

The young sailor stopped in mid-sentence, and a confused look crossed his face. He tried to finish the thought, but no matter how hard he tried, his tongue refused to move. The cook and other crew members also started feeling numbness in their limbs, and it became difficult for them to breathe. One of Morgan's favorites, Mr. Ransom, tried to stand, but fell to the ground. Within a few minutes, the entire work party sat frozen, their eyes wide with fear.

Morgan paced around the crew to observe their distress. What he had heard was correct. The small fish had a most unusual effect on his men. He knew that most who were exposed to it would die. But he didn't know how or in what manner. The paralysis was fascinating. He had the impression that his men were quite lucid and could see and understand him as he walked around the fire. And Morgan was sure that they were fully aware that they had been betrayed.

"Such a waste of good rum, men," Morgan stated as he paced and waited. "I would like nothing better than to preserve that for another celebration, but I'm afraid anything that has touched your lips has been fouled. Perhaps we can use it to stoke the fire!"

It was taking longer than Morgan anticipated, so he sat against the muddy trunk of the large mahogany tree that he had chosen as his marker. Its base was broad and solid, and its canopy provided cooling shade. It stood on the bluff above Port Maria, and he could see the *West Wind* at anchor below. He peered into the horizon but saw no other sails. He knew there would be soon, so this excursion was a necessity.

God willing, he would be able to enjoy the fruits of his labor after the long years of service to the Crown. He had given England much, but if the stories of peace were true, he would have some quick talking to do in order to escape confinement in the Tower of London. Having a spot of this fish stew would be preferable to that, he thought.

Mr. Ransom was the first to stop breathing. His body convulsed as his diaphragm and lungs refused to work. His eyes bulged out as he clung to life, but his efforts were fruitless. One by one, they all met the same fate until the last, the young sailor who had graciously toasted Morgan, took in his last breath.

With the sun setting, Morgan dragged each body into the underbrush at various locations, knowing that the scavengers and native insects would make quick work of their bodies. He made sure that the location was remote enough so that it would be years before anyone other than himself would happen upon the spot.

He finally came back to the cook site. He kicked the wooden bowls into the fire, careful not to touch them with his bare hands or skin. He did the same with the cook's tripod and made sure the remains of the stew burned in the flames. Satisfied that the fire would not spread beyond the cook site, Morgan made the long hike down to Port Maria and the sanctuary of his cabin on the *West Wind*.

O nce on board, Morgan scrubbed his hands with lye soap just to make sure no residue of the fish paste remained. He then hailed young Mr. Dunn and explained that the crew would not be coming back aboard. Mr. Dunn's first task in the morning was to commandeer two pack mules from Port Maria. He was then to take Senora Castillo to Morgan's small plantation house above the town to get her settled. Morgan would follow within the day. But for now, it was time to sleep.

Morgan entered his cabin. Senora Castillo was wearing a sleeping gown and combing her hair. His heart always skipped a beat when he saw her after a brief absence. He had never experienced such a feeling before, and it made him long for more.

"I have made arrangements for you to go to my plantation in the morning," Morgan announced. "In spite of my better judgment, Mr. Dunn will take you there. I just hope your faith in him is warranted."

"He is young and faithful to you, Captain. There is no need to treat him harshly. I am sure he will prove his worth to you someday. In the meantime, I need someone to look after my needs here, and I'm quite enjoying teaching him how to read."

"Read?"

"Of course! He needs to be educated to survive in this world. It is my intention to at least teach him the rudiments of history and politics—even business, although you men seem to think it's beyond the understanding of us women."

"I am coming to believe that nothing is beyond you!" Morgan laughed. "But speaking of history, how much do you know about the ancient local cultures?"

"In what way, Captain?" she asked.

Morgan paused, reaching over to the canvas sack that he'd personally brought aboard. He pulled out the deep-red, heart-shaped gemstone. "In this way, Senora Castillo."

She stopped and stared at the ruby. It was the largest stone she had ever seen. It would have been difficult for her small hands to enclose it entirely. As Morgan moved it in the light, its smooth face and multifaceted edges were breathtaking.

"I've heard rumors of this stone but I never imagined the stories were true. There is truly nothing its equal. This is not of Spanish design, so I am perplexed as to its origin. Perhaps this was the handiwork of the ancient natives of the area. I have also heard my husband say that merchant ships have carried large rubies from the Far East," she said.

"I agree that the craftsmanship is without peer. But I am unaware of anyone being so skilled as to have carved this," Morgan stated.

"It would seem that there is only one other possible explanation, Captain," Senora Castillo offered.

"What would that be?" Morgan asked.

"That it truly is a gift from God."

Morgan personally manned the oars of the longboat as Senora Castillo and Mr. Dunn sat in the rear. They secured their belongings on the pack mules, and soon they were heading along the grassy path up to Morgan's small plantation house.

Morgan returned to the *West Wind* and made his preparations. With effort, he placed casks of powder in the empty hold of the vessel and attached a long fuse to the largest barrel. He then returned to the main deck and headed toward the bow. Taking a boarding ax, he hacked at the anchor hawser until the last strands were severed, setting the *West Wind* adrift. Morgan knew that the ebb tide would take the vessel out to sea. He gathered all of his necessities, including his heart-shaped treasure, and loaded the longboat.

Certain that Senora Castillo and Mr. Dunn were out of earshot, Morgan carefully descended the ladder into the hold with a burning candle in hand. He placed the flame to the fuse. It lit at once and burned rapidly toward its target. Morgan dropped the candle and scrambled out of the hold and into the waiting longboat. He hurriedly untied the small vessel and rowed with all his might to create distance between himself and the *West Wind*.

He had rowed for almost a minute when the first explosion came. He saw a large flash and then heard the roar as black smoke billowed up from the belly of the ship. Two more explosions followed, and the vessel started to founder. Morgan was surprised at how fast the *West Wind* took on water and started to slip beneath the sea's surface. He continued to row as the pieces of the ship slowly sank to the bottom of the bay. By the time he reached shore, all that was left of her were remnants of the main mast and shards of decking floating slowly out to sea.

TWENTY ONE

After they pulled up anchor the following morning, Poole idled the boat to Montego Bay's public dock. Mari kept a watchful eye on him as he guided the sixty-footer slowly toward the pier using the bow and stern thrusters to ease the vessel to the dock. Mari jumped off the stern and tied the mooring line on the nearest cleat, and then raced up to the bow to secure that line. Poole stayed on the flying bridge until they were safely moored and shut down the engines when Mari gave him the thumbs-up.

"Not bad for a first timer!" Mari said, impressed.

Poole tried to act like it wasn't a big deal, but he couldn't help but feel a little pride in handling the boat without embarrassing himself. "Thanks. Piece of cake," he said, grinning, even though they both knew it wasn't.

After Mari scrambled back on board, they sat down in the main cabin to plan the day. "OK," Mari started, "the Montego branch doesn't open until nine. All we have is a key at this point and not much else to go on."

"Well, it's eight o'clock now, so let's go for a walk and check out the surroundings. The bank will open up soon enough," Poole said.

They were preparing to lock up the boat and start their walk into the small business district when they were interrupted. "Ahoy, on the *Rebecca*!" a voice with an Australian accent called out.

Poole looked up and saw a man roughly his height in blue shorts and a white linen shirt, the sleeves rolled up to his elbows. He carried a brown leather satchel, and an almost spent cigarette was balanced between his fingers. His weathered face hid his age. Although his hair was black, he could have been in his forties or his early sixties.

He offered a crooked smile, took one last pull of his cigarette, and expertly flicked the butt into the harbor.

"You're not John Morgan's son, are you?" the dark-haired man asked.

"I am," Poole responded. "And you are?"

"Ryker Wilson, a good friend of your father's," he answered.

"How can I help you, Mr. Wilson? We were about to leave."

"Call me Ryker. In truth, I just wanted to pay my respects. Your dad and I went way back. In fact, we were business partners until a few years ago," he said, squinting into the morning sun.

Mari popped out of the main cabin wearing shorts, sneakers, and a simple, white polo shirt. She thought she recognized the dark-haired man but couldn't place him.

"Mari, this is Ryker Wilson," Poole said, motioning over to the dock. "I guess he used to work with my father."

Mari recognized the name. "Ryker Wilson. Yes. John Morgan mentioned that you two used to work the diving business before I came on board."

"That's right, and you must be Maria Robeson," Wilson said. "John Morgan thought very highly of you."

There was a slight pause as they all looked at each other. Wilson broke the silence. "Listen, let me buy you both a cup of coffee. I couldn't make the service because of a client commitment. If you could tell me about it, I would be in your debt."

Poole looked at Mari and shrugged. "We've got an hour to kill, so why not? You lead the way."

Wilson helped Mari to the dock while Poole jumped down on his own. Wilson led the way to a small, open-air restaurant near the public dock that had been crowded with revelers the night before.

Wilson yelled over to a young, attractive blonde at the serving station. "Morning, Jackie! Three coffees when you get a chance, love!"

Their drinks came, and Wilson continued to lead the conversation. "Your dad was quite a character, he was. We ran the diving business together during the day and had our fair share of cocktails at night. We made quite a pair, especially in the old days."

Wilson dumped two packets of sugar into his coffee and stirred. "I helped him a bit with that Morgan treasure stuff back then too. A couple of times we thought we were this close," he said, spreading his thumb and index finger about an inch apart, "but we always seemed to hit a dead end. Finally, about five years ago he changed. He didn't talk that much about the treasure and didn't seem too interested in sharing anything."

"Was that why you stopped working together?" Poole asked.

"To be honest, we had sort of a falling out when, out of the blue, he buys that boat you sailed in on," Wilson responded. "That bad boy wasn't cheap, and I figured he'd found something and was holding out on me."

Poole's senses were on high alert with Wilson. "Did you ever find out where he got the money to buy the *Rebecca*?"

"No, I never gave him the chance," Wilson laughed. "I punched him right in the nose and walked away. We didn't speak for years. Until a few months ago, that is."

Poole and Mari didn't say a word. They just looked at the dark-haired Australian.

"One night at this bar we used to go to, old John Morgan waltzes in and sits down next to me. He says it's been too long and wants to apologize. I'm not one to hold a grudge forever, so I shook his hand and that was that."

"That was that?" Mari asked.

"That, and he wanted me to help him with the Morgan treasure thing again. He said he was stuck and knew that I might be able to get him going on the right track. So he shared his research with me," Wilson responded. "If you're following that same path, I'm pretty sure I can help you too."

"I appreciate that, Mr. Wilson, but we're not really looking for anything," Poole said. "We decided to take the boat for a cruise. I'm trying to figure out whether I should keep it as part of my inheritance or sell it for the cash."

"It is a mighty fine vessel, that *Rebecca*. He named it after your mother; but I suppose you figured that out."

"Yes, and thanks."

"He told me a lot about you too," Wilson added.

Poole just nodded.

Wilson looked at his watch and stood. "Like I said, if you need any help here's my number." He handed a slip of paper to Poole. "And remember to be careful around this island. There's lots of reefs and shoals out there, if you don't know where you're going."

Wilson gave Poole and Mari his crooked smile, and then walked at a leisurely pace toward the center of town. Poole peered over at Mari with a questioning look. "Who the hell is that guy again?"

"I don't know, but he seemed to know a lot about us," Mari answered.

"And I don't know if I believe all that buddy-buddy stuff with my father," Poole added. "I'm hoping I'm wrong, but I've got a feeling this won't be the last time we cross paths with Ryker Wilson."

Mari looked at her watch. "Hey, it's almost nine. Let's make our way over to the bank."

Within a few minutes, they found themselves in front of a small, stucco building bearing a First Caribbean Bank sign. A young woman, who disappeared into a back room, had just unlocked the doors. Poole and Mari entered the branch and looked for someone who could help them.

They walked up to the first likely suspect, a young man with short braids whose back was to them as he put a backpack into his credenza drawer. As he turned to greet them, Poole noticed the nameplate on the desk, F. Williams.

"Fredrickson!" Poole laughed. "What are you doing here?"

Fredrickson looked puzzled for a second before he recognized Poole and Mari. "Cuba Libres! Hello, sir and ma'am! I trust you made it home OK that day?"

"No thanks to you, my friend. But yes, we did find our way home," Poole answered, extending his hand to Fredrickson. "I'm John Poole and this is my close friend, Mari. So, is this a second career option for you?"

"I have a couple of jobs around here. I work the Cliffs on the weekends and here during the week. I also pick up odd jobs every once in a while, too," he said proudly. "I'm saving my money. My mother wants me to go to college, and I might, but I've read that a lot of rich men didn't bother, or dropped out, like Steve Jobs, the Apple guy. So I'm weighing my options."

Poole smiled. "There's no substitute for hard work, Fredrickson. Good for you."

"Thank you, Mr. Poole. Now, how may I help you?"

Just then, two men walked into the bank and hovered around the small, stand-up desk in the lobby that was used for writing checks and filling out deposit slips. One man was short and the other tall. Both glanced casually over toward Fredrikson's desk, where Poole and Mari were sitting.

Mari noticed them out of the corner of her eye and nudged Poole. "Those two look like the guys who were nosing around the Mustang when your dad was in the hospital," she whispered.

Poole didn't turn his head, but leaned over to Mari and whispered, "I'm pretty sure that isn't a coincidence. Let's put our little scavenger hunt on hold for a bit."

"I'm with you on that," Mari agreed.

Poole stood without looking at the two men. "As it turns out, we have to run a few errands first, Fredrickson. Sorry to take up your time this morning. We'll be back."

"No problem, Mr. Poole. Any man that tips like you is a friend of mine!" he said. They said their good-byes and walked out of the branch, passing the two men on their way out. They ran over to a drug store across the street and pretended to shop while keeping an eye on the bank. The two men left the branch shortly after they did and split up, one heading toward the dock, and the other, uptown.

"What the hell," Poole said under his breath. "What do you think, Mari?"

"You got me. I thought they were just a couple of thieves in Kingston looking to boost the car or steal something out of it. This is a little different now."

"And how the heck did they know we were up here? Are we that easy to follow?" Poole asked.

"Well, it's not like the *Rebecca* is a rowboat, John. Between your dad's Mustang and that boat, we might as well be shooting off flares and carrying a 'Follow Us' banner."

"Hard to argue with you there. We may have to reconsider our modes of transportation."

"In the meantime, what do we do?"

"We ditch those guys. And then we find a way to get back here when nobody's watching, if that's possible," Poole said.

"You lead the way, then. I don't have much experience with this James Bond stuff," Mari said quietly.

"Stick with me, honey. I've seen all his movies."

TWENTY TWO

They couldn't cower in the drug store all day, so Poole decided that the only thing to do was act as if they didn't know they were being followed. He and Mari strolled down toward the docks again, taking their time. Then they stopped back at the small restaurant where they had met Ryker Wilson. The outdoor café offered a great vantage point, so they could keep an eye on the *Rebecca* while watching the passersby.

There was no sign of the two men from the bank. But they both knew they couldn't be too far away. "There's no sense in hanging around here forever," Poole said. "We'd just be playing a stupid waiting game with those guys. And my guess is that they've got all the time in the world."

"We could go back to anchor and maybe sneak in on the dinghy later," Mari suggested.

"That's no good. As long as they can see the boat, they're going to know we're here. We need to regroup and find another way to get back," Poole stated.

"Then we might as well head back down to the marina. At least Robert's there to watch our backs."

"I'm OK with that. But when we get back, we might want to think about getting a rental car and finding another place to stay for a while," Poole said.

"Fine by me. Let's get the heck out of here."

They made their way back to the boat, and within ten minutes they were ready to cast off.

"Need a hand with those lines?" the Aussie voice yelled. Poole looked down to see Ryker Wilson on the dock. "Why are you leaving so soon?"

"Just a day-trip, Ryker," Poole answered, wondering about his convenient appearance. "Thanks for helping with the lines, though."

Wilson untied the bow line and threw it to Mari, then went to the stern cleat and tossed the line onto the aft deck. Wilson gave Poole that crooked smile. "Like I told you, John, I'm here to help."

With the image of Wilson's smug look still on his mind, Poole pulled the *Rebecca* out of the bay and steered east by southeast, staying about half a mile offshore. It was only eleven in the morning, so they reduced their cruising speed to about fifteen knots, which still gave them plenty of time to make it down the coast. They both sat on the flying bridge, trying to figure out what to do next.

"This is getting complicated, John," Mari said. "Do you think we're in danger?"

"I'd be lying if I said no. You saw what happened to my father." He paused and looked at Mari with a serious expression. "You don't need to be part of this. I don't know what I'd do if something happened to you."

Mari returned his gaze. "That makes two of us, John. But I already told you, I'm in it for the long haul. So quit getting all sappy on me. Let's get back to the marina, shall we?"

Poole shook his head with a half smile on his face and turned back to the helm.

They'd been cruising for almost three hours, and the tensions of the morning had started to dissipate. Mari went down to the galley to get a couple of sodas and a snack. When she returned to the aft deck, she noticed a boat far off their stern cruising at twice their speed.

She sat down next to Poole on the flying bridge and handed him his drink. "I must be getting paranoid, but do you think there's anything to worry about with that boat coming up on us?"

Poole looked behind them. "Hard to say, but there's only one way to find out."

He changed their course about ten degrees to port and started to head farther out from shore. Mari looked back. "Damn it, they've changed their course too!"

"What's the top speed on this thing, Mari?"

"About thirty-five knots, I think. You might as well open it up."

Poole pushed the throttle to its limit, and the boat sprang to life. The bow rose up to meet the swells in front of them, slicing through the waves without trouble. Mari looked back, and she could see that the other boat increased its speed as well. The boat trailed less than a half mile behind them. It was a smaller and slightly faster craft than the *Rebecca*, and it gained on them steadily.

"John, you'd better correct our course, or we'll be out in no man's land before we know it," Mari said, pointing to the compass.

Poole changed his heading and aimed for a point about two miles ahead. "How far is the marina from here?" Poole asked.

"We're about twenty minutes out, give or take. We still have a good ten miles after we round that point up there."

Poole tried to do the math, but the only thing he knew was that the boat chasing them would be on them before they got to the marina. Mari pulled out the chart of the north coast to make sure their bearing was safe from the shallows. "John, be careful going around that point, you need to stay at least half a mile off shore!"

"Here, you take the wheel. I'm going to see if Robert is at the marina and also grab a couple things from down below."

Poole climbed down to the aft deck and looked at their pursuers. It was a blue-hulled cruiser about thirty-five feet long. He could see two figures in the enclosed cabin. "It looks like we didn't quite lose those guys from the bank!" he yelled up at Mari, who nodded in reply.

He went into the cabin to call Robert. The reception was bad on the water, but he could hear the number ring in intermittent spurts. Robert didn't answer. Poole left a message, hoping Robert could round up his poker buddies one more time. Then he went into the wheelhouse.

He looked to his right, toward shore, and saw that they were rounding the point. But according to Mari, they were still ten miles from the marina. The blue-hulled boat was less than three hundred yards to their stern and inching closer by the minute. He scanned the horizon; no other boats were in sight.

He grabbed what he needed from the wheelhouse and went back out to the aft deck, watching their pursuers intently. The bow of the blue boat bounced high with each swell, and the white spray against the hull was like the froth on the mouth of a rabid dog. He yelled up to Mari, "Keep doing what you're doing!"

After about five minutes, the blue-hulled boat cut the distance in half. There was no way the *Rebecca* would make the marina before being intercepted, so Poole decided that drastic action needed to be taken.

Just inside the main cabin, Poole had laid out two flare guns and the AK-47. He'd never held an automatic rifle before, let alone fired one. Keeping the gun out of sight, he quickly figured out the safety and made sure it was loaded. Mari hit a couple of swells that made the *Rebecca* shift, and he lost his balance for a moment, but the boat righted itself and continued to slice through the water. The smaller boat hit the swells a bit harder and briefly lost ground. But when the distance between them narrowed to only one hundred and fifty yards, Poole finally decided they were too close for comfort.

He turned back to the flying bridge. "Mari!" he yelled up. "I'm going to try to slow them down!"

Mari turned around and saw that Poole was holding the automatic rifle. She nodded in agreement and turned her attention to their heading. Poole walked back to the stern, careful to keep his balance. He clicked off the safety, pointed to a spot about fifty yards in front of the bow of the blue boat, and pulled the trigger.

The speed and power of the volley surprised Poole, and the AK-47 jumped in his hands.

The blue boat continued its chase in spite of the brief warning shot. OK, Poole thought, maybe these guys think I'm bluffing. He spread his feet wide and braced himself for the recoil. Then he let out a spray of bullets that strafed the bow of the blue boat and came within inches of its enclosed wheelhouse. Immediately, the blue boat slowed and its bow dropped low in the water. Mari kept the *Rebecca* at full speed, and the distance between them increased with each passing second.

Poole breathed a quick sigh of relief and clicked the safety back on the rifle. He lodged it securely inside one of the mooring cleats and scrambled back up to the flying bridge next to Mari.

"Nice shootin' there, Rambo!" Mari yelled, the adrenaline flowing.

"It looks like they weren't expecting that," Poole said as he turned to their pursuers. "In fact, it looks like they're turning around!"

"Thank God!" Mari exclaimed with no small relief. "The marina's only a couple miles up ahead. Did you get a hold of Robert?"

"No answer. But we've got a little breathing room, it looks like. Whatever they wanted to do, they intended to overtake us on the water. I guess there wouldn't be any witnesses out here," Poole surmised.

"One thing's for sure. We've got to gather up all of your father's stuff and find a new place to call home. At this point, I don't even trust either of us getting a rental car in our own names. Whoever those guys are, or whoever they work for, probably can track down that information. Give me that phone."

Mari made a quick call and then gave the phone back to Poole. "All set. We've got a loaner for as long as we need it," she said smugly.

"Another cousin?"

"Cousin," she said, nodding.

"As long as it has a roof and air conditioning, I'll be a happy man," Poole said. "Oh, and brakes. Good brakes."

TWENTY THREE

Robert was waiting at the marina for them. Mari brought the *Rebecca* in faster than normal but docked her expertly with the help of Robert, who tied the lines. Once Mari shut down the main engines, Robert climbed aboard, noticing the automatic rifle wedged upright on the aft deck and the shaken looks on the faces of both Poole and Mari.

"I can't take my eyes off you for a second!" Robert bellowed. "Are you two all right?"

"We've been better," Poole admitted. "I sure wish I knew who was following us, though. This is getting damn old!"

"I'll second that," Mari said, climbing down from the flying bridge.

"What can I do to help?" Robert asked.

Poole sat on the gunnel, pondering the question. "We've got to find a place where we can regroup without being sitting ducks. They obviously know the *Rebecca* and my father's Mustang. Geez, they've probably been following me ever since I've been on the island."

"You two can stay with me, Mr. John," Robert offered. "The missus already mentioned it, even before your little boat chase."

"Thanks, Robert. I can't tell you how much I appreciate that," Poole replied.

"Me too, Cousin," Mari added. "But I don't think that's such a good idea. You and Marthy don't need to be in the middle of this."

Poole nodded. "I agree. This last little episode tells me that someone is getting desperate. So I'm not too anxious to get you involved any more than you already are, Robert."

"OK, I'm not going to argue. But tell me what you want me to do, and I'll try to make it happen," Robert said in earnest.

Poole clapped Robert on the shoulder. "I'll tell you what. We sure could use your local knowledge. And we haven't eaten anything all day. OK if we buy a couple of burgers from you and pick your brain?"

"Sure thing, Mr. John," Robert responded. "Lock up, and I'll meet you up there."

After Robert left, they stowed the guns in the storage locker in the wheelhouse and locked up the main cabin. It was almost five o'clock, and the heat of the day was starting to wane. Poole jumped off the boat first and then held Mari by the waist and helped her to the dock.

As they walked up to the café, Mari stopped and locked at Poole. "We must be on the right track, John, or else those guys wouldn't be chasing after us."

"I was thinking the same thing. The problem is that we still don't know what we're supposed to be looking for. Obviously, it's something of value, but I haven't a damned clue what it could be."

"You know, Robert's a pretty wise dude. Let's bounce a couple of ideas off him and see what he has to say. He knows a fair amount of the local lore too. You never know what he might add to this," Mari said.

Robert seated Poole and Mari at the back of the café even though tables were available on the veranda.

"Thank you, Robert," Poole said. "Please, have a seat and join us."

"Give me a second; I'll be right back," he said and retreated to the kitchen.

Poole scanned the patrons, looking for familiar faces, but came up empty. Robert soon came back, balancing a tray holding three beers and three shot glasses filled with brown liquor.

Robert put down the tray and sat in the metal chair opposite Poole and Mari, which creaked in protest. "I figured you wouldn't mind if I broke out the Jack Daniels, Mr. John."

Poole smiled in approval and made a toast. "To those stupid bastards on that boat. May they burn in hell for scaring the shit out of us!"

Robert and Mari laughed. "Well," Robert interjected. "It's not what I'm used to hearing at the dinner table, but I'll drink to that!"

They all lifted their glasses and emptied the warm liquid in one shot. The nervousness subsided enough for Poole to bring them back to the problem at hand.

"OK, we've got a major issue here. And it's obvious that my father had the same one. He figured out where the Morgan treasure was, and someone else wants that secret. And we've been naively leading them around the island, doing their work for them. I suppose we should have gotten the idea after that Mercedes a couple of days ago, but I still thought it could have been a coincidence. This time, not so much."

"They must have thought we retrieved the contents of that third safe deposit box in Montego Bay," Mari responded. "Why else would they have been so blatant this time? You'd think that they'd still wait and let us lead them to the treasure—or whatever it is we're supposed to find."

"Unless they weren't sure that we could figure the clues out. After all, the only thing we've been doing is going from bank to bank. My father might have left clues that are obvious to someone who's been following Morgan's trail for a while but would escape us totally," Poole said.

"Begging your pardon, Mr. John, but your father was no fool," Robert said. "I'm guessing that he wouldn't leave stuff in those boxes that you couldn't figure out. In fact, probably the simpler the better."

"That's right, John," Mari added. "The only thing he was sure of is that you were smart, and I'd be here to help. Maybe he figured that if you got stuck, you'd find a way to get the answers you needed."

Poole took a sip from his beer and pondered Mari's statement. "I think both of you are onto something. This little goose chase might be serving two purposes. The first is to lead us to whatever my father found, or at least close enough for us to take the last few steps. The second is to let us know who else wants it. Maybe he figured that the competition would do exactly what they've done. Get impatient and expose their hand."

"It makes sense to me, Mr. John," Robert said, nodding in agreement.

"So who else knows about what your dad was working on?" Mari asked.

"There are four people that I can think of that he talked to or collaborated with in the last year or so: Dunbar; Ms. Hattie; Father Michael; and our good pal, Ryker Wilson. But heaven knows who else might be out there."

"I don't know about you, John, but I wouldn't trust Wilson as far as I could throw him," Mari commented.

"Yeah, his offer to help seemed a little too sincere for my taste. And was it a coincidence that those two guys and Wilson happened to be in Montego Bay at the same time?"

"Not to mention the boat chase right after that," Mari added.

"Well, I think we can put him at the top of our list," Poole noted. "I included Ms. Hattie simply because my father visited her with that book. You'd think they chatted about more than just the name of the Spanish woman. She's well read and has been on this island her whole life, so maybe there was more to their meetings than she let on."

"Then there's Dunbar," Mari interjected. "He said that he and your father shared an academic interest in the Morgan treasure. Maybe he knows more than he's telling."

"Perhaps. I have to go see him to start the official paperwork on my father's estate, so maybe I can hint around a bit and see if there's something there. At the very least, he could be a good source of information," Poole said.

"What about Father Michael?" Robert asked.

"I chatted with him for a few minutes at the service," Poole answered. "He mentioned that he and my father would discuss local history for hours on end. I was thinking that maybe they touched on the Morgan treasure at some point. It's worth a shot, anyway."

"How about you, Robert?" Mari asked. "Did you and John Morgan ever talk about his search?"

"Not his search, no. We used to talk about the local legends and where other folks had looked in the past. Hell, I told him it would be easier to ask where folks didn't look!" Robert laughed.

"Well, you've probably seen or heard about a lot of theories," Poole persisted. "What were the most popular?"

"Most folks say his treasure is buried with him in old Port Royal. Others think he may have taken it up north, to present-day Cuba, or even buried it on little Cabarita Island, outside of Port Maria."

"What do you think, Robert?" Poole asked.

"I think there's no treasure at all, that's what I think," Robert answered solemnly. "It's been about three hundred and fifty years. Lots of things could have happened between then and now. Maybe he had something stashed, and someone else found it. Or, more likely, he squandered whatever he had during his last days on the island. It's common knowledge that he drank like a fish in those last years. In fact, I think he died of liver disease or something like that."

"That's right, Robert," Mari agreed. "Cirrhosis of the liver. The guy drank himself to death after he came back from England. That book on the *Rebecca* said that he came back as Sir Henry Morgan and was given a post as lieutenant governor. In fact, he was made governor for a brief time but was relieved of that job because of his drinking. Why in the world would a guy who was that successful screw it all up through drinking?"

"Not a clue, Mari," Poole answered. "But it wouldn't be the first time the bottle has ruined a man. Maybe Robert is right. Once you start that downhill slide, you usually don't stop until you lose everything."

"Or," Robert added, "the slide starts *after* you lose everything."

Their burgers came, and they ate mostly in silence. After finishing off the last of his fries, Poole continued the conversation. "So we've still got to figure out our plan of attack. We need transportation and a safe place to stay so we're not followed. On the other hand, we still need to somehow lead our competition around so we can figure out who they are."

"Would you mind starting with the easy problems first, John?" Mari said sarcastically.

Poole smiled. "We also need to figure out how to get back to the bank in Montego Bay. Again, another easy problem."

"First things first, you two," Robert interjected. "If you need transportation, I can figure something out for you."

"Got that handled, Cousin," Mari responded.

"OK. Then where are you going to stay? As long as your boat is here, my boys and I can keep an eye on it, and on you."

"I thought about that, Robert. But if someone were watching the marina, he'd still see us come and go. No, we need a place where our movements would be a little less restrictive. We can always come back to the boat if and when we want to be followed." Poole pushed his plate away and took a sip of beer.

"That sounds reasonable to me," Mari said. "But what do you have in mind for accommodations, Mr. Poole?"

"I'm not exactly sure, but I came up with a possibility while munching down those fries. Do you have a phone book lying around here, Robert?"

"In the little office next to the kitchen. You need a hand?" Robert asked.

"Nope, be right back," Poole answered as he headed to the kitchen. A few minutes later, he returned with a satisfied look on his face.

"You've got that 'cat that ate the canary' look on your face, John," Mari said.

"I'm not sure I'd go that far, but I think I've figured out a way to kill two birds with one stone."

"Do tell, oh smug one!"

"What do people do when they are being chased?" Poole asked.

"Run like hell? I don't know. Why don't you enlighten us?"

"They seek sanctuary," Poole responded, noting the confused looks of Mari and Robert. "When I spoke with Father Michael at the service, he mentioned that he and my father would sometimes talk until the wee hours. And on some occasions, when it got too late, my father would stay the night in a cottage behind the church. I just called Father Michael to see if that cottage might be available for a few days."

"Great idea!" Mari exclaimed. "It'll certainly keep us out of the mainstream for a while. I'm not sure if anyone would think to look for us there."

"And it will give us a chance to find out what Father Michael and my father talked about. You never know where the next clue will come from," Poole said. "In fact, he's asked you and me to join him for a light snack this evening."

"Good work, Mr. John," Robert said. "But it's not good manners to show up empty-handed. I'll be right back." Robert stood and went back to the kitchen.

Just then, a gorgeous Jamaican woman in her mid-thirties walked into the café and headed to their table. "Hey, Mari! Give your cousin a hug!"

Poole couldn't help but marvel at the similarity between the two women. Both were around five foot seven and had smooth, cocoa-colored skin. The only real difference was that the other woman's black hair was close-cropped in tight curls.

"John, this is my cousin, Abby. She's here to solve our transportation problem," Mari said, smiling.

"Good to meet you, Abby," Poole said as he stood.

Abby held out a set of keys and gave them to Mari. "Just like you asked," she said. "You'll fit right in."

"This will work great. Are you sure Auntie Beth won't miss it?"

"Her eyesight is so bad she hasn't driven in two years. She just bought the damn thing to make her feel young," Abby answered with a small smile.

Poole interjected. "I'm afraid to ask what it is. Remember, we're supposed to be low key, Mari."

"Don't worry, John," Abby responded. "It's a used RAV4 that's been sitting in my auntie's front yard since she stopped driving. I drop by once a week to check in on her and do odd jobs around the house. I also start the car up every time I'm there and drive her around for a couple of miles to make her happy. The only thing I haven't done is wash it."

"That'll be perfect for us," Poole said. "When do you need it back?"

"Not for a while, anyway. I told Auntie Beth I was taking it into the shop for maintenance. So please don't run it into a ditch or anything. If you break it, you buy it."

"Sounds good to me. Thank you," Poole said.

Robert returned and gave Abby a big bear hug. "Hey, Cousin! You're as beautiful as ever. Need a ride home?"

"Got that all taken care of. My new boyfriend, Tommy, followed me over here. He's taking me to dinner."

"Dinner?" Robert asked, arching his eyebrows. "To another restaurant?"

"It was my suggestion, Cuz. You're worse than my father when it comes to my boyfriends!"

"OK, OK. You go have a good time," Robert replied.

"And thanks again for the car," Poole added, extending his hand. Abby ignored the gesture and gave him a hug.

"Ahem," Mari said, clearing her throat. "Tommy, the new boy-friend, remember?"

Abby gave Mari a wink. "Nice meeting you, John," she said with a smile. Then she waved to Mari and Robert and left the café.

"Nice girl, that cousin of yours," Poole said to Mari.

Mari's eyes flashed in mock jealousy as Robert interrupted the scene. "Here," he said as he gave Poole a bottle of wine.

"What's this for?" Poole asked.

"For your light snack with the padre. I've never heard of a man of the cloth turning down a bit of the sacrament."

"Heaven forbid that he think we're unappreciative guests."

Robert nodded in agreement. "There are two things you just can't ignore on this island, Mr. John."

"What are those?"

"Hurricane season and a 2007 Stag's Leap Cabernet."

TWENTY FOUR

Abby had left the RAV4 in the back, near the shed where the Mustang was garaged. It was just as she had described. It sported innocuous green exterior paint that could have used a bath. The windows were tinted, and the tires were almost brand new.

The plan was to park it away from the main parking lot so that prying eyes wouldn't see them get into the car. To make it look like Abby was behind the wheel, Mari had Poole lie down in the backseat until she drove it out onto the main highway. About a mile down the road, after making sure they had no followers, Mari allowed Poole to sit up.

"That was nice and comfy," Poole said.

"Glad you're enjoying your ride, Mr. Poole. Sit back and relax. We should be in Port Maria in no time."

"I love a woman who takes control," Poole replied, smiling. "But seriously, I want to thank you for all the arrangements. It was a nice touch with the look-a-like cousin."

"Abby can be a handful, but we're pretty close. She's the sister I never had."

"It was also smart to arrange to have Robert's wife bring us some clothes once we're at the cottage. You pretty much thought of everything."

"If I had thought of everything, we'd be done with our scavenger hunt by now and be talking about that kiss from the other day." Mari smiled and looked at Poole in the rearview mirror.

"In that case, I'm hoping Father Michael has all the answers!"

"Shame on you, Mr. Poole." Mari shook her head and turned her attention back to the highway. "While we're at the church, you may want to ask the good father for some confession time."

"Amen, sister. Amen."

The church was on the left side of the main highway passing through Port Maria, and Mari guided the green SUV to the back parking area. The small cottage was about fifty paces from where they parked. The rear door of the church was unlocked. They entered quickly so as not to be seen.

"Father?" Poole called in a low voice in the empty sanctuary. "It's John Poole!"

From a side door appeared Father Michael. He was dressed in blue jeans, a white cotton shirt with the tails out, and light-brown boat shoes. "Hi John, good to see you!" he said, extending his hand. "And good to see you as well, Mari."

Father Michael was in his late fifties and had a full head of salt-and-pepper hair. His dark, smooth complexion gave him a movie star quality. And his brilliant smile did nothing to change that perception.

"Please, let's go back to the kitchen. I was just putting together some fruit and cheese," he said.

Poole lifted up the bottle. "I hope you don't mind, but we brought a little thank-you gift. Do you like cabernet?"

A grin came to Father Michael's lips and his laugh filled the sanctuary. "Is the pope Catholic?"

They sat around the sparse kitchen table, picking at the platter of cheese and grapes and sipping on the fabulous red wine. "This cabernet is superb!" Father Michael exclaimed. "I haven't had a red this good since I was in seminary school at Santa Clara. That was my first crisis of faith—continue on to priesthood or start a winery in Napa!"

"Any regrets, Father?" Poole asked.

"Not on days like this," Father Michael answered, lifting his glass to his guests.

"Thanks again for letting us stay at the cottage for a few days," Poole said in earnest.

"That's why we're here, John. Besides, it's the least I can do to honor your father's memory."

"You mentioned that you and my father used to meet and talk on occasion. Can you share what you talked about?" Poole asked.

"Sure, nothing confidential. We mostly talked about the history of this church. And we got into genealogy—what kind of records the church kept, that sort of thing."

"Did he say why?"

"Well, he admitted that he had somewhat of an obsession for Henry Morgan, the pirate. It started out as sort of a search for his roots. I would call it a search for himself, really. He told me that he was abandoned as a child and the only thing he had heard was that he was a descendant of Morgan. He thought that maybe there would be birth records somewhere that would help with his search."

Father Michael studied a grape before he popped it into his mouth. "We also talked about Morgan's land in Port Maria. You know, where it was originally located, what it consisted of."

Mari interrupted. "Did he say that he thought there might be a link between Morgan's old property and his supposed treasure?"

"Sure, we talked about that a lot. But at the end of the day, it was all supposition."

"Did he ever mention a Spanish woman? Teresa Montoya Castillo?" Poole asked.

Father Michael paused to think. "Yes, I remember that name. He was very interested in her and whatever happened to her. He said that he was pretty sure that she lived in Port Maria back in Morgan's time. He even had an odd theory that she was the mother of Morgan's children."

"Why do you think it was an odd theory?" Mari questioned.

"Oh, I don't know, really. It just seemed like a Shakespearean play to me. Morgan was English; she was Spanish. He was Church of England; she was Catholic. Their countries were at war, at least on and off during that time, and it seemed too much like a real-life Romeo and Juliet story to be believable. But, as they say, God works in mysterious ways."

"Did you have any birth records here?" Poole asked.

"No, not here. All of the old records are at Holy Trinity Cathedral in Kingston. It was built in the early 1900s, after the original church was destroyed in an earthquake."

"When was that original church built, Father?" Poole pressed.

"Around 1810, give or take."

"How about in Morgan's time? Were there still Catholic churches on the island then?"

"Absolutely. In fact, that was one of the last conversations your father and I had. Remember, the Spanish Catholics were here way before the English took over the island around 1655. There were small churches all over the place. Even our little church still has rock-work dating back to that time period."

"That's incredible," Mari interjected. "So this was part of the original building?"

"Yes, as far as I know. But I've heard that there were one or two smaller structures that served the faithful back then. I have no idea where, but I supposed Holy Trinity might have some records," Father Michael said.

They emptied the remainder of the Stag's Leap, and Father Michael held up his hand. "Stay seated. Now it's time for me to be a gracious host."

He disappeared into the pantry. Poole and Mari could hear another door open and footsteps descend. When Father Michael reappeared, he held another bottle of wine. "Yes, I think this will do. In honor of my guest from the great State of Washington, I have a nice bottle of Leonetti that you might like."

Poole immediately recognized one of his favorite wines from Washington. "Father, I think this is the beginning of a beautiful friendship!"

"*Casablanca*, right?" Father Michael stated as he opened up the red and refilled their glasses.

"That's right. One of my favorite movies," Poole answered.

Father Michael grinned as he raised his glass. "Well, in that case, here's looking at you kid."

About an hour later, Robert's wife, Marthy, dropped by with some clothes and toiletries for Poole and Mari. After she left, Father Michael led them out to the cottage in the back. "It's not much, but you can call this home for as long as you want. If you need anything, I live in that old stone house farther up the hill," he said, pointing to a structure that looked at least two hundred years old.

Poole and Mari said their thanks, and Father Michael went back to the church to close things up for the night. When they entered the small cottage, Poole felt as though he'd been transported back to the summer camps of his youth. It consisted of three areas, with only the bathroom having walls and a door. The bathroom separated the open galley kitchen and the bedroom, which housed a solitary bed. In front, the main living area contained a small sofa, an old, brown coffee table, and two wooden chairs. On the kitchen side of the room stood a simple wooden table and two more chairs.

"Not quite the *Rebecca*, is it, Mari?" Poole asked rhetorically.

"I've stayed in worse. But let's just hope this is temporary. Really temporary," she answered.

"Well, if we didn't have incentive to get to the end of this, we do now. I'll take the couch; you take the bed," Poole said.

"No way, John. You'll never fit on that thing. I volunteer, and I don't want an argument. There's a curtain dividing the bed from the rest of the room, so we'll have enough privacy," she responded.

"OK. I've learned not to argue with you, so you win," Poole said, smiling. "I'll get ready first."

Five minutes later, Poole drew the sheer curtain to provide separation between the bed and the living area. He was surprised at how firm and comfortable the bed was when he climbed in. Mari came out of the bathroom, shut off the lights, and walked lightly over to the makeshift bed she created out of the sofa. The moonlight shimmered through a side window, giving her an almost ghostly silhouette.

With her back to Poole, Mari slipped out of her shorts and then the cotton blouse she wore. He was taken aback by her figure as she took off her bra, and the moonlight illuminated her breasts. She quickly put on a loose T-shirt and crawled under the blankets as Poole continued to stare.

It took another hour for Poole to slip into a fitful slumber. Even though Mari's steady breathing eventually slowed his racing heart, he couldn't erase the image of her from his mind.

TWENTY FIVE

Poole woke up to the smell of fresh-brewed coffee and the sounds of Mari shuffling about in the kitchen. It was an odd sensation at first. He'd lived on his own for so long that he had become used to silence in the morning. Even though he and Mari had been on the boat together for a couple of weeks, this was different. There was something comforting about the arrangement on dry land.

He rose and padded out to the kitchen where Mari was just pouring two cups of coffee for them. She was still in her T-shirt and had donned her gray sweatpants for the morning. Without thinking about it, Poole walked up behind her, gently grabbed her arms, and gave her a light kiss on the shoulder.

Mari paused slightly and then finished pouring his cup. "You're welcome," she said with a small smile on her face.

They sat down at the wooden table near the kitchen and took a couple of sips without saying a word. Mari finally broke the silence. "What's next, John?"

"I was afraid you were going to ask that," he replied, wiping the sleep out of his eyes. "Eventually, we've got to get back to Montego Bay, and I might have an idea about that. We also know the contents of the first two safe deposit boxes, and that my father was very interested in Catholic church history on the island. Judging by some of the conversations Father Michael described, my father seemed particularly interested in the history of the church around these parts."

"It's obvious that it's related to Teresa Montoya Castillo somehow. It's a safe bet that she was Catholic like all other Spaniards of the day," Mari responded.

"Maybe Morgan built a church for her to worship at or something like that—although he would have had to do it on the sly. Remember, he was still Church of England," Poole said.

"I'm thinking that everything he did with her had to be on the sly. You forget that he was married, and his wife was still on the island. Pirate or not, the English were still a prudish lot," Mari added.

"You're right. So that's why my father concentrated on this side of the island. Remember, Morgan's wife lived in Port Royal. That had to be at least four to five days' ride by horse to his sugar plantation on this side. Most well-bred English women wouldn't even have bothered to make that trip, given that all of the amenities were in Port Royal at the time. My guess is that she didn't like it here anyway and wouldn't have exposed herself to more mosquitoes and unclean conditions," Poole said.

"So, Morgan sets the Spanish woman up on this side, probably at his sugar plantation, and is so smitten by her that he somehow builds her a Catholic church?" Mari asked.

"Well, I'm not sure it was that simple or that blatant. Morgan was pretty sneaky, remember. But I wouldn't put it past him to do something like that."

"Did you see anything on that map that Father Michael showed us last night that looked like a possibility?" Mari asked.

"No, but that map was made probably fifty to a hundred years after Morgan's time. And again, I'm not sure it's going to be as simple as X marks the spot," Poole responded. "We may have to go to the Kingston library to check out some of the old stuff. I suppose while we're there it wouldn't hurt to drop in at Holy Trinity."

Poole checked his watch "But first, I think I need to pay a visit to our lawyer, Mr. Dunbar. He's close by, and I have to start the paperwork on my father's estate eventually. Do you want to come with me?"

"If I ever set foot in that creepy office again, it'll be too soon, John. You're on your own. Besides, I'd like to get this place organized a little and maybe pick Father Michael's brain some more while you're gone," Mari answered.

"Deal. I'll call his office and set something up. And you have fun with the good father. Don't think I don't know what you're up to, by the way. If the guy was any more handsome and charming, he'd give George Clooney a run for his money," Poole said, smiling.

"Don't worry, big boy." Mari replied dryly. "I'm more of a Brad Pitt girl, myself."

Poole arranged to meet Dunbar at ten o'clock that morning. He could have made it sooner but didn't want to give Dunbar the impression that he was in town. Poole quickly crossed the road in front of the church and jogged down a couple of side streets until he felt comfortable enough to slow his pace. The market district was just a few blocks away, and he still had a good hour to kill. A small café appeared on the corner of the next block, so he ducked inside.

A Jamaican in her late teens came to his table. "Good morning, sir. Would you like something to eat?" she asked in the melodic local accent.

"Yes, thank you. What do you recommend?"

"I'm supposed to say it's all good, sir," she said, smiling.

"Tell you what. I've got about an hour, so why don't you bring me what you think is good," Poole said, smiling back.

The young woman left, nodding her head. She returned in a minute or so with a cup of Jamaican hot chocolate. "You'll like this, sir. It's cacao boiled with nutmeg and a cinnamon leaf. Very good for the digestion."

She disappeared again as Poole took a sip of the dark brew. The taste was unique and much better than the American version. In a few minutes, she returned with a plate of local favorites.

"This is ackee and saltfish," she said, pointing to the various colors on the plate. "The green stuff is callaloo, and I've thrown in a couple of johnnycakes."

"This looks and smells wonderful!" Poole said, his mouth watering.

"I just hope you like the taste as much as the looks and smells," she replied, as she walked over to another customer.

Poole ate in silence, enjoying each bite. This was nothing like the typical ham and eggs he usually ordered. He cleaned his plate, using the last johnnycake to sop up the remains of the callaloo. His server returned with a huge smile on her face.

"And the verdict is?" she asked, knowing the answer already.

"You're hired!" Poole grinned. "If I ever have another tough decision to make, I'm calling you."

"Why thank you, sir! It's been my pleasure. I hope to see you again soon."

Poole paid the tab and confirmed that he still had ten minutes to make his way to Dunbar's office. The morning heat was rising, and the town was now fully awake. He walked through the now-familiar market district and spotted the blistered blue door. The flower vendor next door was setting out his wares, but the bright colors did nothing to improve the drabness of Dunbar's office.

Poole opened the creaking door right at ten, and Dunbar appeared from his back office as if he'd been shot out of a cannon.

"Mr. Poole! So good to see you again! Please have a seat over here."

Poole took the chair he'd occupied the last time he was there. "Thanks for seeing me on such short notice, Mr. Dunbar. I'm not sure how much longer I'll be staying on the island, so I thought I'd better get the legal paperwork started."

"Very good, Mr. Poole. I've actually been anticipating this meeting and have had the preliminary paperwork prepared for a couple of days now." With that, Dunbar produced a manila folder containing legal-sized documents that were numbered on the side.

"Please give me a moment, Mr. Dunbar. As you know, I'm an attorney in the States, but I specialize in maritime law, not estates," Poole said, peering over the paperwork. "So this petition is a request to the magistrate to grant me authority to administer the estate, correct?"

"Yes, that's right. You'll see in that one section there that I took the liberty of appointing myself as your resident agent, since you don't live here. This will allow the government to contact my office when it's time to pay death taxes," Dunbar offered.

"That sounds reasonable. How much are the taxes down here?" Poole asked.

"Usually around 5 percent. It's based on the fair market value of the inheritance. Once you are appointed, you need to appraise your father's property and get back to me."

"How long does this whole process take?" Poole asked.

"It really depends on you, Mr. Poole. Many times it can take as long as eighteen months. I don't believe your father owned any real property here, so the administration will most likely be much shorter," Dunbar answered.

"Fine," Poole said as he signed the petition and other documents Dunbar had prepared. "When do you expect that I will have the letters of authority for his estate?"

"Within a few days, Mr. Poole. Lucky for you, I had a couple of cancellations, so I can address your matter right away."

"Excellent," Poole replied. "While I'm here, do you mind if I ask you a couple more questions about my father?"

Dunbar looked up from the paperwork. "Certainly. Anything you want."

"I was wondering how much you and my father worked together on his research. I've come across some things relating to the pirate, Henry Morgan, but I'm not sure what they mean."

Dunbar sat up in his chair and inched closer to Poole. "What things are you referring to?"

"Did you two ever discuss the existence of a Spanish woman who may have been a mistress of Morgan's?" Poole asked.

"Well, of course," Dunbar responded cryptically. "The woman from Panama."

"What ever happened to her?"

"Good question. Your father and I looked at all the usual texts and were convinced that he loved her. There would have been no other explanation as to why he freed her in Panama," Dunbar answered.

"Would it surprise you that he may have brought her to Jamaica instead of releasing her?"

Dunbar sat up in his chair, dumbfounded. "Yes, I would be surprised. Your father and I never found any records that would suggest that. Although the theory would have had some merit, from your father's point of view."

"Why is that, Mr. Dunbar?"

"Well, your father was on a quest for his identity. He was somehow convinced that he was a descendant of Morgan. In order for that to happen, Morgan would have had to have children, which did not occur with his wife, Mary Elizabeth," Dunbar stated. "So I suppose it would make sense that he thought Morgan had children with that Spanish woman. Grasping at straws, if you ask me."

"What about a ruby? Did you ever discuss some sort of precious gem involving Morgan?"

"What kind of ruby?" Dunbar asked, as he pulled out his handkerchief and dabbed his forehead.

"I guess it was heart-shaped. Did you two ever discuss that?" Poole asked.

"You're talking about 'Madonna's Heart.' At least, that's the name we gave it. A large heart-shaped ruby that was last seen in Panama City before the Morgan raid. What do you know about it?" Dunbar asked intently.

"Not much at all, really," Poole responded. "I just saw a vague reference to a large ruby in one of my father's journals. Did you two track it to Jamaica?"

"We both believed that it had to have come back with him, but neither of us could find any direct evidence for that assumption. Of course, if that gem were found today, it would be priceless," Dunbar said, again dabbing his forehead. "Damned heat!"

"One last thing, if you don't mind. Have you ever heard of a fellow named Ryker Wilson?"

Dunbar froze for a moment and then quickly answered. "Yes, I've heard of the name. He's an old partner of your father's, if I'm not mistaken. I believe they shared the same interests in Morgan, but that's all I can tell you."

"Thank you for your time, Mr. Dunbar. I appreciate your enlightenment on some of this Morgan stuff as well. If I have any other questions, I trust that I can count on your input and discretion?" Poole asked as he stood and took Dunbar's hand.

"Absolutely, young man. I'm here to help in any way!" Dunbar answered with a weak smile.

Poole quickly left the dingy office to breathe in the fresh air of the market. Dunbar didn't follow him out this time, saying he wanted to start working on the estate paperwork right away. Poole took his time strolling through the market, looking for familiar faces. He checked his watch, and it was still shy of eleven. To make sure he wasn't being followed, he went back to the café where he had breakfast and took a discreet seat by the window.

His young waitress came over with a large smile. "Back for more, sir?"

"How about a nice cup of that Jamaican chocolate. I think I might give up coffee for that," Poole responded with a smile of his own.

Once the chocolate arrived, he scanned the passersby while he hid his face from the window. It only took two sips to see Dunbar scurry past the café, walking at an urgent pace. Then, out of the corner of his eye, he noticed a tall, dark-haired man coming out of a shop on the other side of the street. The man was watching Dunbar, and followed his path from a distance. He paused to light a cigarette and glanced briefly toward the café where Poole was sitting. Then Ryker Wilson continued on the opposite side of the street until he disappeared from view.

TWENTY SIX

"That Wilson guy keeps turning up like a bad penny," Poole said to Mari after discussing the events of the morning. "To be honest, I'm not sure if he was watching me or Dunbar. I swear he looked my way, but walked after Dunbar instead. What's with that guy?"

"I think you're right not to trust him. My guess is that he's still a little bitter about the falling out with your dad," Mari responded.

"Then why would my father go back and make amends with him a few months ago?"

"If you believe that, then I've got some swampland to sell you. That was his story, not your father's," Mari replied.

"OK, you're right. All I know for sure is that lately it seems like he knows where we are or where we're going to be. And that doesn't make me feel all that safe," Poole admitted.

Mari nodded in agreement. "At least we've answered one more question, John. Now we know that it wasn't 'my Donna's heart,' it was 'Madonna's Heart.'"

"Yeah, it was all I could do to keep my mouth shut. Dunbar seems harmless enough, but you never know who might force him to talk," Poole said.

"You mean like Ryker Wilson?"

"That's exactly who I mean," Poole replied.

"What was Dunbar's reaction when you mentioned it?" Mari asked.

"I don't know. Matter-of-fact, I guess. Like it was old news," Poole responded. "He did say that it would be priceless today."

"Then that would give more than a few people enough incentive to find it. Maybe to the point of making sure that we don't," Mari said warily. "What do we do now?"

"Follow my father's lead. He didn't spend time with Father Michael just to get religion. My guess is that he narrowed the location of Madonna's Heart to around here somewhere. Maybe the answer is in that last safe deposit box. Or it could be in the records of Holy Trinity," Poole replied.

"My vote is Montego Bay. At least we know there's something there worth finding. At Holy Trinity, it would be like looking for a needle in a haystack."

"I'm with you. Now that we have the new car, maybe we can go in unnoticed and get what we need."

"That's good in theory, but if Ryker Wilson is following us, or if those two guys are still casing the bank, we're not going to fool anybody," Mari responded.

Poole pondered that for a bit. "I think I may have a possible solution to that problem. It'll require a little trust, though."

"Hell, that's all we've been going on since you got here. No need to change in midstream, John."

"Do you have a digital camera around here?"

"Sure. There's one in the wheelhouse."

"Then grab the camera and the keys. I want to make sure we get there before lunchtime."

Again, Mari drove, and Poole slid down in the backseat until she felt the coast was clear. Poole made a quick phone call while they were on the road. When he ended the call, Mari looked back at him in the rearview mirror with questioning eyes.

"I just made sure that our friend was working today," he answered.

"Fredrickson?" she asked.

"Yep. He takes lunch at twelve thirty on Fridays. He's agreed to meet with us as long as I spring for a sandwich," Poole replied.

"We've got about an hour, so we should be good for time. Where are we meeting him?" Mari asked.

"The Cliffs, of course. There's a private employee dining area where we can meet."

"Good. Montego Bay is too small to have a private rendezvous," Mari said. "So what's the plan?"

"I'll let you know when it's fully formed. It's in the idea stage right now," Poole said.

"You really know how to instill confidence in the troops, John."

About fifteen minutes later, they pulled into the valet area of the Cliffs. Poole jumped out immediately and walked into the restaurant without looking up. Mari took care of the attendant and followed him in. They waited in the lobby for Fredrickson, who rode up a minute later on a light-blue Vespa.

Fredrickson entered through a side door and met them in the lobby. "Hi Mr. Poole, Ms. Mari. Follow me downstairs," he said.

They sat down in the employee lunchroom. Again, Poole whistled as he looked out the window. "Even the employees get a great view! Not bad at all."

"If I could afford the stuff on the menu, I'd enjoy the view too, sir," Fredrickson said, smiling.

"Well, this one's on me, so order what you want. But more importantly, thanks for meeting us, Fredrickson," Poole continued, getting down to business. "I know you don't have much time, so go ahead and order and let us pick your brain for a bit."

Fredrickson nodded. He called the kitchen and put in his order. "I'm the one to thank you, Mr. Poole. How can I help you?"

"Do you remember yesterday, when we came into your branch, we decided against getting into our safe deposit box?" Poole asked.

"Yeah, I thought you left pretty fast. What happened?"

"We think that someone has been following us around for some reason. And whatever is in that safe deposit box might be why," Poole answered.

"OK, but I don't see how I can help," he answered truthfully.

"I'm not sure if you can either, really. But is it possible for you to help me see what's in the box?" Poole asked.

"It would be bending the rules, but I guess it's possible. I'd need the key and your authority to open the box for you," Fredrickson said.

"Do you need that in writing?" Poole asked.

"Yes, or else it would be as if I was stealing. There's no way I would take that risk, sir."

Fredrickson's lunch arrived—a strip steak and warm-water lobster. Poole nodded with approval. "Good, eat up. The favor I'm asking is big."

Poole put his elbows on the table and leaned toward Fredrickson. "I'll sign whatever you need, Fredrickson. I don't know you, but I trust you. And that's sort of the theme for the day around here."

Fredrickson smiled between bites. "Opening it is one thing, but I don't think it would be cool to take anything out of the vault."

"We don't want you to. I have a digital camera here. I want you to take pictures of everything. If there is a sack with gold coins, for example, I want you to take a picture of the sack and then its contents. I also want you to make sure you separate and count the coins in the sack for good measure," Poole said.

"Sounds easy enough," Fredrickson responded.

"And if there is any correspondence, we need you to photograph the page or pages. The contents of those may be important."

Poole leaned back in his chair and looked intently at Fredrickson. "Finally, if there is another safe deposit box key I'll need that or at least I'll need the key number to figure out what branch to go to next. Do you think that's doable for you?"

"Sure, Mr. Poole. But how can I get that authorization to you for signature?"

"Do you have one more break before the end of the day?" Poole asked.

"Yes, at three thirty. Then I close up at six," he answered.

"Good. You know that drug store across the street?"

"Yeah, sure."

"Just meet me there when you take your break. I'll sign the authorization and give you the key to the box. We'll rendezvous after you get off work. By the way, Fredrickson, I'm going to make this worth your while," Poole said earnestly.

"I have no doubt, Mr. Poole. Once a good tipper, always a good tipper."

After Fredrickson left, Poole and Mari were allowed to hang out in the employee's dining room for the next hour. Poole bought Mari a small lunch, but he was still stuffed from the ackee and saltfish he'd eaten for breakfast. When she was finished, she went to get the SUV. After paying the valet, Poole quickly exited the restaurant and climbed in the backseat.

"So what do you think of my plan?" Poole asked Mari.

"It's pretty harebrained, if you ask me, but I don't have anything better, so let's go for it," she answered.

"Well, that's not exactly a ringing endorsement, but I'll take anything I can get right now," Poole said.

By three fifteen, they were in Montego Bay. Mari parked the car a couple of blocks behind the drug store and waited. After scanning the surrounding area, Poole exited the SUV and walked to the drug store. He entered quickly and hung out toward the back of the store, but still kept an eye on the street.

On cue, Fredrickson came out of the bank and headed over to the drug store. He picked up some gum and grabbed a Coke from the cooler in the back, where Poole stood. As he passed by, Poole handed him the key. At the same time, Poole signed the slip of paper Fredrickson gave to him. They spoke briefly, then as smooth as could be, Fredrickson paid for his items at the register and walked casually back to the bank.

"That kid's an operator," Poole said under his breath. "I'll be working for him one of these days."

Poole waited to make sure he didn't see any familiar faces. Satisfied, he slipped out the front door and quickly turned down the alley to meet Mari.

A block away, a short Jamaican man with long dreadlocks sat on a bench and watched Poole leave the drug store. He picked up his cell phone and made a call. "I saw him. But he didn't enter the bank."

"Stay there. He'll probably be back at closing time. He has to go in there sometime."

"The sooner, the better. This wig is making my head itch."

"Patience. He's smart, so I have confidence that he'll figure it all out. Let him find what he's supposed to find. Then we'll let him lead us right to the treasure."

TWENTY SEVEN

September 1671

M organ paced on the veranda of the plantation house. Mr. Dunn sat in one of the rocking chairs on pins and needles, hoping that all went well that afternoon. Morgan had entreated the old priest in Port Maria to summon his nuns with birthing skills, and they had come to the plantation. They had been with Teresa for several hours, and his mind was racing.

It had been a difficult six months for Morgan. It took all of his cunning to convince the acting governor that he had lost his ship in a squall just off Portland Point and that he was fortunate to have saved himself in one of the longboats. No, he couldn't account for the crew, God rest their poor souls.

His good friend, Thomas Modyford, had been arrested for allowing Morgan to raid Panama City after the peace accord was reached between England and Spain. Modyford already had returned to England to face charges. In spite of Morgan's attempts to plead ignorance of the treaty, which, ironically, was true, a decision was pending on whether he must follow Modyford to England. In the meantime, Morgan was allowed to put his affairs in order on the island. His wife, Mary Elizabeth, was anxious to get back to civilization, but Morgan had more important things on his mind.

"Mr. Dunn. Some tea, lad," Morgan commanded. Dunn scampered into the kitchen to comply.

Morgan was worried. Teresa was a strong, young woman, but the conditions here were primitive. Many things could go wrong during the birth of a child, and he thought about every one of them. He shook his head and laughed silently. You're as troubled as an old woman, he told himself. You wouldn't feel this way if it wasn't Teresa.

Mr. Dunn came back with Morgan's tea, and he sat down in one of the rockers. It was cooler than usual for the time of year; a storm had just blown through, and the air was less humid. Morgan figured that he had about six months, at the most, before he had to go back to England. And he wasn't sure he would ever be allowed to come back. Unlike his wife, he didn't want to leave. He'd been in Jamaica since he was a young man. This was home. And now, he truly felt that he had a reason to stay.

He had grown to love Teresa over the last few months, and he felt that she was at least gaining more and more acceptance of her new life with him. He heard the first scream from inside the bedroom, and it startled him. When he heard the second, he bolted to his feet, spilling the remains of his tea on his trousers.

Morgan became more agitated as he heard his lovely Teresa struggle. He knew that he was supposed to stay on the veranda, but he couldn't remain there any longer. He burst through the front door and headed to the master bedroom, where the midwives were attending to her. As he strode across the floor, he heard her scream one more time and then there was silence. He stopped, frozen. Then he heard another cry, the cry of a small voice new to the world.

He slowly entered the bedroom to see Teresa holding a small bundle next to her chest. The baby was still red with blood. Teresa was sweating and exhausted, but she looked up at him and smiled.

"It is a girl, Henry," she said. "I hope you aren't disappointed."

He looked at the exquisite woman and her newborn child, and a wave of pride swelled inside him. "I am far from disappointed, Teresa. You have brought me an angel today."

"Then perhaps that will be her name."

"Angelica?" Morgan suggested.

"Angelica." She nodded. "Our little angel."

TWENTY EIGHT

P oole walked back to the SUV and jumped into the backseat. "All
set," he said to Mari.

"OK, what's next?"

"We meet Fredrickson at a place called The Dive in Negril around
seven. We've got a couple of hours to kill, so do you have any sug-
gestions?" Poole asked.

"As a matter of fact, I do. I told you that Negril is my favorite part
of the island. There's a great beach there."

"As long as there's a Red Stripe dispenser close by, I'm in," Poole
said.

Mari laughed. "Then it's your lucky day!"

Mari started the RAV4 and took side streets until they were out
of the central part of Montego Bay. Then they headed west on the
highway toward Negril. Mari pulled over at a roadside store, picked
up a six-pack of Red Stripe, and then continued for a few miles until
they reached a turnoff on the right. The sign read Cousins Cove.

"Cousins Cove? Really?" Poole said sarcastically.

"Don't worry, John. It's just a name. No relatives in this neck of
the woods. I know about a great, secluded beach down here. And
you can even dip your toes in the surf, if you dare."

"OK, you're driving, and I'm at your mercy. Cousins Cove it is."

They drove off the paved road and followed dirt tire tracks down
toward the water. At the end of the road was a small, secluded beach.

"Grab the beer. I've got a blanket in the back," she said.

Poole and Mari walked out onto the sand and found a shaded
area beneath a couple of intertwined palm trees. The sand was as
fine as sugar, and the beach was protected by outcrops of black rock

on either end, like sentries on guard. It was late afternoon, and they had the beach to themselves. After laying out the blanket and opening the beer, it was almost as if Poole was on vacation.

"How funny is this, Mari? We look like a couple on holiday, but we're involved in a treasure hunt, and bad guys are chasing us. The folks back home will never believe it," he said.

"Well, I have to say that you're not dull. If we didn't have this scavenger hunt, what would we talk about?" Mari asked.

"I'd ask a lot more about you," he said honestly. "I'd want to know as much as I could."

"What would you want to know?" she asked, looking at him intently.

"I'd want to know what your plans are. Whether you plan to spend the rest of your life in Jamaica or if that was just the plan for now."

"Anything else?" she prodded.

"And I'd want to know if there was someone serious in your life, or if you had room for someone like that."

She smiled. "I guess I would answer those questions with some questions of my own. My plans are mine until they involve more than me. Since I don't have someone in my life right now, then my plans are what they are. Is there room for someone like that? Sure, if the right guy comes along. How about you?"

"I've been thinking about it more and more. And I guess my answer is the same as yours," Poole replied.

They held up their beers and touched the bottles lightly. "Here's to making room for the right one," Mari said.

Poole nodded in agreement without taking his eyes off hers. "I'll drink to that."

The sun went down, and they made their way back to the SUV. Mari steered the Toyota back to the main highway and drove straight to The Dive, which was just a few miles away. They parked on the other side of the street and waited for the light-blue Vespa to arrive. The Dive was nestled in a grove of palm trees, and its yellow glow lit up the night like a firefly. Steel drum music lilted across the road to the parking lot, carrying with it the smell of cooked meat and the laughter of the patrons inside. In spite of the restaurant's inviting atmosphere, it was ten minutes past seven and they were starting to get concerned.

"I hope something didn't happen to Fredrickson," Poole said.

"I shouldn't say this, but I'm just hoping he's as trustworthy as you think," Mari replied.

Just then, they heard the high pitch of the Vespa's engine, and ten seconds later it pulled into the parking lot. Fredrickson had his backpack with him, and he entered the restaurant without delay.

"We're on!" Poole said. They crossed the street to meet with their new friend.

The Dive was an open-air restaurant with a long bar on the left, just past the front door. Fredrickson was sitting at the far end of the bar, with an open stool on either side of him. Poole and Mari joined him, and Poole ordered drinks for them all.

"I can't tell you how much I appreciate this, Fredrickson," Poole said seriously.

"No problem, Mr. Poole. I might have broken a couple of banking laws, but it was worth it just to see what was in the box," Fredrickson responded. "Here's your camera and the key. I took pictures of everything."

Poole took the camera and started looking at the pictures in the view finder while Fredrickson described each one.

"I started with the leather bag. It was there, just like you said, with the drawstring and everything. I opened it up, and there were two gold coins and one pretty big emerald inside. Here's a good picture of it," Fredrickson said, pointing to an image of the coins.

Poole and Mari looked at the photograph. It showed the same type of bag that they'd found in the other two safe deposit boxes.

The emerald looked large, like the others. But the gold coins were larger, with Spanish writing on them. "I'm guessing these have a little value, but I don't have a clue as to what it might be," Poole said.

"Those are old Spanish doubloons, Mr. Poole," Fredrickson chimed in. "In great shape, so they're probably worth a thousand US dollars each."

"But there's only two of them, so we can't retire yet," Mari added.

"Then there's the emerald, just like the first bag. I'm sure there's a pattern, but I don't see it yet," Poole commented. "What's next, Fredrickson?"

"This next shot is of a map, or at least part of one. Check out the edges. It looked like the entire thing was ripped from a larger map," Fredrickson pointed out.

They all looked closer. The edges of the paper were roughly torn, almost as if it had been done in a hurry. The section that was left was just a simple sketch. Broad pencil strokes suggested hills and valleys; a dotted line implied a trail, and there were several trees. There were also two small rectangles, perhaps indicating structures. The one on the left was circled in red.

"You don't suppose this is where your father was leading you, do you?" Mari asked with wide eyes.

"It's not an X, but it's pretty damned close," Poole replied. "But it doesn't mean a thing unless we know where this ripped-out section fits. There's no way to get a reference as to where it might be on the island."

"Why not just give us the whole damned map?" Mari demanded. "It's the least John Morgan could have done!"

"My guess is that it was some sort of fail-safe precaution. If someone got hold of this one section, he would only know as much as we do. And if he got hold of the other part, he wouldn't know where to go exactly. I think he was counting on, or hoping, that we would be the only ones to get both parts," Poole answered.

"OK, I'll buy that. What else do you have, Fredrickson?" Mari asked.

"Two more things. One was a copy of an old letter. I freaked out when I saw it was signed by H. Morgan! Like Henry Morgan, the pirate?"

"One and the same," Poole answered. "Go on."

"And the other was a slip of note paper addressed to you, Mr. Poole. I was careful to take pictures of both," Fredrickson reported. "And I checked the backs of both of them to make sure I didn't miss anything."

"And nothing else was in the box?" Mari asked.

"Nope, that was it, and I put everything back, like you asked."

"Thank you, Fredrickson," Poole said, extending his hand.

They shook, and Poole pressed five one-hundred-dollar bills into Fredrickson's palm. "This is for your time today. I want you to know that you still have a tip coming, so I'll be looking you up when we're through. Deal?"

Fredrickson nodded with a smile. "Deal."

"Good. Now you should take off, just in case an unwanted visitor walks through the door. We'll be in touch," Poole said.

Fredrickson stood and gulped down the last of his drink. "Always a pleasure, Mr. Poole and Ms. Mari," he said and turned toward the door.

Poole and Mari could hear the little Vespa whir to life, and the high-pitched whine of the engine receded into the night as Fredrickson rode away.

"It was good that you sent Fredrickson on, John," Mari said. "The less he knows, the safer he'll be."

"My thinking exactly," Poole replied. "Now, which letter should we read first?"

"Age before beauty, I always say," Mari answered.

"OK, Captain Morgan it is," Poole said as he took the phone and scrolled to the picture of the Morgan letter. "Damn it all!"

"What's wrong, John?"

"The flash. This letter was encased in some sort of plastic. The flash just made the whole photo a big, white reflection. The only thing I can make out is the date, January 10, 1681, at the top of the correspondence and H. Morgan at the bottom," Poole said dejectedly.

"Poor Fredrickson, I'm sure he didn't know," Mari replied, consoling him.

"Yeah, it wasn't his fault. Everything else looks like it came out great. We'll just have to figure that one out later. The banks will be closed for the weekend, so I guess we'll just regroup on Monday and go from there."

"What about the other letter?" Mari asked.

"At least this one I can read," Poole responded. "Let's see what it says." Poole enlarged the text and held it out so they could read it together.

> Dearest John:
>
> I hope this letter finds you well, as I am sure you've had an interesting few days on the island. I'm sorry for the little scavenger hunt I've led you on, but I felt it was necessary. Some of the things that I have discovered are of great value to me and our family. Other things I've found are of great monetary value to others—so much so that I felt it important to be cautious on how, and when, you learn what I have learned.
>
> My hope is that the people who caused me to create this will make themselves evident to you before you reach the end of your journey. If I knew for sure who they were as I write this letter, I would tell you. I can only surmise who those "interested" parties are. Concentrating on finding them will not get you any closer to your goal, so please don't worry about them. I have faith that you will be looked after.
>
> I have to apologize for the crudeness of the map I left for you. Obviously, it is part of a larger map,

but, again, I've done this to make sure that the entire answer would not fall into the wrong hands. Of course, the correspondence from Henry Morgan provides the final pieces of the puzzle. You must promise me to heed the words of Morgan, as I truly believe there is danger lurking for the unwary once you get close.

As you can see, I have no more safe deposit box keys for you to use. In order to find the final piece, you'll need to hit the books. Then sit down and think awhile. Only then will an answer reveal itself.

Lastly, remember to follow my woman. That's what I should have done from the start. All that's left now is her memory.

Dad

Poole and Mari looked at each other in puzzlement. "You're kidding, right?" Mari asked incredulously.

"I think my father thinks I'm a lot smarter than I am. There might be some clues or something in this letter, but I sure don't get them right now," Poole said. "In order to find the final piece, we have to hit the books. What, go to the library?"

"Don't look at me. You're the lawyer. I'm just a little old diver girl," Mari responded.

"Thanks. It sounds like the rats are jumping off this sinking ship."

Mari gave him a nudge. "The ship's not sinking, John. But we might want to think about bailing some water soon."

TWENTY NINE

Poole and Mari made the long drive back to the cottage in the darkness of the Jamaican evening. Poole scanned through the photos again while Mari drove, looking at the coins, the map, and the letter.

"At least we know one thing," Poole said. "There're no more safe deposit boxes in our future."

"OK. What else do we know?" she asked.

"Well, we know that all three boxes had coins and gems in them. So, we know that wasn't by coincidence. If we find a pattern, then perhaps that's something we can build on."

Poole scrolled back to the map. "We also know that there is a larger part of this map. And as soon as we go to the library, we'll be able to figure it all out," he said sarcastically.

"Don't be so negative, John. I'm sure there's an easy explanation. It just hasn't hit us on the head yet. Maybe Father Michael can help?"

"Maybe, unless he's one of those interested parties my father was talking about."

"Oh, ye of little faith. If Father Michael is an interested party then I'm joining the other side. I'd like him at least to look at the cutout of that map. Maybe he'll recognize it. Or maybe he might know what that reference to 'hit the books' means," Mari said.

"Sorry, Mari, you're right. I'm just a little frustrated with my father. Why give us a cryptic clue like that right now?"

"I'm going to give him the benefit of the doubt. We just have to think in terms of how you would interpret that letter as opposed to someone else."

"Good point. But right now, I think we should sleep on it and see if the letter looks different in the morning," Poole said.

"Sorry, John. I'm not sleepy yet. Let's at least talk about the gold coins," Mari replied as they drove along the A-1.

"You missed your calling, Mari," Poole laughed. "You remind me of Ms. McCallister, my fifth-grade teacher. She wouldn't let me slough anything off."

"Well, good! Glad I can help bring back your bad memories for you," Mari teased.

"Not bad memories at all," Poole said. "Ms. McCallister was hot!"

"Enough, you pervert!" Mari cried.

"Funny, that's what Ms. McCallister would say."

"Gawd!"

"OK, OK. Back to the coins," Poole said as he pulled out his phone and scrolled through the pictures of the other leather bags. "The first one had eleven small gold coins and an emerald."

"Eleven plus one. Twelve total. OK, what was the next one?"

"That one had a bunch of smaller gold bits. There were twenty-six in total, plus this gorgeous ruby," Poole answered.

"Twenty-six plus one. Twenty-seven in total. And the last box had an emerald and two large gold doubloons. Three in all."

"Clear as mud," Poole responded. "Could it be coordinates or something? Latitude and longitude?"

"Maybe. We'll have to get out a chart to see what it lines up to," Mari replied. "There are charts on the *Rebecca*, but I imagine we can get what we need on your tablet as well."

"There's got to be something with the emeralds and ruby, too," Poole said.

"I guess. They could mean stop and go. It could also mean plus and minus. Maybe we're supposed to add and subtract some coins," Mari guessed.

"Could be, but until we line it up with a map, we could go round and round with this," Poole said.

"You're right, John. We might as well put this to rest for a while."

"At least for tonight. Tomorrow I want to look at the letter with fresh eyes. And I want to talk with Father Michael, if he's around. We may be making a trip to Kingston to the main library," Poole said.

"I wonder if Holy Trinity has a library," Mari said. "Father Michael mentioned that they had records there for all the old churches and stuff."

"If that's the case, they probably have maps too. Good a plan as any, Mari."

"Thank you, Mr. John." Mari said in a deep voice, attempting to imitate Robert.

Poole shook his head. "I think I like you better as Ms. McCallister."

The next morning, Poole woke up to the smell of coffee and the rustling of papers. He opened his eyes to see Mari huddled over the wooden table next to the kitchen. Even through the gauze of the makeshift curtain, he could tell she was deep in thought.

"Hey, good morning!" Poole said, sitting up in bed. "How long have you been up?"

"Maybe an hour. I heard Father Michael shuffling around out-side, so I got up to talk to him before he got too involved with his day."

"How is the good father?" Poole asked.

"Handsome and charming as ever," Mari replied.

Poole rolled his eyes as he got out of bed. "I'm sure there's a consequence for those thoughts you're having. You'd better say a Hail Mary or two."

"Just get your fanny out of bed, you smart aleck," Mari responded. "I got some maps from Father Michael, and I need your help to figure this out."

Poole let out a big yawn and pulled back the curtain. "At least let me wake up for a minute, would you?"

"Two minutes, lazy bones. Coffee's made," Mari responded.

Poole grabbed a cup of coffee from the kitchen and sat down opposite Mari at the wooden table. She was already in shorts and a button-down blouse. Her dark hair was up in its familiar ponytail.

"So what are you looking at?" Poole asked.

"These are maps of the Port Maria area supplied by Father Michael, thank you very much," Mari said smugly. She turned the map around so Poole could get a better view. The map was old, maybe from around 1800. Unfortunately, it didn't show much detail other than a general outline of the coast and the parish divisions on the island. But it did show Port Maria, in the Saint Mary parish, and a marking that could have been Cabarita Island.

Poole looked at the picture on the camera and tried to match it to the map, but there were no distinguishing marks to use as reference points. "Did you show him this picture, Mari?"

"Yes, but he didn't have a clue either. He did confirm that there are archives at Holy Trinity, though. In fact, he called one of his friends and made arrangements for a private tour for us," Mari said.

"What time?"

"Eleven sharp. We've got a couple of hours. Father Michael has invited us for a little breakfast before we go."

"Good. I've got a hankering for ackee and saltfish," Poole said, smiling.

"You've been here for less than two weeks and you already think you're a local. Brother," Mari said, shaking her head.

Poole quickly cleaned up, and then transferred the pictures from the camera to his cell phone before they went over to the church. Father Michael was waiting for them in the kitchen. "Good morning, John. I've got some more coffee, if you want some."

"Thank you, Father," Poole replied.

"I trust you looked at the map I gave you two," Father Michael started. "Did you find anything?"

"Nothing at all, Father," Mari answered. "It looks like we need to make that trip to Holy Trinity."

"Fine. Like I said, ask for Brother Thomas. He'll be able to help you," Father Michael said. "You shouldn't have any problem figuring out who he is."

"Why is that?" Poole asked.

"He's the only brother there who used to be an offensive lineman in the NFL. He's six foot six and weighs over three hundred pounds."

"Who did he used to play for, Father?"

"San Francisco. So do me a favor."

"What's that?"

"Don't tell him you're from Seattle."

A t just past eleven, they entered the Holy Trinity Cathedral. By Jamaican standards, the foyer was cavernous. Outside, it was eighty-five degrees, but it felt fifteen degrees cooler inside. It took about two seconds to spot Brother Thomas. He was wearing a black cassock and filled the entire doorway of his office.

"You must be John Poole and Mari Robeson," he said in a lilting Jamaican accent. "I'm Thomas."

Brother Thomas towered over them. Father Michael had been kind when he said that Thomas weighed around three hundred pounds. Four hundred was closer to the mark. In spite of his girth, he had a kind face and smiling eyes. "Thomas, thank you so much for seeing us on such short notice," Poole said as he watched his hand disappear in Thomas's.

"My pleasure, Mr. Poole. Father Michael said that you would like to visit the archives. Do you know what you're looking for?"

"I wish we did, Thomas," Poole replied. "To be honest, we're hoping for a stroke of inspiration while we're in there."

"Then you've come to the right place. We specialize in inspiration around here," Brother Thomas said as he led the way to the archives.

Poole and Mari spent the rest of the afternoon immersed in the archive room of the cathedral. They started in the map section, going over every ancient map and chart the archives had to offer. Then they looked through volumes of texts on the early Catholic churches of the period, learning when they were built and where they were located on the island, but found no link to Morgan or Teresa Montoya Castillo.

"This is more than frustrating, John," Mari said, as loose strands of her hair danced free from her ponytail.

"I'm with you on that," Poole said in a whisper. "We've 'hit the books' and there's nothing here. I suppose we could go to the Kingston library, but I'm convinced it would be another waste of our time."

"But where does that leave us? Have we reached a dead end?"

"No. There's always the last bank in Montego Bay. We can read that Morgan letter and maybe that will give us something to go on. But I can't ask Fredrickson to bend the rules for us this time. It's something I need to do on my own," Poole said.

"But that's a big risk. Someone's probably watching the place so they'll pick up our trail again."

"Listen, Mari. If there was another way, I'd do it."

Mari thought for a moment. "Maybe there is. Fredrickson may not have taken a good picture of the Morgan letter, but I'd put money down that he read it. It wouldn't hurt to ask him. If he did, maybe he can remember enough of the details to give us something."

"That's a great idea, Mari," Poole said. "We know where he works on Sundays, so let's take a quick trip up to the Cliffs tomorrow."

"Sounds like a plan, John. In the meantime, I want to go over that letter from your father again. There was something in there that's been bugging me."

"What's that?"

"It was that phrase 'remember to follow my woman.' Something about it sounds odd to me. Every other reference was about following *the* woman. But this letter says follow *my* woman."

"He probably was thinking in the possessive with Senora Castillo after chasing her for so many years," Poole offered.

"Nope, I don't think so. Give me your phone for a second."

Mari scrolled through the photographs until she came to the letter from John Morgan. "Here. It says, 'Lastly, remember to follow my woman. That's what I should have done from the start. All that's left now is her memory.'"

Mari handed the phone back to Poole. "What if he wasn't talking about the Spanish woman?"

Poole paused, stunned. "You're absolutely right, Mari. My father's 'woman' was my mother! In a way, it's a confession. He's saying that's what he should have done—follow her instead of letting her go."

"And all that's left now is her memory?" Mari asked, knowing the answer.

"The *Rebecca*. He was trying to lead us back to the *Rebecca*."

"My thoughts exactly, Mr. Poole!" Mari agreed.

"Well, the sooner the better. Let's get out of here."

"Not so fast, John," Mari said.

"What now?"

"Look at the mess we have around us," Mari said. "We'd better put this stuff back where we found it or we'll have to answer to Brother Thomas."

"Good point, Mari," Poole agreed. "The last thing we need is to get on the wrong side of that guy."

"I'm sure there were a lot of guys he played against who said the same thing."

THIRTY

March 1675

M organ stood on the bow of the naval frigate as it left Hispaniola, the last leg of his passage from England back to Jamaica. It had been almost three years since his arrest in the summer of 1672. As he suspected, the Crown was covering its embarrassment for his taking of Panama City. His poor friend, Thomas Modyford, the first to go, had been forced to spend a short time in the Tower of London. Fortunately, Morgan's reputation allowed him more freedom, and he managed to avoid that vile place.

The wind refreshed him, as he knew within a few hours he would be back home in Jamaica. Politics, he thought. One moment you're a scoundrel and the next, you're a celebrity. Morgan shook his head, thinking of the past years in England. All of the lords and dukes had invited him to their parties so that he could regale them with tales of his piracy. The worst "punishment" he ever suffered was to pay for his own food and lodging when he wasn't playing the celebrity.

The Crown accepted his explanation that he was unaware of the treaty between Spain and England at the time of the raid. Although he wasn't certain, Morgan suspected that the Crown might be lenient under the circumstances, since he had brought significant contributions to its coffers. Ironically, the King had even sought Morgan's opinion as to how best to protect England's interests in the Caribbean, now that the Dutch were making some headway in the region. And instead of having to spend the rest of his days in dusty old England, good King Charles II had knighted him and named him lieutenant governor of Port Royal, in charge of the island's defenses.

Morgan didn't care about the post or the knighthood. He was actually perturbed that he would have to spend precious time setting things up in Port Royal. Instead, his entire focus was on the other side of the island and his plantation in Port Maria, where his beloved Teresa waited. He'd sent word of his return on a merchantman a few months before and hoped that it had found its way to Mr. Dunn. This time, his stay would be different. His wife, Mary Elizabeth, had elected to remain in London. Although he feigned disappointment and said he would return as soon as his duties were completed, they both knew that it was the last they would see of each other. His life and his future were now going to be with the woman he loved.

The Blue Mountains loomed in the distance and rose higher from the sea the closer they sailed toward Port Royal. Morgan could make out the sails of several ships in the harbor and could see the bustle of activity in the town. He was on the first longboat to shore after they anchored, and was greeted by Mr. Dunn, now a young man of fourteen, once he landed.

"You've grown, Mr. Dunn!" Morgan exclaimed as he clapped him on the back. "It seems like only yesterday you were barely up to my chin!"

"And you look the same, Captain. We've all missed you here," Dunn said truthfully.

Morgan smiled, knowing that Mr. Dunn was placating his ego. During the voyage, Morgan had turned forty, and he knew that he was now an elder statesman in Jamaica, rather than a man of action. "Thank you, Mr. Dunn. I see that you are learning the language of diplomacy."

With Dunn in tow, Morgan walked past the customs house on Queen Street toward the governor's residence. "I have a few days here to reestablish myself and my new post. It would seem that I've become a politician, Mr. Dunn. So I have to keep up appearances before I make my way back to the plantation. Please tell me, how is everything in Port Maria?"

"The plantation is thriving, and the mistress has been managing the sale of crops in your absence. I believe that you will be quite pleased when you return," Dunn said.

"And how has she fared with the child?"

"The senora is a marvel. She has raised the child with so much love and care that it has saddened me that you have not been here to see it," Dunn replied. "And your sweet Angelica is learning to speak both English and Spanish. It's quite remarkable."

Morgan's chest filled with pride as Mr. Dunn spoke. Of course things would flourish under Teresa's hand. She was truly remarkable. "And the senora's health?"

"Begging you pardon, Captain, but I think she is probably more beautiful than when you left. Her smile has returned."

The image left him breathless, yet a feeling of trepidation ran through him. "And of me? Is the senora looking forward to my return?"

"There is no doubt, Captain. She wanted to make the trip to Port Royal with me, but I told her your instructions were clear that she stay on the plantation. I'm not so sure she was happy about that, sir. She has a way of raising her chin and making her eyes flash that makes it difficult to say no," Dunn answered.

Morgan laughed. It was the first deep, hardy laugh he'd had in months. "I know that look well, Mr. Dunn!" He reached into his pocket and gave Dunn a gold coin. "Here. This is yours for following my orders. Lesser men would have broken."

Teresa Montoya Castillo stood on the veranda of the plantation house as Morgan and Mr. Dunn rode up, followed by two pack mules with Morgan's belongings. In spite of the heat, she wore a long, green flowing skirt with a tight-fitting, white cotton blouse buttoned to her neck. Her dark hair was pinned up, accenting her cheekbones. Her bright smile lit up her tanned face, and Morgan readily returned it with a smile of his own. Morgan dismounted and gave the reins to Mr. Dunn as he strode over to her. He took her hand and stared into her dark eyes, becoming lost for the briefest of moments. He felt like a schoolboy as he fumbled for words.

"I...I can't tell you how I have looked forward to this moment, Teresa," Morgan said, more formally than he wanted to.

"I am glad you have returned, Henry. I feared that you would not. This is no place for a woman on her own."

Morgan smiled. "Mr. Dunn tells me that you've done well on your own."

"The plantation of the great Captain Morgan has done well. I have only been a caretaker while you've been gone."

"And our daughter? How is she?" Morgan asked.

"The little angel is growing fast. You will be so proud of her!" Teresa smiled. "She is playing with her dolls right now. You know that she will probably not recognize you since you've been gone so long."

"That was my initial fear, but I hope my love for her will get us reacquainted quickly," Morgan said, holding Teresa by the waist.

"And your love for her mother?" Teresa asked.

"There is no treasure in the world that would exceed it," he replied as he bent down and kissed her fully on the lips.

THIRTY ONE

Poole and Mari said their good-byes to Brother Thomas and made their way back to the north side of the island. Poole insisted that they stop at Moncrief's for jerk chicken and sodas.

"I think our creative juices flow better on full stomachs," Poole said as he bit into a chicken leg.

"I think you're just looking for an excuse to eat. This island has a way of doing that to you," Mari laughed.

"Then how do you keep so trim? You've been with me every step of the way!"

"Like I said, I chalk it up to good breeding. You should have seen my mom. She was in shape all the way to the end," Mari answered, pausing to let the memory pass.

"Sorry, Mari."

"No worries, John. It just hits me every once in a while. She was a great woman. Just like your dad, really. I hope you're starting to appreciate that he was a decent man."

"Yeah, I'm there, Mari. I can't help but feel a little guilty about the whole thing. He and my mom gave up what they had for me, and it's weird thinking that I was the reason they gave up a life of love."

"You know, I've been thinking about that too. I don't think they did. Just because they weren't even in the same country didn't mean that they loved each other any less. In fact, I think they grew to love each other more because of the absence. There's probably nothing more powerful than that, in my opinion."

"I hope you're right, Mari. It would make me feel a little bit better. That's why I'm doing what I'm doing, you know. For their sake, not mine."

"I know. But it's OK to be a little selfish too. Are you in that big of a rush to go back to your law practice?"

"Funny thing about that. There have been only one or two times that my practice has even crossed my mind since I've been here. I wonder what that means?"

"It means that you need to finish this and then reassess your priorities," Mari said. "Who knows, maybe there's a pot of gold waiting with your name on it."

Poole smiled. "Right now, I'd be happy with just a rainbow."

"Then let's finish up here and head back to the cottage. In the morning, we can sneak down to the *Rebecca* and have a look around."

"Fine by me. I just hope we can find what my father was talking about."

"Stick with me, John. I think I may have already figured that one out."

"You're really not going to tell me?" Poole asked as they walked into the cottage several hours later. It was close to six, and the sky was turning a pale orange.

"Nope. Not yet. It's just a vague theory, and I don't want to look like an idiot if I'm wrong," Mari replied.

"Well, two can play that game," Poole said, smiling at Mari. He picked up his phone and read the letter from his father again. He sat at the wooden table and recited the words of the next-to-last paragraph. "I have no more safe deposit box keys for you to follow. In order to find the final piece, you'll need to hit the books. Then sit down and think awhile. Only then will an answer reveal itself."

Poole recited the line three times before he stopped in midsentence. "The flippin' bookcase?"

"You men can be so dense sometimes," Mari said, shaking her head sarcastically. "What's the only difference between the two staterooms on the *Rebecca*? The bookcase in your dad's cabin. I should have figured that out from the start."

"It sure makes sense now. He couldn't make it so difficult that we wouldn't get it. It just wasn't that obvious to me at first."

"Me either, to be honest. As soon as we figured out the *Rebecca* reference, it all fell in place for me," Mari confessed.

"Let's hope we're both right. If so, we may be close to the end of this hunt," Poole said.

"I guess that depends on what we find. Remember, we're supposed to 'hit the books,' then sit down, think, and the answer will reveal itself. Based on our track record, that may take a while."

Poole nodded. "If it's anything like law school, we could be there for days."

It was still dark when they left the cottage the next morning. Mari filled a couple of to-go cups with coffee for the ride to the marina. Since they hadn't spotted anyone tailing them in the last couple of days, they were more confident about driving, and Poole sat in the front seat.

"I wonder what we're going to find on the *Rebecca*?" he said.

"I'm hoping the rest of that map—or at least directions to it."

"Geez, I was hoping for a bunch of gold coins and that Madonna's Heart ruby. That would make my decision about going back to my law practice a little easier."

"OK, that solves your problems, but what about me? You're not the only one who's been chased around this island. I've invested a little of my time in this fiasco too, you know," Mari said, hitting Poole on the shoulder with the back of her hand.

"Don't think I haven't thought about that. I couldn't have gotten anywhere on this island without you. Whatever we find, we're finding together, fifty-fifty. Deal?" Poole asked.

"Deal."

Ten minutes later, they pulled into the marina. The café was closed, and there was no activity on the docks. Mari said that she expected Robert to come rolling in around six, so they had about thirty minutes to check out the *Rebecca* before he arrived. They parked the SUV behind the café. The early morning air was silent, so they decided to simply run down to the boat and hop into the main cabin—hopefully without being seen.

Poole's breathing was heavy as they unlocked the main cabin and disappeared into the darkness. "I've only been here two weeks, and I'm getting out of shape."

"It's the heavy air, John. Even in the morning it's hard to get enough oxygen. But, yes, you may be a little out of shape." Mari teased.

"Shhh," Poole cautioned. "Please hold the compliments until we get out of here, would you?"

"You're just no fun in the morning, Mr. Poole," Mari complained. "You go down below, and I'll go up to the wheelhouse to get a couple of flashlights."

Mari joined Poole down in his father's stateroom. Poole closed the curtain covering the small cabin window on the dock side of the room, and Mari turned on both flashlights. The room was as he had left it, including the unmade bed.

"OK, time to hit the books," Poole said. "Let's do this systematically. I don't want to pull all these books out of the case and find out later there was a pattern we had to follow or something. Grab that notepad on the shelf over the bed, and let's do an inventory."

Poole and Mari painstakingly listed each book and their order on the shelves. Luckily, the case wasn't very big, only about three feet high and maybe thirty inches wide. The case held three shelves that were about a foot deep, and a removable guardrail secured the books on each shelf.

"OK, now what?" Mari asked.

"Let's take off all of the guardrails first. Then maybe we can pull each book out like a lever. You know, like in the movies," Poole replied.

They went through that process without any luck. "It looks like my dad wasn't a big moviegoer," Poole said with frustration. "Maybe it's what's inside the books?"

Each picking a shelf, Poole and Mari perused each volume, looking for margin notes, highlights, or even book titles that would strike a chord with either one of them. Still nothing.

"Well that's strike two. He did say to 'hit the books,' so maybe he meant it literally," Poole suggested. With that, he started punching each volume with the back of his hand, but nothing happened. "Screw this. Let's start pulling them all out, maybe there's something behind the books."

After all of the books were neatly stacked on the wood decking of the stateroom, Poole and Mari examined the bookcase. There were no visible seams or cracks behind the shelves, nor were there any scrape marks on the decking or the wall that would suggest movement. Then they tried to pull the bookcase away from the wall, but it was solidly affixed. Attempts to pull it up were also to no avail. "This can't be right, John. All the clues lead to the *Rebecca* and this bookcase. There's no other place where he kept books on this boat," Mari said with disappointment in her voice.

"I don't know, Mari. Maybe he meant something else. Chart books, cookbooks, logs, journals, diaries. Shall I go on?"

"We're here. We might as well bring down every book on this boat and look through them all. Maybe there's something we're missing."

"Fine. I'll search the main cabin and galley, you check out the wheelhouse. There're also those boxes in the stern storage locker, but I don't remember seeing books in any of them. Let's leave them be for now."

Within five minutes, they had piled another dozen books on the bed of the stateroom. "The chart books are all standard. We used those every day when we were diving. But we can at least leaf through them to see if there's a special notation or something," Mari said.

After going through the six chart books that covered each sector of the shoreline around Jamaica, they were left with six books from the galley and main cabin. Five of these were cookbooks with no distinguishing marks or notes. The last book was the biography of Henry Morgan that Poole had left in the main galley several days earlier.

"This one might take some time, since he marked the hell out of it. What time is it?" Poole asked.

"Just six o'clock now. The sun won't rise for another half hour, but I'm guessing that Robert will be showing up at the café pretty soon."

"OK, sit next to me. You take all the left-side pages and I'll take all the right-side pages."

"Got it, Captain." Mari saluted. "I've got port; you've got starboard."

It took them about thirty minutes to go through each page of the two-hundred-page biography. They concentrated on every note, highlight, and scribble but still didn't find anything remotely connected to books, coins, or treasure that would correspond with their search. Eventually, Poole tossed the biography on the bed with the other loose books.

"Damn it! This doesn't make any sense!" he said in frustration, smacking the top shelf with his balled up fist. The shelf moved downward ever so slightly with the blow and then returned to its original position.

"John! Did you see that?" Mari exclaimed.

"No, what?"

"I thought I saw the shelf move a little—just slightly—when you hit it from the top!"

Poole stood up and examined the bookcase and the decking more closely with the flashlight. Then he looked at the inside of the bookcase to check the joints where the vertical sections met the shelves. "I'll be damned. If you look really close, it looks like there's a little wear in these vertical joints!" Poole said, whistling. "Stand back a little. I hope I don't break this thing."

Poole looked at Mari as he placed both of his palms on the top shelf and quickly put his full weight on it, forcing it down. The three shelves sunk in unison about a half an inch, and they heard a distinct click. Then, when Poole took his weight off the top shelf, the entire structure rose.

"Holy secret compartment, Batman," Mari exclaimed. "I think you've figured it out!"

They both sat on the bed and watched the shelves rise up. "It's on some sort of hydraulic or pneumatic system," Poole said.

Under the bottom shelf, they could see the metallic top of some sort of box attached to the substructure of the bookcase. It didn't take long to see that it was a small safe, complete with a combination lock in the front.

"Wonderful," Poole said. "Now we have to go through every one of those books again to find the combination."

"Maybe not. I have a hunch your dad may have already given us the combination."

"Sorry, I need more coffee to follow you."

"What did we consistently find in those safe deposit boxes?"

Poole paused for a second. "The coins? Sure, of course! Where are those pictures again?" Poole pulled out his phone and scrolled through the pictures of the contents of each safe deposit box. "OK, we've got eleven coins with the emerald. We've got twenty-six coins with the ruby, and two coins with the other emerald."

"Your dad was something, John. Emerald, ruby, emerald. Green, red, green."

"And?"

"He lived on a boat almost his entire adult life. What do the colors red and green mean to a sailor?" Mari asked.

"Port and starboard," Poole answered. "Left and right!"

"It's a wild guess, mind you. And I know you're in charge here. But you may want to try going right to eleven, left to twenty-six, and right again to two."

Poole reached over and dutifully tried the combination. As soon as the tumbler landed on the two, he grabbed the handle, looked at Mari, and gave it a twist. The handle moved effortlessly down about two inches, and the safe clicked open.

"I have to remember to listen to you a little more often," Poole said with a nod.

He opened the safe door and carefully shone his flashlight inside. He first pulled out a roughly drawn map with a center portion missing. "Looks like we have the match, Mari. Let's take a picture of this one too. I just don't fee that comfortable walking around with the original."

They pulled the map out and unfolded it on the bed. It showed the general coastline around Port Maria, complete with a small round circle in the middle of the bay denoting Cabarita Island. The missing piece looked to be roughly a mile or two south of the shore-line of Port Maria. They took several photographs of the entire map, and of detailed sections, before they folded it back up and placed it on the bed.

"There're a couple more things in here, Mari," Poole said, reach-ing into the safe. First, he pulled out a folded-up document of medium thickness that was bound with a rubber band. The scrollwork on its face clearly indicated that it was a life insurance policy.

"Dunbar might need to know about this as part of the estate," Poole said as he tossed the bound paperwork on the bed. He reached in one more time and pulled out an old-style key made of solid gold with rubies embedded in the handle.

Mari whistled. "Now, that's pretty cool. And I'm betting that's not something you can buy on eBay," Mari said.

"Do you think? I hate to even ask if there's a lock for this bad boy," Poole added.

"Let's take a couple of pictures of this. Maybe someone can tell us what it is," Mar replied. "Anything else in there? Any more notes from your dad?"

"That's it. My father must have thought this is all we would need. I guess we're supposed to use what he's given us and find what we're supposed to find."

"That's a lot of 'supposes,' John."

"Yeah." Poole paused. "I suppose you're right."

THIRTY TWO

"You two took a chance by coming back to the marina," Robert scolded. "There's no telling who's been on the lookout for you here."

"We had no choice, Robert," Mari said. "The clues finally led us back here. I'm sort of surprised that no one else had the idea of checking the boat."

"Maybe it was too obvious, Mari," Poole responded. "You wouldn't think about putting something as critical as that on a boat that could sink."

"Oh no?" Robert responded. "If that was the case, you'd never have heard the term sunken treasure!"

"OK, you've got me there," Poole admitted.

"So what brilliant plan do you guys have now?" Robert asked.

"We thought we'd grab a quick bite here and then make our way over to Montego Bay. We have a friend who might be able to tell us about a letter that we weren't able to read," Mari answered.

"Fine. At least you have a plan," Robert responded. "Mr. John, can I get you anything?"

Poole was looking out at the parking lot as a red CJ-5 Jeep pulled up. Its canvas top was missing and a familiar, dark-haired man was behind the wheel. "I'd ask for a cloak of invisibility but it might be a little late for that," Poole said as the man spotted Poole and walked toward the café.

"Damn," Mari whispered.

As he walked through the door, Robert leaned down next to Poole's ear. "Do you know this guy?"

Poole stood as the man approached the table. "Robert, this is Ryker Wilson."

Ryker extended his hand and shook Robert's. "Hello, mate. Nice to meet you. You wouldn't happen to have a spot of coffee around, would you?"

"If you're paying, I'm pouring," Robert responded.

"Then let's make it three coffees, Robert."

As Robert went back to the kitchen, Wilson pulled out a chair and joined Poole and Mari. "So," he started, "fancy meeting you two here."

"Quite a coincidence, Ryker," Poole said. "What brings you to our little neck of the woods?"

"Just checking in on your dad's boat. Wanted to make sure it was on the right side of the waterline."

"That's awfully neighborly of you."

"Just doing my part. Like I told you, your father and I went way back."

Poole didn't say a word. He just stared at Ryker without expression. Robert brought their coffees and stood behind the counter, pretending to mind his own business.

"So how'd you two get here this morning?" Ryker asked, looking at the empty parking lot. "It wouldn't have been in that nice little RAV4 out back, would it?"

"I'm sorry, Ryker. I'm trying to figure out why that would be of interest to you," Poole responded.

"Just looking out for your best interests, mate. There's a lot of bad guys on this little island. Lucky for you, I'm one of the good guys," Ryker said.

"That's reassuring, Ryker. But isn't that what all the bad guys say?"

Ryker laughed. "You may have a point there, John. You may have a point," he said as he took three huge gulps of the steaming black coffee. "You just have to know that I'm here to help if you need it. Like in your little search, for example."

"I'm not sure if I know what you're talking about, Ryker."

"Then John Morgan was telling me a little white lie when he said that he'd found the Madonna's Heart?" Ryker asked.

"What's that?" Poole answered with a straight face.

"Just a little ruby about the size of my fist. It's probably only worth tens of millions of dollars to the right buyer," Ryker said.

"Madonna's Heart!" Robert interrupted. "That old wives' tale? Good luck with that one, Mr. Wilson. I wouldn't be quitting your day job any time soon to find that thing."

"Do you believe that, John?" Ryker asked.

"Look at him," Poole said, pointing to Robert. "Would you like to tell him he's a liar?"

"You're full of good points this morning, John." Ryker smiled. "Like I said before, I'm here to help if you need it. All you need to do is ask."

"Thanks, Ryker. I still have your number."

"Good then," he said as he stood, drank the last of his coffee, and threw a few bills on the table. "I'll probably be seeing you around. Good to see you again, Mari, and nice meeting you, Robert." With that, Ryker turned on his heel and exited the café. As he drove out of the parking lot, he stopped, honked his horn, and waved before he turned onto the highway.

They all sat in silence for a few seconds processing the "chance" meeting. Mari was the first to speak. "Boys, I hate say it, but our smarmy friend now knows the car we drive and that we're on this search. He even pegged the Madonna's Heart. How he knew that is beyond me."

"That guy knows a lot more than he's letting on," Poole added. "The fact that he knows we're on a little hunt tells me that he's the one who's been following us, too."

"Great. Then how are we going to get rid of him?" Mari asked.

"Maybe we don't. Remember, my father said that part of this hunt was to draw out whoever the interested parties were. We know

Ryker Wilson is one of those guys. Maybe there are more," Poole said.

"So what do we do now?"

"We have breakfast. And then we go to Montego Bay to have a bit of lunch later. After that, we need to find another car," Poole answered.

"I can help you with that, Mr. John," Robert said. "I've been looking at one of those RAV4s for Marthy, so maybe we can do a swap for a little while."

"Are you sure, Robert?" Mari asked. "Marthy loves that car of hers. She'll kill you if she finds out."

"It's only temporary, Cousin," Robert replied. "Besides, her car is pretty impractical when you've got a couple of young ones at home. They can hardly fit into the backseat."

"It's your funeral, Robert. Just warning you in advance," Mari said.

"Um, I'm sort of afraid to ask, but what kind of car is it?" Poole interjected.

"You don't want to know," Robert and Mari replied in unison.

THIRTY THREE

August 1680

Morgan had been on the road for three days and was finally nearing his plantation. He hated being away, but affairs of state required his attention. He was responsible for the defense of the island and the other English holdings in the Caribbean and was in constant communication with the former privateers in the area. For their years of service to the Crown, most had been branded as outcasts and enemies of the realm. Morgan knew better than to treat them as such. They knew all of the trade routes and were invaluable in his attempts to quell the expansion of Dutch interests in the Caribbean. The fact that he surreptitiously shared in the take was beside the point.

The plantation house appeared on the rise. It had been about thirteen months since the last cutting, so it was harvest time. The slaves were carefully burning the fields to clear the grass and scare away the snakes. Then skilled men cut the stalks with machetes and laid them in rows. Women with carts followed, placing the stalks neatly on the beds to transport them to the holding sheds.

The sickly sweet smell of the burned fields filled the air, and Morgan put a handkerchief to his nose to lessen the stench. He knew that Teresa would be in the plantation house avoiding the foul air as well. It was a necessary evil. The few days of discomfort were worth the English pounds that each crop put in their coffers.

Morgan dismounted and handed his horse's reins to one of the stableboys. He strode over to the plantation house and entered through the kitchen door. "Hello! Is the mistress of the house in?" he bellowed as he walked into the sitting room.

"That wouldn't be the infamous pirate, Morgan, would it?" a familiar voice replied in a perfect English accent. Morgan looked to his left to see Teresa enter the room. Even after nine years, she still took his breath away.

"I've heard about this scoundrel, my lady. But I'm afraid that the English navy finally caught up with him, and he was hanged from a yardarm as an example to the rest of the scalawags."

"Such a pity. I heard that he was a nice man once you got to know him."

"Of course, the stories I've heard could just be vicious rumors. If I ever run across the man, I'll make sure to send him your way, my lady."

"That is very kind of you, sir. If it's not too much trouble, I would be in your debt if you ran into him soon!" Teresa said, finally letting down the pretense and rushing over to greet Morgan.

"Your pirate has returned, my lady." Morgan whispered as he kissed her deeply. He could feel her stomach meeting his, knowing another life was forming inside her.

"Oh, Henry, my stomach is starting to meet you before the rest of my body. How repulsed you must be!"

Morgan looked into her eyes and smiled with his. "You couldn't be farther from the truth, my love. You get more beautiful each day, with or without child. I am blessed that you are in my life."

"By the New Year, our second child with be with us. I am hoping it will be a boy for you," Teresa said honestly.

"It is no matter. I wouldn't trade our little angel for the world. In fact, where is that precocious young lady?"

"She's out with William inspecting the harvesting. She has such a curious mind, just like her father. She wants to know how the cane grows and why it's burned before harvesting and a multitude of other questions. William was kind enough to take her when I was too tired to answer her questions."

"She'll be running this place before we know it," Morgan said, shaking his head. "I'll ride out as well just to let the workers know that the master of the house is back. You rest, and then we'll have a nice supper."

"Don't be gone too long. This house needs protection!"

"My lady, the only protection you'll need is from me when I return!" Morgan whispered as he gave her a tender kiss. Teresa gave him a gentle tap on his shoulder and sent him out to the fields.

The sugar plantation had thrived under Teresa's hand. There were over a thousand acres in production. Because of the long growing cycle of the cane, Teresa suggested that they divide the land so that when one part was being harvested, the other would be halfway grown. That way, workers were busy all year long. It also gave them some insurance: in the event of a bad storm, they'd lose only half of their crop. This proved invaluable when the terrible hurricane of the previous summer had swept over the island. While most other plantations were wiped out, Morgan's cane procured exorbitant prices.

Morgan could see Mr. Dunn's horse in the distance and trotted out to meet him. Angelica sat behind Mr. Dunn with her arms wrapped tightly around his waist, and he explained the harvesting process.

"Good afternoon, Mr. Dunn!" Morgan hailed. "I see you have an assistant today!"

"Papa!" Angelica squealed as she waved to Morgan. He couldn't believe she was almost nine years old. She looked more like her mother every day.

Morgan reined in his horse as he came abreast of Mr. Dunn and Angelica. "Hello, my little angel. Please tell me, how is the harvesting going?"

"Splendidly, Papa! William and I think that we should be done by the end of the week!"

"Excellent news!" Morgan replied, nodding. "Mr. Dunn, do you concur?"

"Why yes, Captain. I believe Miss Angelica is completely correct."

Morgan reached over and tousled her hair. "Take care of this precious cargo, Mr. Dunn. I believe she'll be running this plantation in no time!"

Angelica beamed and returned her father's smile.

"Mr. Dunn, after you're through, please report to me in my study. I've been thinking about a small building project that I would like to discuss with you."

"Very good, sir," Dunn replied.

"By the way, when we're through, please be our guest for supper, would you?" Morgan added.

"Thank you, sir. It will be my pleasure."

M organ was in his study looking over a simple drawing he had just created when Mr. Dunn knocked on the study door. "Sorry to interrupt, sir. You wanted to see me?"

"Yes, Mr. Dunn. Please have a seat," Morgan replied, motioning to the chair opposite his writing desk. "I've been drawing a few sketches of a building that I am considering for the property. I would like your opinion as to the design and location."

Dunn was taken aback. Morgan had never asked his opinion before, and he didn't know what to say.

"Don't be shy, man. You're eighteen years old now and have a good head on your shoulders. You've looked after my family in my absence, and I've grown to trust you. Trust on this island is a rare thing," Morgan said sincerely. "It's something that is not given lightly, and can be broken quickly."

"Thank you, sir," Mr. Dunn responded, his pride swelling. "If it's another outbuilding, we could use a larger barn if you're considering expansion."

"No, nothing like that. I've been thinking about doing something for the mistress of the house and my family. You know that I am not a religious man by nature. You've been witness to the acts committed in my younger days, and I am resigned that my entry into the next life will not be to heaven."

"But that was a long time ago. It was war, sir," Dunn interjected.

Morgan held up his hand to stop Dunn. "We both know what that was, Mr. Dunn. We called it war for convenience. But discussing the past is not why I brought you here. What I want to do, and what I am tasking you to oversee, is to build a small chapel on the property. In fact, I want you to build two chapels. One would be for my family, including you, of course, and the other for our workers."

"I'd be honored to oversee that project, sir," Dunn said sincerely. "What design did you have in mind?"

Morgan gave Dunn the sketches he had just prepared. "Nothing fancy. Just something large enough to house a few family members. The other one, for the workers, should be much larger, of course. My thought, actually, was to have them help with the building project once the harvesting is complete and the fields are replanted."

"Very good, sir. And the location?" Dunn asked.

"I will defer to your judgment with respect to the chapel for the workers. However, I do have a location in mind for the family chapel. There's a large mahogany tree near the bluff that overlooks the harbor," he said, pointing to a map of the plantation. "We can ride out there tomorrow to see if it is a suitable building site."

THIRTY FOUR

It was just past noon when they pulled up to the valet at the Cliffs. Poole and Mari decided to drop the pretense of stealth since Ryker Wilson already knew what car they drove. Mari flipped the keys to the attendant, and they both walked out to the beautiful deck that was becoming their second home.

"Three times in a week. I wonder if they have a frequent-dining card?" Mari asked rhetorically.

"The heck with dining. I'd be a happy man if they just gave us a discount on the cocktails!"

"Not with this view they won't, John."

They looked around and spotted Fredrickson at the outdoor server's station. He saw them and immediately walked over with a smile on his face. "Mr. Poole! Ms. Mari! How can I help you today?" he asked cheerfully.

"Just seat us in your section, Fredrickson. And when you have a moment, we were hoping to ask you a few questions about the other night," Poole responded.

"Always my pleasure. Follow me," he said as he took them to a table with a prime view, yet offered some privacy from the other guests.

"Two Cuba Libres coming right up!" he said with a smile and retreated to the bar.

"That kid is damned good," Mari observed. "What company did you say he was going to run?"

It was another beautiful day on the island—not a cloud in the sky. They settled in and waited for Fredrickson's return. Mari insisted that Poole wear some sun block, even though his skin had turned a golden brown over the past two weeks.

Fredrickson returned with their cocktails but excused himself to serve his other guests. "Do you think he can remember anything else about that letter?" Mari asked.

"I've stopped being surprised by that kid. I'll bet he remembers enough to give us something to go on. If not, we might as well just go to the bank tomorrow and look at it ourselves. I'm tired of play-ing cat-and-mouse with these guys, whoever they are."

Fredrickson returned after seeing to his other customers. "So what's up? Did the pictures work out for you?"

"Yes and no, to be honest. I think we're almost there, but one of the pictures didn't come out," Poole replied.

Fredrickson looked deflated. "Shoot! It must have been that old letter. I was wondering if the plastic would be a problem, but I didn't want to take too long in there, if you know what I mean."

"Understand completely, Fredrickson," Poole said. "But did you have enough time to read the letter by any chance?"

"Sure, who wouldn't?" he answered truthfully. "It was in that old English text, but I got the gist of it I think." He looked up and was hailed by another table. "I'll be back in a minute."

They took a sip of their drinks and were enjoying the view when Poole felt a tap on his shoulder. "Excuse me, Mr. Poole. I saw you walk in and wanted to say hello. Sorry if I'm intruding," Warren Dunbar said in a timid voice.

"Mr. Dunbar, very nice to see you. How are you?"

"Very well, thank you. Do you mind if I join you for a few min-utes?" he asked.

Poole glanced over at Mari with the briefest of looks.

"Mr. Dunbar, please take my seat. I have to go to the powder room," Mari said as she stood.

"Why, thank you, Ms. Robeson," Dunbar said.

As Mari left, she stopped Fredrickson briefly to appear as if she was asking directions to the restroom.

"She's quite attractive, Mr. Poole," said Dunbar. "A lovely woman."

"Yes, I have to agree, Mr. Dunbar. I'm glad to see you enjoy this restaurant. It has a marvelous view. So do you have news on the estate?"

"As a matter of fact, I do. The paperwork has been filed, and you're now able to start collecting assets and valuating the estate. Of course, I would be happy to help with the process, if you like."

"Thanks, but I still need to get my head around what is there. I suppose I could start with getting the certificate of authority from you so I can access my father's bank account. I'm sure there are bills to pay, including yours," Poole said.

"Well, yes, that would be nice," Dunbar said with a weak smile. "There will be hospital bills as well, I would assume."

"You're right. I hadn't even gotten that far. He probably has a bunch of mail stacking up, and I don't even know where he gets it," Poole admitted.

"Oh, I believe he had a post office box down in Port Antonio. That's where I would send correspondence from my office."

"Thanks for letting me know. That will save some hunting around. I've been doing enough of that as it is," Poole said.

"Hunting? Hunting for what, Mr. Poole?"

"Oh, nothing really," Poole said, backtracking. "He just had a couple of safe deposit boxes with some valuables and personal mementos that I've been gathering."

"If there's anything of significant value, we'll have to include that on the estate inventory. What did you find?"

"Oh, uh, a couple of rings and watches, pictures, things like that. Does that have to be disclosed?"

"Not that, no. Now if he happened to have that Madonna's Heart in one of those boxes, that would be another story!" Dunbar stated as he looked at Poole and dabbed his forehead with his handkerchief.

"Nope, nothing that exciting. Sorry to disappointment you," Poole said, smiling.

"That would be quite a find, wouldn't it?" Dunbar said. "Lots of folks have been looking for that over the years."

"It's funny; a friend of my father's brought up that ruby this morning," Poole said.

"Really? Who was that?" Dunbar asked inquisitively.

"That Ryker Wilson fellow we spoke about before. He's been showing his face quite a bit lately."

"Interesting. I wonder why?"

"I was thinking the same thing, Mr. Dunbar. You don't think I have anything to worry about with that guy, do you?" Poole asked.

"I really don't know. I don't know him that well, only that he and your father worked together for a while. Do you think that he was involved in your father's death?"

"I don't have an answer for you. But I wouldn't put it past him, I guess."

"Well, if I can be of help, you let me know. I have some friends on this island who could keep an eye on him for you," Dunbar stated.

"If we do, I'll let you know. In the meantime, is it possible for me to drop by tomorrow to pick up the certificates of authority?"

"Certainly. I'll be in my office early tomorrow, so feel free to drop by anytime," Dunbar answered.

Mari returned from the restroom and stood by Poole's shoulder. "Ah, Ms. Robeson!" Dunbar exclaimed as he stood and wiped his forehead one more time. "Thank you for letting me borrow your chair. I was just leaving."

Poole stood and shook Dunbar's hand. "Thanks for dropping by, Mr. Dunbar. I'll take that last offer under advisement."

"Please do, Mr. Poole. I hope you both enjoy the rest of your Sunday," Dunbar said as he returned to his seat.

"Two interesting characters in one day," Mari chimed in. "You'd think Mr. Dunbar would consider a different climate, though. The guy always looks like he's just run a marathon."

"I agree he's not in the best of shape. That heart of his must be working overtime."

"With him sitting in the corner, I feel a bit uncomfortable chatting it up with Fredrickson now. We'll have to make some other arrangements with him," Mari said.

"You're probably right," Poole agreed. "But maybe we can sneak in a little conversation here and there if we order something to eat and take our time."

Poole motioned Fredrickson over to their table and briefly told him about their situation. They agreed to discuss the Morgan letter throughout lunch.

"No worries, sir. I've got it handled," Fredrickson said as he left for the kitchen. In a few minutes, Fredrickson returned with two blackened-chicken Caesar salads for them, while keeping a wary eye on Dunbar.

"Here you go. It's one of my favorites," Fredrickson said. "So what do you want to know about the letter?" he asked as he held up the pepper grinder.

"For starters, can you just give us a sense of what it was about?" Poole asked.

"Well, it was a letter to a friend of his, and he was really bummed out. It said that the lady of the house had died."

"Go on," Poole urged

"He said that it wasn't fair that he survived her and that he was the one that should have died. I think it said 'died many times over' or something like that."

One of Fredrickson's customers asked for his check, so he went to attend to him. Poole and Mari thought about what Fredrickson had said. "So in 1681, he said that the lady of the house died," Poole recited.

"That has to be the Spanish woman. I think I remember reading that his wife, Mary Elizabeth, died in England several years after Morgan did," Mari said.

"That sounds about right. So Ms. Castillo dies in 1681, and Morgan is distraught. This was the love of his life, so I get it," Poole agreed.

Fredrickson came back to their table. "Can I get you another cocktail?"

"How about some wine," Poole responded. "What do you have in a white?"

"There's a good chardonnay that I can bring in a minute," Fredrickson said as he picked up the wine list. "As for the rest of the letter, it said that he was going to use the new chapel as a crypt or something like that. And he said that his heart was hers to take since he didn't have a need for it anymore."

Mari pointed to the wine list to stall for time. "Did the letter mention the name Madonna's Heart?"

"Uh, sort of, I guess. He called her his "Madonna", and said that it was the only way he could think of to thank her."

"Anything else you can remember, Fredrickson?" Poole asked.

"Oh, yeah. The end was a little creepy. He said that he would make sure that only she could have his heart, and that anyone who tried to take it would be surprised at what they found, or something like that," Fredrickson said. "That's all I can remember off the top of my head."

"Thanks, Fredrickson. You're the best," Poole said.

"No problem, Mr. Poole. I'll be back right away with your wine," he said, tipping his head slightly.

Poole and Mari finished their salads as they sipped the excellent chardonnay that Fredrickson brought to their table. "If Fredrickson is right, and I'm pretty sure he is, that heart-shaped ruby is buried with Ms. Castillo," Poole surmised.

"And presumably, we now have the map that will lead us to the site," Mari added.

"Now that we know, should we even be looking for it? Wouldn't we be grave robbers?"

"Only if it's in her grave. The least we can do is find the spot and snoop around. If we end up thinking it's in her grave or casket or whatever they did back then, we can notify the authorities and call it a day," Mari suggested.

"I'm good with that, Mari," Poole said as he raised his glass. "A toast, to the Madonna and her heart."

Dunbar watched from his corner table as Poole and Mari touched their glasses together. After paying his tab, he stood up and walked out of the restaurant. As he waited for his car, he couldn't help but wonder what in the world Ryker Wilson was up to.

THIRTY FIVE

January 1681

The oil lamps were lit throughout the plantation house as Morgan again was relegated to the veranda with Mr. Dunn. Teresa had been with the nuns for much longer this time. The wait was excruciating, but he knew that his place was outside.

"Please tell me about the family chapel, Mr. Dunn," Morgan requested. "I need something to take my mind off this infernal wait."

Dunn cleared his throat, worried for Morgan. "We laid the foundation right where you requested, sir. It's a simple structure, fifteen by twenty feet, but it should be enough room to fit your family comfortably. I was fortunate to salvage hewn rock from an old Spanish church that was destroyed by the hurricane two years ago. We used that for the walls and raised a simple truss roof made out of mahogany to keep out the weather. And we've put in paving stones for the floor. I hope you'll be pleased, sir."

"It sounds just fine, Mr. Dunn," Morgan said, distracted.

"All that's left is the placement of the pews and the construction of a small altar. I thought I would leave that last detail to you and Senora Castillo because of its personal nature."

"Very good, Mr. Dunn. Excellent thinking."

A scream interrupted their conversation. Morgan hadn't heard that sound since their first child, Angelica, was born, and it still curdled his blood. A second scream came soon after.

"Damn it, Mr. Dunn, this part is unbearable."

"Aye, sir. Is there anything I can get for you?"

Morgan appraised the young man before him, thinking back to when Dunn was just ten years old. "I think we both need a spot of rum, William. Be off with you now!"

Dunn went to the pantry to fetch some local dark rum and two cups. He returned and handed Morgan a cup, pouring his captain's and then his own. "Sir, if I may," he said, raising his cup. "To your family, sir."

Morgan raised his cup and nodded his head to Dunn. "And to yours, William, when that time comes." They drained their cups and were leaning against the railing of the veranda when the next scream came, longer and harder than Morgan could recall from Teresa's last birthing.

"My God, man! What in heaven's name is going on in there?" Morgan fought the urge to go into the bedroom. The nuns told him it wasn't his place, but it still gnawed at him.

There was one more scream and then silence. He waited for the cry of a small voice, but the night air was quiet. He paced the length of the veranda but could no longer wait and barged through the front door and into the bedroom filled with midwives. The birthing had occurred, and Teresa was holding an unmoving child wrapped tightly in small cotton towels. The nuns were working furiously to stem the bleeding as Teresa visibly weakened before his eyes.

Morgan rushed over to Teresa's side, ignoring the stillborn child in her arms. Her breathing was shallow and her eyes had a vacant, faraway look about them. "Darling, darling can you hear me? It's Henry," he whispered in her ear.

Teresa turned her head toward him slightly, studying his face and searching for words. Her exhaustion was palpable, and she couldn't respond.

"Please, stay with me, Teresa. You are the strongest woman I've ever known. We have a lifetime left to build our lives together. You must be strong."

The vacant look in her eyes disappeared for a moment as she finally recognized Morgan. Tears rolled down her cheeks, and she tried to speak. The life was draining from her.

"Yes, darling, I'm here. What can I do for you? Please tell me!" Morgan urged.

Teresa took a long steady breath and looked intently at Morgan. "Henry," she whispered faintly. "You once asked me to do something for you." Her voice trailed off to a murmur. She took another long breath and continued. "You asked many years ago."

Morgan was in a panic. His heart was racing, and he didn't know what to do. He didn't know what she was talking about and didn't want to upset her. "That can wait, darling. You need to rest and get better."

"No, Henry," she said, stopping him. She took another shallow breath. "You need to know that..."

Morgan moved his ear next to her trembling lips. Her eyes were weary, and Morgan could see the life draining from them.

"I forgive you."

Morgan sat there, stunned, as Teresa closed her eyes and let out her final breath. He gently held her hand and stared at the face of the only woman he had ever loved. She was still the most beautiful, even in death.

THIRTY SIX

Mari steered the SUV into the drive and parked out of view, behind Father Michael's church. Once they entered the cottage, they decided to compare the photographs of the map Poole's father had made with the local maps that Father Michael had given to them. They rolled out the physical maps on the wooden table, and studied the picture of the large map from Poole's phone to see if they could line up any familiar landmarks.

"See there?" Mari pointed out as she ran her finger along the coastline of Port Maria. "It looks about the same as the sketch your father made."

Poole looked at the coastline and nodded. "OK, and it looks like if you line up that point with the center of Cabarita Island," he paused, fishing out a pencil from underneath the map, "it goes straight to the little rectangular building that he circled in the smaler cutout."

"Yes. It's almost directly south, as the crow flies, and about two miles from the shore," she agreed.

"We're sitting only about a quarter of a mile from the water right now, give or take. Do any of the modern maps show any roads or trails that lead back, farther away from shore?"

Mari pulled out a topographical map from the stack Father Michael gave them. "It looks like there might be a little hiking trail just to the west of here," she said, pointing. "Does that correspond with that dotted line on the sketch?"

"Could be, if you use your imagination," Poole said. "But who knows, my father might have been terrible at drawing."

"Since his map looks like a third-grader drew it up, I'd put my money on that," Mari said.

"How much light is left, Mari?" Poole asked.

"We probably have three hours, give or take."

"Then why don't we get a little exercise. Are you up for it?" Poole asked.

"I'm game if you are. Let me put on some sneakers, and I'll be right with you."

After grabbing a couple of machetes from the church's gardening shed, they found their way to what looked like the trailhead. It was overgrown, but a faint path was distinguishable. They slowly made their way up the trail, hacking through the overgrowth. After about a half hour, they came to a small clearing.

"I can see the church and cottage down below," Poole said as sweat poured off him. "We must be half a mile away, tops."

"According to this sketch, we still have another mile or so," Mari said. "At least we can still see the trail. How are you holding up, John?"

"I'm fine. But there's going to be a Red Stripe with my name on it when we get back to the cottage."

They continued on, climbing steadily as they cut away the fronds and underbrush. Finally, they reached a clearing at the top of the bluff overlooking the bay. Poole was drenched in sweat. The light breeze coming off the ocean did little to cool him down.

"How is it that I'm sweating like a pig and you're fresh as a daisy?" Poole panted. "No, don't answer that. Good breeding, I know!"

Mari chuckled as she put her hands on her knees. "You're just not used to the humidity yet, John. I was born here."

"Well, if I have to go any farther, I might just die here," Poole said, trying to catch his breath.

Mari looked at the angle of the sun and then checked her watch. "We've only got about an hour and a half before the sun starts going down. So we have about a half hour up here to look around."

"Let's look at that sketch again to get our bearings," Poole said. He pulled out his phone, and they both looked at the picture of the larger map. "This is a guess, but I think we're right about where that dotted line ends."

"I'll buy that," Mari agreed.

"So it looks like we'd have to go east about a half mile or so before we get to the cut out section."

"But it looks like this clearing can't be more than a couple of hundred yards wide, at the most. It looks pretty thick in there too," Mari said.

"A lot of things change in three hundred and fifty years. I wouldn't be surprised if it was all an open clearing at one point. Nature just reclaimed the land."

"Fair point. But there's no way we can search around in there at this time of day. We're going to have to go back to the cottage and regroup. We also may want to think about bringing more than just these machetes next time," Mari said.

"OK, let's head back down. And I'm with you, let's plan this out so if there is something to find, we're prepared."

They made their way down the trail in about half the time the ascent had taken. Poole was dripping with sweat when they finally reached the trailhead. The sun had just set, and the sky had turned from a brilliant orange to a deep red. Clouds in the distance carried a purple cast as they lazed across the horizon.

"You take the first shower, John," Mari said as they entered the cottage. "I'll try to think of things we might need."

"Good. I'll take that shower. And for the next fifteen minutes, I'm not going to think about anything."

The next morning, Poole got up at the same time Mari was stirring. He felt surprisingly well considering the exhaustion he'd felt the afternoon before. He put his head under the tap of the bathroom sink to wake himself up. Mari was already in the kitchen making coffee.

"You're an early riser today. Good morning," Mari said.

"Same to you," Poole said with a yawn. "I want to go down to Dunbar's office early and get those certificates of authority so we can start taking care of the estate. I can't be down here forever."

Mari looked at him sideways. "I can think of worse things."

Poole returned her gaze. She looked stunning, even first thing in the morning. "A lot worse things," he replied.

"How long are you going to be?" Mari asked, ignoring Poole's comment.

"I can't imagine it will be more than an hour, with walking time. When I get back we can get an early start on that trail."

"OK. I'll put together our supplies while you're gone. I'm pretty sure I can find everything we need in these outbuildings."

Poole drained his coffee and headed down to the Port Maria market district. He stopped a couple times to look into shop windows to see if there was anyone following him, but he was confident that he was not being watched. It was a quarter after eight when he was once again in front of the blistered blue door. He could see Dunbar moving around through the grimy front window. Poole knocked before he opened the door, and Dunbar was there to greet him.

"Good morning, Mr. Poole. I was just making some coffee. Would you like a cup?" Dunbar asked.

"No, thank you. I really don't have that much time. I just wanted to pick up the paperwork and then I have some errands to run."

"Very well, then. Give me a second, and I'll be right back." Dunbar disappeared into his office briefly and came back with a manila envelope. "This has everything you need. You can present the certificates to the bank or the licensing office if you decide to sell your father's boat. Of course, you can call me at any time if you run into a snag."

"I really appreciate it, Mr. Dunbar," Poole said. "We'll be in touch."

Poole left the office and headed back up to the cottage. Like before, he stopped to see if he was being followed, but he didn't see anything unusual.

As he made his way toward the church, a tall Jamaican man spoke on his cell phone. "He's heading up toward you, Jimar. I'll get back on the main road and be ready there."

Poole passed the café where the other man was sitting. He had just ended the call from the tall man. He pretended to read something on his smartphone instead of looking out the window at Poole. As Poole passed, he dialed another number. "He passed by here, sir. It looks like he's heading toward the road."

When Poole finally reached the main road, he didn't notice the car parked on the opposite side, about fifty yards to the west. He waited for three cars to pass before running across the road and down to the driveway of the church.

The man in the car called the now familiar number. "He didn't drive, sir. It looks like he's staying at the church."

"Good, I'm getting tired of tracking him down. I think it's about time we put an end to all of this."

THIRTY SEVEN

January 1681

Morgan was numb from the rum he'd been drinking. He had spoken briefly with Mr. Dunn the night before and requested that he arrange for Angelica to stay with the nuns. The midwives took the stillborn baby, but Morgan insisted that Teresa remain in the house. He held her hand for more than an hour, studying every feature of her face. Silently, he thanked her, both for her love and her forgiveness, knowing that she was a better woman than he ever deserved. Finally, he pulled himself away and closed the door gently behind him without looking back.

The darkness of the morning was waning and a hint of dawn approached. Morgan had been sitting on the veranda in Teresa's favorite rocking chair the entire night. The bottle of rum next to the chair was empty and lying on its side.

Riding back from Port Maria, Mr. Dunn dismounted from his horse and carefully approached the veranda. He stood motionless, waiting for Morgan to address him when he was ready.

Morgan raised his head and looked out toward the fields. "Is Angelica in good hands?"

"Yes, sir," Dunn replied. "They have agreed to look after her for as long as is necessary."

"Good. She is a good girl. She is too young to lose her mother."

"Yes, sir."

"I have been thinking about the family chapel. I have a different purpose for it now, Mr. Dunn," Morgan said vacantly.

"Whatever you say, Captain," Dunn replied.

"It is my desire to bury Senora Castillo there now. Will that be possible?" Morgan asked.

Mr. Dunn nodded. "We just need to pry the paving stones up. They were placed directly on the earth floor."

"Very good," Morgan said. "I also would like you to build an appropriate casket. She deserves something befitting her, so if you could fashion it out of mahogany, I would be in your debt."

"Is there anything else, sir?"

"Yes. When the casket is complete, I want you to bring t here along with a hammer and nails to seal it. I will prepare Senora Castillo myself," Morgan ordered.

"Begging your pardon, sir, but it might take a day or two to have everything prepared for you," Dunn said with trepidation.

"I understand, but my preference would be sometime tomorrow afternoon, if that is possible. I have some preparations of my own as well, and I should be ready by then," Morgan said. "Now be off with you."

M organ rode down to the shoreline and spoke with several fishermen. He promised to pay extraordinary sums for the particular fish he was seeking. The fishermen were well aware of the unusual fish, one that they had learned to avoid at an early age. But they were more than willing to throw their nets in the waters for the gold Morgan was willing to pay. Morgan said he would be back at dusk, and the fishermen wasted no time in launching their boats.

While on the shore, he stopped to pick up a small fallen coconut. The shell was oval-shaped, and slightly larger than the size of his fists clasped together. This will work just fine, he thought. He then rode up to the family chapel to inspect Mr. Dunn's work. The chapel was as described by Mr. Dunn: small but well built. The paving stones were still fresh on the earthen floor. Morgan paced the breadth of the building and was satisfied that it would suit his purpose.

By noon, he was back at the plantation house. He made sure that the servants were still out of the house and that he was alone. Going into his study, he slid back the silk rug that was under his writing desk, revealing a small trap door. He opened it and reached down, pulling up a familiar canvas sack. He closed the door and replaced the rug, fighting his growing weariness. He reminded himself that there would be no time for sleep until he was done.

Canvas sack in hand, Morgan then walked out to the workshop and spoke with his carpenter, who assured him that they had the materials for plaster casting and offered some instruction in its use, as Morgan had never attempted the art. Morgan then made sure that the materials were left for his use later that evening.

Morgan walked back into the plantation house and uncorked another bottle of rum. A long drink from the bottle strengthened him. He decided that he had time to write a letter to his good friend, Thomas Modyford, who was now living a comfortable life in England after his stay in the Tower of London. In his grief, he related the passing of Teresa and his plans for her interment. The more he wrote, the more resolved he became that his plans were correct.

He then wrote another letter to Mr. Dunn. He laughed to himself as he wrote, knowing that it would be read upon his death. At least he had the choice, he thought. Most of his enemies never had the chance to plan their fates. When he was done and had sealed both letters, Morgan went back to the veranda with the canvas sack and the bottle of rum. He had a few more hours before the fishermen would return with their catch, so he sat in Teresa's chair and waited.

THIRTY EIGHT

"I met with Father Michael this morning, and I think we're all set," Mari said when Poole returned. "I didn't tell him what we were doing, but told him that we were going to walk the property."

"Was he even curious about it?" Poole asked.

"Not at all. He just said that he kept some machetes in the tool-shed and gave me a key. I didn't have the heart to tell him that we already pilfered a couple from another outbuilding."

"So was there anything worthwhile in the toolshed?"

"Everything that we would need, I guess. There were some pick-axes and shovels, things like that," Mari answered. "I don't want to be too obvious when we head out. I'm guessing those and the machetes are all we'd really need. What do you think?"

"Sounds good to me, but let's not advertise it. Maybe we can wrap up a couple of those things in a blanket and make it look like we're going for a picnic or something," Poole said.

"Right, like someone would believe that!" Mari said sarcastically. "I think we're at a point where we're probably not going to fool Father Michael. I think we just grab the stuff and go over to the trailhead like we know what we're doing."

"The old 'hiding in plain sight' routine. Good as any," Poole responded. "Let's make some sandwiches and take some water this time. I don't want to lose it like I did yesterday."

"Already got that covered. While you were visiting the lawyer, I filled my backpack. We're all set," Mari said proudly.

"Remind me to keep you around," Poole kidded.

"That *was* a reminder. Now quit procrastinating. Let's go!"

The church grounds were empty as they casually made their way to the trailhead. Without hesitation, they entered the dense foliage and disappeared from view. Even though it was just past nine in the morning, Poole started to sweat after just a couple of minutes of climbing.

"It's not even eighty degrees yet, and I'm going to be drenched," he said.

"I might get there with you, John. I checked the weather report, and it will be over ninety with no winds today. The humidity is going to be a killer too."

"Well, we might as well take our time then. No need to go crazy on the way up. Besides, we're carrying more stuff with us now."

"I'm not going to argue there. We just need to remember to drink our water," Mari reminded him.

There wasn't a cloud in the sky, and the sun beat down on them once they emerged from the canopy of the trail. They decided to rest at the first clearing. Poole eagerly drank from the water bottle, and Mari followed suit. After ten minutes, they decided to continue the climb and rest again when they reached the top of the bluff.

Poole's red T-shirt was stained under the arms and down his back as they slowly marched along the trail. Mari, in her tight shorts and snug tank top, finally glistened as the heat and humidity took its toll. The foliage smelled like it was slow cooking in an oven as they pressed upward and the heat of the day climbed.

They finally reached the clearing at the top of the bluff, and Mari was the first to grab the water bottle. "There's a crack in her armor!" Poole said, relieved he wasn't the only one suffering.

"I didn't want to make you look bad, John," Mari said.

"Just another reason I should keep you around."

Mari passed the water bottle to Poole, and they sat down as they caught their breath. They emptied the water bottle and pulled out another as Mari brought out the sandwiches. "We might as well have an early lunch here. There's no telling what we're going to find in the underbrush over there," she said, pointing to the dense foliage on the other side of the clearing.

They ate and rested for another half hour before they decided to traverse the clearing. "You know," Poole said looking down at the bay from their vantage point, "I'm surprised that this area has never been developed. The view up here is spectacular."

"I think it has to do with money more than anything else," Mari responded. "Father Michael said he would like nothing more than to build up here, but the folks at Holy Trinity told him there wasn't enough money allocated for building a new church."

"Couldn't they just sell some of this land to rebuild the existing church?" Poole asked.

"I suppose, but I've never heard of the Catholic Church doing that, at least on this island. Once they have land, they tend to keep it."

"Well, it's a shame, if you ask me. I always thought the Catholic Church was loaded and could afford anything. To build a road up here and erect a proper church would be something you'd think they'd want to do," Poole stated.

Mari nodded in agreement. "But Father Michael didn't seem too concerned. He just gave me the old company line—the Lord will provide."

"The man definitely has faith, I'll give him that," Poole said as he stood up. "Shall we?"

Mari looked across the clearing and nodded. "No time like the present."

Poole put the pickax and shovel on his shoulder, while Mari put on the backpack. They both carried their machetes as they quickly traversed the clearing. Poole checked his phone to get their bearings.

"I'm thinking it's going to be due east from here. I can't really tell the distance, but it could be as little as a half mile to a mile and a half," Poole said.

"We just have to make sure we mark our trail so we don't get too lost," Mari replied.

"We should be OK if we don't run into any snags. One thing about these smartphones is that you can get almost any app you want. Don't ask me why, but I've had a compass on this thing forever," Poole said. "Now I finally get to use it."

They picked a spot that was less dense and hacked their way across the bluff. The overgrowth consisted mostly of long grass and overhanging foliage. Once they worked their way into the brush, it became less congested, and they found themselves in a wooded area covered by a canopy of large, old-growth mahogany.

"Not to worry you, John," Mari said. "But we should probably keep an eye on any vines that move."

"Now you tell me! It's enough I have to deal with your jetliner mosquitoes!"

"Nothing's poisonous. I just didn't want you to worry."

"Geez, I wasn't worrying until you told me. Why did I want to keep you around again?"

"Because you're fascinated by me. Any other questions?"

"Yes. Are we there yet?"

Mari shook her head as they continued to hike deeper into the brush. They briefly stopped for a water break and checked the time. It was almost one o'clock, and the heat under the canopy was at sauna levels. Even Mari was starting to drip sweat. Poole checked the maps on his phone. "We have to be getting close, by my rough calculations. I just wish we knew what exactly we were looking for."

"Whatever it is, it's got to be pretty rustic. You have to think that back in the 1600s, they didn't have the best building materials," Mari replied.

"But there still has to be evidence of it if my father was able to create a map of its general location. My bet would be to look for piles of stones or something like that."

"You mean like that pile over there?" Mari asked, pointing to a glade on their right.

"Good eye, Mari!"

They turned just south of their heading and went to inspect the site. "This looks like it was probably something back then," Poole exclaimed.

Stones were strewn throughout the site, and a flat, mossy layer suggested a floor. Poole took the shovel and jabbed it into the ground, hitting some kind of rock on the first blow. "There must be paving stones or something like that under this moss."

"Let's pace off this area to see how big it is," Mari suggested. After several strides around the perimeter she said, "It looks like thirty feet by sixty feet, give or take. I suppose it could have been a church back in the day."

"Probably," Poole said, looking at the maps on his phone. "Now, if this is the large rectangle shown on my father's sketch, then the smaller one circled in red is about a quarter of a mile east by northeast from here."

"Let's have another drink of water first," Mari said.

"You read my mind."

They rested for a minute more and then continued east. The overgrowth was sporadic, making it evident that at one time, this area was all part of the clearing on the bluff. The mahogany trees provided shade from the midday sun, but the lack of breeze made the canopy as hot as an oven. Luckily, the walking was easier on the level surface, and the need for machetes was minimal.

Poole was the first to spot it. "Hey, look over there! It's a small, stone building."

"You're right!" Mari exclaimed. "That must be what your dad found."

They approached the small structure. Its stone walls were remarkably intact. It couldn't have been more than ten or fifteen feet wide and twenty feet long. Its wooden roof appeared to have caved into the center of the structure; remnants remained inside the walls. Over the centuries, a few stones had fallen from the tops of the walls too. Mari paced the exterior of the structure and confirmed that it was markedly smaller than the other.

"This is definitely it, John," Mari said. "I know this sounds stupid, but now what?"

"How about if we knock and see if anyone's home?"

THIRTY NINE

January 1681

Morgan refused to sleep. With Teresa still in the bedroom, he was compelled to complete his task before resting any further. The sun was getting low in the sky, so he summoned his horse from the stable and rode down to Port Maria to meet with the fishermen.

As he reached the shoreline, the first boats were making their way back. He waited patiently as they each carefully unloaded their catches on the sand before him. What an unusual little creature, Morgan thought, quite harmless by its looks, but deadly. The fishermen had done well and brought back more than he needed. He paid them all handsomely and motioned them to place the lot into the canvas sack that he'd brought with him. He secured it on his saddle next to the smaller canvas sack before he rode away.

His horse climbed the steady rise to the bluff and slowly plodded to the plantation house. Morgan rode with hardly a move, his glazed eyes fixed on the path ahead. Mr. Dunn was waiting for him on the veranda as Morgan dismounted and untied both canvas sacks.

"Good evening, sir," Mr. Dunn said cautiously. "The arrangements have been made as you requested."

"Very good, William," Morgan replied. "Where is the casket?"

"In the living room, sir."

"Fine. Please come back at first light with a horse and cart. You and I will handle this on our own."

"Yes, sir. Anything else, Captain?" Dunn asked.

Morgan shook his head in reply and turned away, carrying the canvas sacks as he did. Dunn watched him as he walked inside the house and felt sorry for him. Over the past few years, he had never seen him in better spirits. Now he was a walking corpse, a shell of his former self.

As Dunn left to attend to the final matters at the family chapel, Morgan went to the kitchen to prepare. He pulled a washing bowl from a cupboard and carefully emptied the wet canvas sack into it. The small, round fish had pale-gray skin and yellow fins. Small spikes protruded from their bodies. Morgan put on leather gloves and found a wooden spoon to crush the fish, careful not to splash any offal on his skin or face. He mashed the fish, bones and all, until he created a sickening gray slurry.

After carefully picking out the bones, he added some fresh ground flour to the mix and slowly blended it with the slurry to make a thick paste. Satisfied with his work, Morgan went out to the workshop with the small coconut he had picked up on the shore. He wedged it securely between two pieces of lumber and took a tree saw to it. Concentrating on the angles, it was a matter of a few brisk strokes to cut an opening in the top of the shell.

Morgan dropped the saw on the earthen floor of the workshop and returned to the kitchen. With the steadiness of a surgeon, Morgan slowly scraped out the coconut meat with a kitchen knife until the brown husk remained. He stopped to consider his handiwork, satisfied that the top of the shell fit snuggly on the cleaned-out body, and thought about how best to complete his task.

For a moment, weariness started to overtake him, but a quick pull from the rum bottle brought Morgan back to life. He walked back to the workshop and found the bucket, water, and powder his carpenter had left for making the plaster. He slowly mixed the materials together until he created the white, sticky substance in the bucket. He carried the bucket into the kitchen, pleased with his first plaster mixture. Once in the kitchen, he took three linen napkins and ripped them into strips. He gauged their lengths and nodded. This will do, he thought.

Morgan smiled. Now let's put this little package together, he said to himself. First, he placed the body of the coconut shell on the counter with the open end up. Then he filled it almost to the top with the thick fish paste he'd created. Finally, he opened the small canvas sack and removed his coveted, blood-red, heart-shaped ruby. "It's the only thing I can give you now, my darling," Morgan whispered.

He slowly wedged the gem into the shell, careful not to spill its contents, until it was securely nestled in place. The displacement brought the fish paste up to the top of the opening. So far, so good, Morgan thought. He then caked the top of the husk with more fish paste until it was coated to the edges. In a quick but careful motion, he placed the top on the body of the shell without spilling a drop, keeping pressure on the top to hold it in place.

Now for the tricky part, Morgan thought. While still keeping pressure on the shell, he lifted up the bucket of plaster and placed it on the counter. He dipped a linen strip into the mixture until it was completely covered, and then he carefully wrapped the coconut where the two sections met. He repeated the procedure in different directions until the entire husk was covered in the white, plaster-soaked strips. He then took a small handful of plaster to cover the coconut in a second layer and waited for the plaster to set.

After about a half hour, Morgan added a bit more water to the bucket and started adding more plaster to the coconut husk to fashion the shape he desired. Morgan was close to delirium by the time his creation was finished, and he was certain that his Teresa would be pleased.

He disposed of the remaining fish paste, cleaned the kitchen, and washed his skin with lye soap. He then went to the living room to prepare the casket. He placed their finest bedding in the bottom of the mahogany box and placed two feather pillows at its head. He took a deep breath to consider what was next. Deciding, he went to the closet and returned with Teresa's favorite green dress.

After putting the dress on Teresa, he gently washed her face and combed her hair. Slowly, he picked her up, walked to the living room, and lovingly placed her in the casket. The sun had been down for at least an hour, and he made the final preparations in the light of the moon. He went out to the foot of the veranda and picked a few bunches of jasmine, Teresa's favorite flower, and placed them with her in the casket.

Finally, he went to the kitchen and carefully carried his plaster creation back to the casket. He placed it on her chest and gently placed her hands over it. "You can have my heart until I come to meet you, my love, and I've made sure it will be no one's but yours," he said as he stared at her one last time. With tears streaming down his face, he placed the wooden top on the casket and nailed it shut for eternity.

The next morning, Mr. Dunn found Morgan on the veranda, fast asleep. He was slumped in Teresa's favorite chair, and he held a sprig of jasmine close to his chest. Dunn hesitated to wake him, but he knew that Morgan would be upset if he did not.

He stomped heavily on the wooden planks of the veranda as he neared Morgan. Morgan stirred slightly and then bolted from his slumber with a start. He blinked his eyes a few times and stifled a yawn. "Mr. Dunn," he said in a dry voice. "Please fetch me some water, and then we can get to work."

Somewhat refreshed, Morgan instructed Dunn to bring the cart to the steps of the veranda. They carried out the sealed casket and placed it on the cart, securing it with ropes, and proceeded to the family chapel. Within a half hour, they reached their destination.

The evening before, Mr. Dunn had loosened the paving stones on the right side of the structure's interior and dug a grave several feet deep. Morgan examined the work. "You've done well, Mr. Dunn. This is exactly as I instructed. Had I still been on the sea, you would have earned your own vessel by now."

The compliment took Dunn aback. "Thank you, Captain."

"You're welcome, William. Now, let us finish this, shall we?"

With some effort, they picked up the casket, carried it into the chapel, and set it down next to the grave. "Get the ropes. We'll place them under the casket," Morgan said.

Dunn did as Morgan instructed. With Morgan on one side holding the ropes and Dunn on the other, they carefully picked up the casket and slowly lowered it into the grave. Once it had settled on the earth, they released the ropes and let them fall next to the casket. Two shovels were propped up against the stone wall. "I've said my good-byes, Mr. Dunn. Hand me a shovel, and we'll make short work of the task."

After filling in the grave and replacing the paving stones, Morgan was satisfied that the task was complete. Mr. Dunn took the shovels back to the cart and left Morgan inside the chapel for a moment.

Morgan knelt at the foot of the grave. "My dearest Teresa, my last gift to you will be to reunite you with your church. You were an angel that walked this earth, and now you must be returned to your heaven. Mr. Dunn will know what to do when I come to meet you. It's the least I can do to repay you for your forgiveness, and your love."

FORTY

Poole and Mari walked over to the open doorway of the small stone building and peered inside. The decayed trusses from the old wooden roof filled up most of the structure. Poole grabbed one of the beams, and it crumbled in his hands. A small rodent scampered out the doorway between his legs.

"Jesus, I hope its mother isn't in there!" Poole exclaimed. "You know, I'm surprised that there's really no evidence of disturbance. You'd think my father would have rooted through here."

"Maybe he knew that there wasn't anything to find inside," Mari offered. "Or maybe he wasn't the grave-robbing type either."

"Let's check around the building. Maybe we can find something."

As they walked around to the east side of the building, Poole noticed that bare spots of packed dirt randomly dotted the verdant ground surrounding the structure. "Look there!" he said as they walked to the first spot. "It looks like a hole was dug here within the last month or so."

"So your dad wasn't looking inside the building; he was looking for something buried around it?" Mari asked.

"It sure looks that way," Poole answered. "There must be more to this riddle than we're aware of right now."

"Maybe it was something in that last Morgan letter we didn't read. There could have been parts that Fredrickson didn't think were important," Mari said.

"You have to think so. But the way these holes were dug, I'd say my father was sort of hunting and pecking his way around here. My guess is that he didn't know exactly where to look."

"It seems a waste not to even look inside, though," Mari said.

"Yeah, but remember that in my father's last letter, he said that Morgan might have left a trap for the unwary or something like that," Poole cautioned.

"That's right, but I highly doubt it involved that rotten wood in there. We might as well clean it out and have a look-see."

"What the hell. It'd be crazy not to at least look around inside," Poole agreed. "Why don't you hang out here, and I'll throw out what I can. Then you can toss the stuff out of the way."

"Sounds like a plan," Mari responded.

"If I don't come out in five minutes, you can assume I found Morgan's trap," Poole smirked, as he entered the small building and started grabbing the debris. "Man, it's hot in here!"

"Quit crying! It's hot out here too!"

Twenty minutes later, Poole emerged completely soaked in sweat and covered with wood chips and dust. He grabbed the shovel and reentered the oven. Mari could hear the scrapes of the blade against the stone floor and stood clear as Poole started tossing shovelfuls of debris through the doorway. Poole finally walked out, looking like he had wrestled a bear in a sawdust pile.

"Madam, your castle awaits," Poole said with a flourish of his hand.

Mari shook her head at Poole as she entered the now barren enclosure. Although the roof was gone, with no breeze to speak of the heat was suffocating in the confined space. Poole followed her in, and they slowly inched their way around the walls.

"It doesn't look like anything more than an old shed, John," Mari observed.

"Yeah, I would have thought that there might be some markings on the walls or even a plaque. Whatever signs that might have existed are now long gone."

"If there were any to begin with," Mari speculated. "If I'm Morgan, I don't want anyone but a few trusted people to know about this place."

"You're right," Poole agreed. "He still had some enemies, and I'm sure there were more than a few people out there who were looking for his loot."

"So it probably was disguised as a shed for storing supplies or some other innocuous purpose. The question is, what do we do now?"

"I've been thinking about that, Mari," Poole answered. "We're not grave robbers. And even if that ruby is in here, it wouldn't legally belong to us anyway. This land belongs to the Catholic Church now, so the ruby would probably be their property, or at least the church and the country of Jamaica would arm-wrestle over the rights of anything found. The best we would get is a firm handshake and a warm thank you for our efforts."

"Don't forget our pictures in the paper," Mari added, smiling.

Poole was about to respond when a shadow crossed the doorway, and he heard the click of a safety being released from a firearm. Mari whirled around to see the two Jamaican men whom they had first seen in the hospital parking lot.

"There will be no need for pictures in the paper," the taller one said in a deep Jamaican accent as he pointed the handgun at them. "Please toss over any weapons you may have on you. I also want your cell phones."

Poole and Mari slid their phones over to the shorter man, who stuffed them into his cargo shorts. He then dialed a familiar number on his phone and waited for the connection. "We have them, and we found the burial site," he said, pausing for the response. "Not that long, about an hour and a half. We can make sure everything is ready when you arrive." The shorter man paused again, staring at Poole and Mari. "Very good, sir. It will be done," he said, with a broadening smile, as he ended the call.

The taller man gave a quick look to the other, wondering what the instructions were. "He'll be here soon enough," the shorter one said. "Let's start on the right side, farthest from the doorway." He disappeared for a moment and brought back the pickax and shovel that were resting against the outer wall. "Here!" he said, as he tossed them into the structure.

Poole and Mari looked at each other in confusion. The taller man jutted the gun toward Poole and Mari. "You heard the man. Dig!"

Poole picked up the pickax, and Mari grabbed the shovel. They looked at each other and knew their fate would be the same as that of Poole's father unless they could think of a way out of the predicament. "Let's just get this over with, Mari. Maybe something will come up," Poole whispered.

Mari stayed clear as Poole raised the pickax and brought it down hard on the floor of the structure. His hands stung as the ax bounced off the stone. Scraping off the moss, he found a small joint and levered the broad end of the ax into the crack. Heaving against the ax handle, Poole was able to lift the flat stone and dislodge it. Mari looked briefly over at the two men before she ran over to grab the edge of the stone and work it away from its resting place.

"Good!" the tall one said. "Keep going, we don't have all day!"

Within a half hour, Poole was able to dislodge most of the paving stones on the front, right side of the structure. Mari helped move them over to the left side of the enclosure, and the shorter man instructed her to stack them neatly in the far corner. "No sense making a mess," he said.

Poole was exhausted from the heat and exertion. "Shovel time, Mr. Poole. Hopefully, you're going to be more cooperative than your father was," the tall one said. Poole stared at the tall man as he grabbed the shovel. He turned to face him and started to dig.

"John, let's alternate. You're tired enough as it is," Mari said.

"I'll let you know when I get tired," Poole said, still staring at the tall man.

Poole cut out a rectangular outline about six feet wide and eight feet long. He then slowly started digging along the outline, throwing the dirt along the left side of the structure. Mari gave Poole a breather after about twenty minutes, but Poole took over again ten minutes later. The sweltering heat slowed their efforts, but within an hour, they had managed to dig down a good three feet.

"We need some water," Poole said to the tall one.

He thought about the request for a moment and then relented. "Get their water bottle," he said to the shorter one. "Better they dig than us."

The shorter man tossed the bottle over to Poole, and he drank thirstily. He gave the bottle to Mari, who sat quietly in the corner, drinking her share. "Back to work, Mr. Poole," the tall one commanded. "We don't have all day!"

Poole looked at his watch. It was nearing three in the afternoon, and he knew they only had about three more hours before it would be getting dark. He looked for an opening, but the tall one had his full concentration on Poole, and his gun was at the ready.

In resignation, Poole began to dig again. He continued his pattern of taking shovelfuls from around the perimeter of the hole and slowly digging deeper in shallow layers. Poole was about to grab the pickax when the smaller one spoke.

"Did you hear that?" he said to the tall one. "It's probably him. I'll go see if I can find him."

The tall one nodded without taking his eyes off Poole and Mari.

Poole started swinging the pickax to loosen up the deeper layers of dirt when he hit something solid. The tall one jumped up and focused his attention on the rectangular hole. "Keep digging!"

Poole raised the pickax and brought it down with more force. This time, it dug into the solid surface. When he pried the ax away, a splinter of wood stuck up from the dirt.

"Stop!" the tall one said.

Poole rested on the edge of the pit, now four feet in depth, and drank again from the water bottle. "Now what?" he asked the tall one.

"We wait," he said. He then pointed at Mari. "In the pit with him."

Mari climbed down next to Poole. He grabbed her hand to give her strength, but he didn't have a clue as to how to get out of their situation, other than to make a mad bull rush and hope the first bullet didn't hit them.

"Jimar, call the man! We're ready!" the tall one said, but there was no answer. "Jimar!" After about twenty seconds, he picked up his cell phone, careful not to take his eyes off Poole and Mari. He pressed the speed dial and placed the phone to his ear. He waited, but there was no answer.

"Jimar! Come, now!" the tall man yelled straining to hear a response in the looming silence. He thought about calling the boss, but decided against looking incompetent. Once more, he yelled, "Jimar!"

Growing impatient, he slowly backed out through the doorway, keeping his gun trained on Poole and Mari. As he stepped over the threshold, Poole and Mari could see the butt of a rifle swing from behind and land with full force on the back of the man's head. A sickening crack reverberated in the enclosure, and the tall one's eyes grew wide as he fell face-first toward them and his handgun pitched forward.

Poole leapt up the side of the pit to grab it. He pulled Mari behind him, pointed the gun at the opening, and waited.

"Do me a favor. Don't do anything stupid, OK?" said a familiar voice as he waved a white handkerchief across the opening of the door.

Poole and Mari looked at each other in confusion. "Show yourself. Now!" Poole yelled.

Slowly the outline of a man came into view. His hands were in the air. "Is that anyway to greet your old pal, Ryker?"

Forty One

"Wilson!" Poole exclaimed. "What are you doing here?"

"Looking after you, John. Your old man told me that you might be needing my help. So here I am," he replied.

"But how did you know we were up here?"

"I didn't, really. I just knew those two goons were following you, so I followed them." he said.

"So this whole time, you had our backs?" Poole asked.

"I told you I was here to help. It's not my fault you didn't believe me."

"Sorry to be so cynical, Ryker, but why should we trust you now?"

"Because your dad trusted me. Around these parts, that should be good enough for you," he replied as he propped his rifle against the side of the structure. "Now we could debate this issue until the cows come home, but it's damn hot out here, and I need some help tying up this guy."

Mari returned Poole's questioning look. "I hate to admit it, John. But I think he's on our side."

Poole nodded and climbed out of the pit, pulling Mari up behind him. They gratefully exited the oven of the stone building but got only minor relief outside.

"I've got a bit of rope," Ryker said. "Let's tie him up to that tree over there." He pointed to a healthy copperwood a few paces away.

"Where is the smaller guy?" Poole asked.

"He's decorating a tamarind tree about fifty yards from here."

"It looks like Mari and I are in your debt," Poole said as he helped drag the tall one over to the copperwood.

"That's right, Ryker," Mari added. "I have to say that I had a different impression of you."

Ryker laughed. "It wouldn't be the first time a woman has said that to me!"

"Seriously, Ryker," Mari continued. "We thought you might have been the guy behind these two thugs."

"Me? Nah," he said. "John Morgan asked for a favor, and I said yes. He did all right by me after all those years, so I'm trying to make it even. Besides, I like you two. A man can't have enough friends to share a pint with on this island."

Poole and Ryker had just finished securing the tall one against the copperwood when Poole stopped short. "Do you have any idea who they work for, Ryker? The shorter one called his boss a couple of hours ago, and I'm pretty sure he said that he would be coming here."

"In that case, we should be getting out of here to a safer—" The metallic sound of a cartridge being loaded cut Ryker's response short.

"There's no need to rush away now that we're all here, Ryker," a man's voice said.

They all turned to find that Ryker's hunting rifle was trained on them. "There's still so much to be done! Since we already have the tools, we might as well put them to use. Wouldn't you agree, Mr. Poole?"

A sinking feeling came over Poole as he stared at the handgun that was now lying by the man's hiking boots. "It's never a good idea to leave your weapons lying around. You just never know when you might need them," the man said, his red face drenched in sweat. "Imagine how fortunate I feel to have a strong body to help with the rest of the digging. Now, if you wouldn't mind securely tying up Mr. Wilson and Ms. Robeson, I believe there's some unfinished business to take care of."

"Anything else?" Poole said.

"Why yes, Mr. Poole, as a matter of fact, there is," he said as he dabbed the sweat off his forehead with a dirty handkerchief. "As of today, I'm resigning as your lawyer."

FORTY TWO

July 1688

Morgan had summoned Mr. Dunn to Port Royal. Dunn had heard that Morgan's health was deteriorating and that he had fallen ill. Ever since Senora Castillo's death, Morgan drank in excess and was a shell of his former self. He couldn't stay at the plantation because of the memories, and spent more and more of his time attending to his life in Kingston. At first, he spent some time with his daughter, Angelica, but as the months turned into years, his contact with her became sporadic.

The virile, swashbuckling man had turned into an overweight drunkard. His position of power as lieutenant governor—and at one point, governor—was stripped from him once he became less attentive to his duties. And it was clear that Morgan didn't care. To the casual observer, it merely seemed as if Morgan was on a mission to accelerate the moment of his death.

As Dunn rode toward Port Royal, he came to the realization that civilization had caught up with Jamaica. Building was rampant, and more Europeans were streaming into his homeland daily. Looking out at the spit protecting the harbor, Dunn saw that the city was rife with sails, and the bustle of commerce was evident everywhere.

Dunn passed by the governor's residence and into the more sordid part of Port Royal. There were several alehouses along the waterfront, and Dunn knew he would find Morgan in one of them. His third try was a pub called The Shipp. Morgan was holding court at a table in the back, surrounded by old salts reliving the glory days of the Caribbean. Although Dunn was only eight at the time, he clearly remembered the raid on Portobello that Morgan was retelling. The old sailors were rapt as Morgan spun the story of the disabled ships and the ruthless and successful raid by land that rewarded his men with vast treasures.

Morgan stopped when he saw Dunn in the light of the doorway. "Gents, may I introduce a young man that was there manning my ship during the battle! Mr. Dunn, come here!"

Dunn cautiously approached the group of drunken sots. "Sir, good to see you," Dunn said.

Morgan stood and reeled. He focused on Dunn's features and smiled at the young man. "William, I'm glad you've come. There is much to discuss. Gentlemen, I must ask your leave! I have business to attend to with this young fellow!"

Despite the groans from his drunken cronies, Morgan grabbed Dunn's coat and walked unsteadily out of The Shipp with Dunn in tow. "Look at you, man!" Morgan exclaimed like a proud father. "You're a far cry from that boy in Panama."

"That was many years ago, sir," Dunn replied.

"Yes, many years. Those days seem like yesterday and yet a lifetime ago."

"How are you, sir? You are missed on the plantation."

"I am of no use on the plantation, Mr. Dunn. You are doing well in my stead."

"Yes, the sugar production is fine. I'm speaking more of Angelica," Dunn said cautiously.

"Angelica," Morgan said with a distant look on his face. "So much like Teresa, so much like her mother."

"She asks about you often, sir," Dunn said honestly.

"That is good for an old man to hear," Morgan mumbled. "But I am no father anymore. She is better off living her life without me."

Dunn studied Morgan's face, seeing the resignation and sadness in his eyes. "Begging your pardon, sir, but she is there waiting for you to be her father."

Morgan coughed. Then the cough turned into an uncontrollable gag, but he didn't respond. His yellowed eyes were vacant as he looked out to the horizon. He stank of rum and fetid ale and hadn't changed his clothes in a week. The buttons of his waistcoat strained at the pressure from his girth, and his double chin hid his once commanding profile.

"Sir, I've come at your request," Dunn said. "How can I be of service?"

"Always to business, Mr. Dunn." Morgan sighed. "Then to business it shall be."

Dunn waited patiently as Morgan gathered his wits. "Mr. Dunn, I've called for you because you are the only man on this island I can trust," Morgan began. "As you have surmised, I am not well, and I have some favors to ask of you."

"Favors, sir? I am at your service. You need not ask me for a favor."

"To the contrary, Mr. Dunn, you are no longer at my service. It is time that you get on with your life and leave me to mine."

"I'm sorry, sir?"

"The physicians say that I am dying, Mr. Dunn. But any fool can see that from a distance."

"No sir, you just need some rest. Perhaps the plantation—"

"Yes, I have been thinking that as well. But not for the reason you suggest," Morgan said, coughing as he finished the words.

"Is there nothing the doctors can do, sir?"

"The doctors say I have dropsy and gout. I am in constant pain, and the only thing that soothes me is the rum." Morgan became silent for a moment before his attempts to stifle his cough failed. Recovering, he continued. "But that isn't why I called for you, Mr. Dunn. I have made arrangements, and I want to make sure that they are carried out."

Dunn listened intently as Morgan inhaled slowly. He could hear the rasp as if Morgan's lungs were half-filled with water. "I have prepared a will. It is in my study at the plantation. I have also left you a letter that I ask that you open when I am gone. Now listen carefully."

Morgan paused, his yellow eyes as sharp as a hawk's for that moment as he grabbed Dunn's forearm and looked him in the eye. "The will gives most of what I have to my two godsons; nephews by marriage. I do this because society warrants it. However, I want you to honor two wishes for me."

"Anything, sir."

"Also in the desk in my study is a deed giving part of my plantation property to the Catholic Church. This must be done quickly before my will is published so that there is no confusion."

"Which part?" Dunn asked, knowing the answer.

"That section of the bluff that looks down over Port Maria. The place where Senora Castillo is buried. I had the property surveyed several years ago, and the description will be accurate."

"And the other request, sir?"

"I suspect that when I die, the Jamaican Counsel will want to put on some sort of elaborate memorial and bury me in Port Royal," Morgan said.

"That would certainly be warranted, sir. Befitting a man of your status."

"Yes, I suppose. But it is my wish to be buried someplace else," Morgan said, staring intently at Dunn. "Do we understand each other?"

"Perfectly, sir."

"Good. Now let us find a nice bottle of rum to seal our pact. I believe it's time for my medicine."

FORTY THREE

"Make sure those bindings are secure, Mr. Poole," Dunbar said. "I really don't want any funny business going on now. There's a good man."

Poole tied Ryker and Mari to the same tree that once secured the tall man, who was still unconscious and lying facedown on the earth a few paces away. The blackened mat of blood on the back of his head suggested that it would be hours before he woke up, if at all.

Poole completed tying Mari to the side of the copperwood tree opposite Ryker. He looked into Mari's eyes and could see that she was looking for answers. He shook his head slightly without saying a word and walked back to the doorway. "Now what, Dunbar?"

"Come to think of it, I'd rather not be disturbed during our work," Dunbar said as he pulled several stained handkerchiefs from his pocket. "Please gag our companions so that we can fully concentrate on the task at hand."

Dunbar threw the handkerchiefs to the ground and Poole did as instructed, stuffing them in the mouths of Mari and Ryker.

"Now, please take that extra bit of rope over there and make sure those gags don't fall out."

Poole tied the ropes to secure the gags and stared with malevolence at Dunbar. Dunbar simply smiled in return. "Thank you. I'd appreciate it if you would stand by the structure while I take a look at your handiwork."

As Poole walked over to the building, Dunbar cautiously moved to the tree and made sure that the ropes binding Mari and Ryker were properly tied. "Excellent job, Mr. Poole! Now, why don't you show me the way in. I'd love to see what you've done to the place," he said, the stagnant air making him sweat even more.

Dunbar replaced the rifle with the handgun and pointed the barrel at Poole as he followed him into the structure. "You've made marvelous progress in spite of the conditions. Quite stifling in here, isn't it?"

"Enough of the chitchat, Dunbar. What do you want?" Poole asked as he crawled into the pit.

"Please, there's really no need to be impolite, Mr. Poole. This entire island needs to become a bit more civilized, in my opinion. Now, please pick up the shovel and dig. While you do that, at least humor me with a little adult conversation."

Poole weighed his options as he looked up at Dunbar. He had the shovel and pickax at his disposal, but they were no match for the handgun. Even though Dunbar was sweating profusely and the excessive heat made him pant for fresh air, Dunbar was focused on Poole and any odd movements that he might make.

Poole picked up the shovel and started digging again. There was at least another eight inches of earth remaining to uncover the hard surface that the pickax had found earlier.

"I have to give you credit, John. I'm sorry, may I call you John?" Dunbar asked.

"You have the gun, Dunbar. You can call me anything you want."

"Why thank you, John. See? We can have an adult conversation," Dunbar continued. "You and your friend, Ms. Robeson, really helped with the last few conundrums that had plagued me in my search for Madonna's Heart."

"So that is what this is all about?" Poole asked as he continued to scrape off the dirt.

"Of course. What else would there be, John? Conservative estimates would value a ruby of that size to be worth at least fifty million dollars US. That's a game changer, as they say in your country," Dunbar laughed.

"What if it's not here?"

"Oh, it's here. Your father and I figured that out several years ago. All of the old Morgan correspondence suggested nothing but this possibility. The only problem was finding the location."

"Why was that such a problem, Dunbar?" Poole asked, stopping to catch his breath.

"Because the Morgan correspondence didn't tell us where the location was. We had to look in another direction."

"What do you mean?"

"Really, it was as simple as following someone other than the infamous Captain Morgan."

"Like Teresa Montoya Castillo," Poole stated.

"Yes, to start. At least that led us to an interesting discovery about the descendants of Morgan, much to your father's surprise."

Poole hit the wooden surface with the shovel blade and continued to scrape along the length of the wood as he uncovered the casket. "I'm sorry. What surprise?"

"That he wasn't a direct descendant of Henry Morgan, of course," Dunbar answered. "You should have seen the look on his face when we discovered that fact. He was convinced that once he found out about Senora Castillo, he would be able to prove his lineage once and for all. When the link to Morgan wasn't there, his focus seemed to change."

"But yours didn't, correct?"

"Quite observant, John. For your father, it was more about finding his roots, validating himself somehow. For me, it has always been about the Heart. My validation will come with the dollar signs that stone will bring."

"But you two were still working together. Why did you turn on him?" Poole asked.

"On the contrary, John, it was your father who turned on me," Dunbar answered. "He came into a little money after your mother passed away. Life insurance I believe. After that, he said his priorities had changed."

"That probably explains the boat," Poole said.

"Oh, yes, the *Rebecca*. That vessel wasn't cheap. Of course, that's what severed your father's relationship with Mr. Wilson."

"I'm sorry, I don't understand," Poole said, trying to keep Dunbar talking.

"He thought John Morgan was holding out on him. To be honest, I thought he was too," Dunbar explained. "As it turns out, my impressions were right. Your dear old father found some things he decided that he didn't need to share with either one of us. Quite frankly, that didn't sit too well with me."

"Wilson said the same thing."

Dunbar nodded and wiped the pouring sweat from his brow. "I've never trusted that Aussie, especially after his falling-out with your father. He could have fouled up all of my plans if he found the treasure first. Almost did, as it turns out," he said dryly.

"But why involve me, Dunbar? You had access to most of the records and could have discovered the rest."

"I wouldn't have had to if it wasn't for your father. As soon as he had me name you as the executor and sole beneficiary in his will, it all changed. Your father had no idea that he sealed his fate, and yours, once that will was made."

"For God's sake, why?"

"Because I should have been the one to get access to everything! I put in the years of research, the sweat, and tears. Not some kid in Seattle who didn't want a thing to do with his father anyway!" Dunbar yelled, shaking the gun at Poole.

"So you decided to accelerate the process."

Dunbar let out a slow breath and regained his composure, the gun now steady in his hand. "That wasn't my original intent, John. I just wanted to get the information and be done with it. But, as it turned out, your father's death had its benefits."

"How do you figure that, you sick bastard?"

"Because then I could just follow you around as you did my work for me," Dunbar gloated. "But I digress. That's ancient history, and we now are on the cusp of a great discovery."

Dunbar pointed the gun at Poole and motioned for him to continue digging. Poole wiped his forehead with the sleeve of his T-shirt, picked up the shovel, and started digging around the exposed edges of the casket. The heat seemed to climb to the high nineties in the enclosed space, and Poole was getting weak with the exertion.

"Just a few more inches, John. I want to make sure you've properly exposed the edges."

Poole did as Dunbar instructed and dug a ditch around the casket about a foot in depth. "Now what, Dunbar?"

Dunbar stood up, walked over to the water bottle near the doorway, and tossed it over to Poole. "Please, take a drink. You've done a fine job so far."

Poole grabbed the bottle and took a few sips while Dunbar walked back to his perch at the foot of the burial site. "Now, if you don't mind, why don't you take that pickax and see if you can't pry the lid off the casket."

Poole tossed the water bottle over to Dunbar. He hefted the ax and quickly surveyed his situation one more time before addressing the lid of the casket. You've brought a pickax to a gunfight, John, Poole thought as Dunbar trained the pistol at him.

"Please, John, it's quite warm in here, so the sooner you do what I ask, the better."

Poole stood on the hard wood surface of the casket and took a full swing toward the lip of the lid with the flat end of the tool. It sank into the wood with little resistance. He pried back on the ax and heard the groan of the coffin nails as their grip on the mahogany loosened slightly. Poole repeated the process until the left side of the lid was free, and he repeated the process on the right side until the lid was completely loose.

"Excellent work, John. Excellent! Now, if you would be so kind, please remove the lid and throw it over to the far end of the room. I'd appreciate it if you would do so slowly and not think about anything heroic."

Standing on the side of the casket, Poole grabbed the lid and placed it where Dunbar had instructed. When he turned around, he saw a brown, decaying skeleton covered in remnants of a green silk dress. The woman's hands were folded neatly on her rib cage, holding a rough, heart-shaped object.

Dunbar stood up from his perch and froze as he stared at the object. Poole stood back, waiting for Dunbar's next move. "John, I believe I have found what I've been looking for. I so much appreciate your help. I have one last favor, if you would be so kind. Carefully remove Senora Castillo's hands from the Heart and gently place it on the edge over here."

Poole reached down and tried to loosen the petrified hands of the woman, but they were wrapped tightly around the object. "It looks like she doesn't want to give it up that easily, Dunbar," Poole stated.

"Then with a bit more force, John. No funny business, please."

Poole knelt down again and grabbed the right hand of the skeleton. With more pressure, he started snapping away the bones until he was holding the remains of her hand. He gently placed the hand in the casket and turned to the other hand. Again, exerting just enough pressure, he snapped off the other hand, leaving what appeared to be some sort of plaster casting exposed. Poole looked along the entire interior of the casket to see if there were any booby traps or anything else that would suggest that the taker of the Heart would be in danger. But nothing was evident to him.

He carefully picked up the object, walked it over to the foot of the pit, and placed it on the paving stones a few feet from where Dunbar was perched.

"Marvelous job, John. Now, please go over to the other end and keep Senora Castillo company."

Poole slowly turned away from Dunbar. He knew he was running out of time. As he passed by the upright shovel, he grabbed the handle and, in one swift motion, swung it toward Dunbar. His throw was errant and the shovel just glanced off Dunbar's left leg. Unfazed, Dunbar pulled the trigger of the handgun and shot Poole in the shoulder. The force threw him back into the pit as blood began to stain his T-shirt. Poole sat there in disbelief, and for a moment, all he could hear were the muffled cries of Mari and Ryker.

"I would have expected a better attempt, John. Lucky for you, I'm not a very good shot. If it was one of my men, you would be dead right now," Dunbar said.

"I'll be dead soon enough, Dunbar," Poole replied, wincing at the pain in his shoulder.

"Soon, perhaps. But right now, this discovery deserves to be shared, don't you think? After all, if it wasn't for you and Ms. Robeson, this treasure might have been lost forever."

"You're sick, Dunbar. Is that ruby worth killing for?"

"I'm just the last in a long line of men who've killed for Madonna's Heart. By the time someone discovers you're missing, and then finally discovers where you are, if at all, I'll be long, long gone."

"It's only money, Dunbar. You're a lawyer, you'd be throwing your life away."

"What life? A shabby law office wedged between street vendors. Clients who don't pay, sweltering heat...every day I sweat like a stuck pig. That's a life I'll gladly throw away."

"You're not a killer, Dunbar. Your henchmen may have done your dirty work for you in the past, but this is different," Poole said.

"John, it's time for you to stop talking and conserve your energy. I would like your full attention as we finally reveal Madonna's Heart after all of these centuries."

As Poole sat slumped in the pit next to the skeletal remains of Teresa Montoya Castillo, Dunbar picked up the plaster object to examine it. He turned it over. Finding no discernable opening, he knelt and placed it on the hard stone surface. Grabbing it with both hands, he applied pressure on the plaster until it started crumbling. Within a few seconds, he was left with the preserved remains of a small coconut shell.

"Curious container, don't you think John?" Dunbar asked rhetorically. Sweat was dripping from his face, and his heart was beating faster as he anticipated the treasure inside. "There's no way I can just crush this with my hands. It looks like we'll have to do this the old-fashioned way."

Hunched over the coconut shell, he picked it up with both hands and brought it gently down on the paving stone beneath it. A small crack appeared, and Dunbar lost patience. He raised the shell higher and brought it down on the flat stone with as much force as he dared. The shell shattered. A large cloud of white powder spewed out of the shell, covering Dunbar's face and hands. His head was so close that he inhaled some of the powder, causing him to cough uncontrollably for several seconds. The cloud surrounded his head, caking in his eyes and nostrils. In his excitement, he paid no attention to the hovering particles. Beneath the fragments of coconut shell, sitting in a bed of powder, was a sparkle of red. He licked his lips in anticipation and picked up the stone. It was as large as his palm and every bit as grand as the ancient accounts had described. He brought it to his lips and kissed it gently, as if it were his lover.

Poole sat in the pit in pain, his shoulder throbbing with each heartbeat. He peered toward the other end of the enclosure as Dunbar fondled the heart-shaped ruby. The cloud of dust continued to hover over his head in the hot, stagnant room. He looked like a ghost with the powder clinging to his sweaty face and hands. Dunbar was oblivious to everything except the stone and kissed it one more time before looking up at Poole.

"You should consider yourself a very lucky man, John," Dunbar stated. "This is a discovery of a lifetime, quite possibly the most unique and valuable gem in the entire world." Dunbar's excitement increased with each breath, and new beads of sweat ran down his face, turning it into a striated mask. The sweat reached the corners of his mouth, and again he licked away the salt and powder from his lips.

"You should see yourself right now, Dunbar. You don't look like much of a conquering hero," Poole said, wincing. "And the sad part about it is that you can't tell a soul."

"I'll console myself with that fact as I'm sitting in a quaint café in Paris, drinking a nice g ass of wine. But I will think fondly of you when I'm there. It will be our own little secret discovery, John. What do you think?" Dunbar asked as his breathing got heavier.

"I think I'm getting bored. I also think you're a spineless weasel. So why don't you pick up that gun and get it over with so I don't have to listen to your tripe any longer."

Dunbar glared at Poole and fumbled around for the pistol while still on his knees. He turned his head slightly and located the gun to his right. "John, we were having a nice, civil conversation until you went and started calling me names. Now you've hurt my feel—" Dunbar stopped talking suddenly, his lips feeling numb.

"You've..." He tried to continue, but for some reason, his lips wouldn't cooperate. He thought it was probably the effects of heat exhaustion, so he tried to get up from his knees to get to the open air. But he couldn't move.

Poole saw the look of panic in Dunbar's eyes as he fell to his side. His breathing became labored almost immediately, and he could only grunt as he struggled to move his limbs. Dunbar tried to blink his eyes, but they, too, were frozen open.

Poole stood up carefully and inched over to the foot of the pit. Dunbar stared at him the entire way, but did nothing to stop him. It was clear that he was incapable of movement, and Poole was free to climb out of the pit and kick the gun away. Careful not to breathe in or touch the powder in any way, Poole nudged the stone within a foot of Dunbar's face, directly in his line of sight.

"It appears that your friend, Captain Morgan, left a final surprise for you, Dunbar. You would have known about it if you had read all of his letters," Poole said. He walked to the other side of the pit so Dunbar could see him. "I have no idea what it is, but it appears to be something quite effective. I'd call for help, but unfortunately, one of your men took my phone. I guess we're just going to have to sit here and see if you get better."

Dunbar's breaths became quick and shallow as the paralysis appeared to take hold of his lungs. His eyes were wide with fear.

"You were saying something about drinking a nice glass of wine in Paris when I rudely started calling you names. You're right, that was uncalled for and completely uncivilized of me. To make it up to you, I've decided to go to Paris and have a drink in your honor."

Poole waited a few more minutes as the life drained from Dunbar. As Poole sat on the other side of the pit, Dunbar took his last breath. His eyes were wide open. The last thing he saw was the heart-shaped ruby that took his life.

FORTY FOUR

Poole staggered out of the building trying to put pressure on the wound in his shoulder. He slumped against the stone wall and tried to breathe, but the humidity and ninety-degree heat made it difficult. It took him a few seconds to get his bearings, and then he slowly walked over to the tree and removed the gags from Mari and Ryker.

"John! Oh, my God, are you all right?" Mari yelled, struggling with the ropes.

"What happened to Dunbar, mate?" Ryker chimed in.

Poole didn't respond but did his best to untie the ropes. After he'd freed Mari, he sat down on the ground and tried to gather himself. Strangely, his lips were slightly numb, and he began to worry. Mari untied Ryker, and they both knelt down to check Poole's wounds.

"It's a through and through, John," Ryker said. "If it hit a main artery, you'd already be dead. We just need to stem the bleeding, and you'll be all right."

Mari grabbed him around the neck and held him tightly. "I thought you were gone, John. I'm so happy to see you!" she said as tears flowed down her cheeks.

"Where's Dunbar?" Ryker interjected.

"Inside. Dead," Poole responded. "Poison, I think. He stopped breathing."

"What happened in there, John?" Mari asked, still holding his neck.

"We found Madonna's Heart. It was in some sort of powder that flew up when Dunbar broke its casing. My lips are numb," Poole said absently.

Ryker's ears picked up. "Your lips are numb? When did this start?"

"A couple of minutes ago, I guess."

"Anything else? How's your breathing, mate?"

"Fine. I'm just tired right now. It's more my shoulder that's hurting than anything else."

"OK. As long as you're feeling pain, that's a good thing. But we better get the hell out of here in case you got some of that poison in your system."

"I'm good with that," Poole said with a grimace.

They all stood and gathered their belongings. Mari and Ryker dragged the tall henchman back over to the copperwood tree and secured him there, just in case. Ryker disappeared into the stone building to check on Dunbar.

"Dead as a doornail," he reported. "The damned fool looks like he's wearing a Halloween mask gone bad."

"We should grab that gun and the ruby," Poole said. "We just can't touch any of that powder."

"Here," Mari replied as she emptied her backpack. "Kick them in with your shoe. Hold your breath though, and try not to disturb the dust."

Ryker grabbed the backpack and disappeared into the building. A few seconds later, he emerged, zipping up the backpack as he did. "OK, I got everything. Let's go check on that other bloke I tied up and then get our behinds off this bluff."

They found the shorter man still tied to the tamarind tree where Ryker had left him. He was conscious and struggling mightily to get free. Ryker calmly walked over to the man, raised the butt of his rifle, and whacked him across the bridge of his nose. The blow stunned the shorter man, and he stopped struggling.

"He has our cell phones, Ryker," Mari said.

"Stealing phones are we, mate?" Ryker asked the stunned man. "There're laws against that sort of thing around here."

Ryker dug through the man's pockets and took all of the cell phones. He then glared into the man's eyes. "There're also laws against killing a man's friend, you asshole!" he cried as he brought the butt of his rifle across the man's temple. The short man slumped forward into unconsciousness.

Poole walked over and gently grabbed the rifle. "I think he got your message, Ryker," he said, steadying himself. "Now, unless you've got other plans, I wouldn't mind taking a stroll down the trail and finding a nice cold Red Stripe to pour down my throat."

Mari called ahead and Robert, Marthy, and Father Michael were waiting for them at the trailhead. Robert had brought water bottles for each of them, and they drank the contents eagerly. Father Michael looked at Poole's wound and declared that he would have to go to the hospital right away.

"You've lost a lot of blood, John. I'm going to call for a medic to come," he said.

"Fine, just let me take a shower and grab a beer first. After that, I'll go anywhere you want."

"Stubborn like your father, I see," Father Michael scolded. "Then you've got exactly twenty minutes because I'm making the call now."

Ryker went into the church with Robert, Marthy, and Father Michael, while Poole and Mari went into the cottage. Poole immediately went into the bathroom and started the shower. Mari came in with two open Red Stripes from the kitchen. "Here, drink this so you quit whining," Mari said, handing him a bottle.

"Quite an adventure today, Mari," Poole replied, raising his beer to hers.

"I'll give you one thing, John. You sure know how to show a girl a good time."

Poole smiled and started to bend down to give her a kiss but stopped short. Mari looked up at him with questioning eyes. "It occurred to me that I better get checked out first," Poole said. "I don't want to go poisoning you."

"Do you use that line often?"

"Only for the girls I really like."

"In that case, I'll take a rain check on that kiss. Now take a shower before the medics get here, will you?" Mari said, closing the bathroom door behind her.

Poole stood in the shower for ten minutes, letting the dust and grime roll off his body. The wound had clotted, but he was careful not to touch the area for fear of reopening it. He emerged from the shower, dried off, and put on the shorts Mari had left on the sink. Not two minutes later, there was a knock on the cottage door and the medics entered.

They dressed Poole's wound but insisted that he go to the hospital for the doctors to examine the extent of the damage and to suture the wound properly. Poole finished his Red Stripe, and he and Mari walked out of the cottage toward the ambulance.

Ryker was standing with Father Michael. "How are you doing, mate?"

"I'll live. But they want to give me a little limo ride to Kingston to get checked out."

"While you're taking it easy, the good Father and I are going to take this backpack down to the police to get a chemical analysis on that powder. And for the time being, that ruby is going to be held as evidence until the rightful owner is determined. Then I get to go back up there to show them the building and where those other two fellows are."

"I'm going with him," Father Michael chimed in. "It's church property, after all."

"Is there anything I can do?" Robert asked.

Poole clapped him on the shoulder. "Maybe you can drive your cousin down to the hospital for me. She's had a long day," Poole said.

"Consider it done, Mr. John." He looked over at Mari. "Marthy's car is here. Do you want to take that to Kingston or the RAV4?"

Poole looked over at the bright-red Porsche 911 and then caught Mari's eye. "We could have switched the SUV for that?"

"She won it playing slots at one of the resort casinos," Mari said. "Robert's going to have to pry that baby out of her cold, dead hands."

Poole laughed, even though the movement sent a stabbing pain through his shoulder. "Stick with the RAV4. We've had enough bloodshed for one day."

Poole was taken to the Kingston Public Hospital, where his gunshot wound was cleaned and sutured. He was ordered to stay overnight for observation, not only for the wound but also for his incidental contact with the powder. Mari stayed with him, even though he insisted that she go home to get some rest. The painkillers did their work, and he was able to sleep through the night with little discomfort.

"Good morning, sleepyhead," Mari said as Poole looked over at her smiling face.

"Hey, there. Good morning to you, too." Poole smiled back as he tried to sit up.

"You're not supposed to push it, John. The doctor will be here in a second and will let us know if you can check out of here."

Just then, the door opened and the stoic face of Dr. Martine stared at Poole. "Well, Mr. Poole, we meet again," she said in her version of humor.

"Dr. Martine, to what do I owe the pleasure?"

"Luck of the draw this morning, Mr. Poole. If I had my druthers, I would be having breakfast with my husband right now," she said as she scanned his chart.

"What do think, Doctor, am I going to live?"

"For several years, unless you get shot again or poison yourself good next time."

"What kind of poison was it?"

"Believe it or not, the lab analysis came back saying that it was the same toxin found in puffer fish."

"Puffer fish?"

"Yes, and that's not something to trifle with. Puffer fish are one of the most toxic vertebrates known to man. Their skin and organs carry a poison that's over a thousand times more deadly than cyanide," she said. "We see one or two cases here each year."

"So that's what the numbness was on my lips?"

"That's where it starts. In fact, puffer fish is considered a delicacy in Japan. People eat the meat with just enough contact with the toxin to create that numbness. Too much could lead to paralysis and a complete shutdown of the system. It is said that victims are completely aware of what is happening to them but are unable to stop the process."

"The substance I was exposed to must have been over three hundred years old. How can it be possible that it still had the potency you're talking about?" Poole asked.

"That's a good question, Mr. Poole. And I'm afraid I don't have a good answer, since this is the first instance of a powdered version of puffer fish toxin I've seen. However, I suppose that in a properly enclosed environment, the potency of the toxin might even increase over time. All in all, I would say that you are a very lucky man."

"Lucky enough to get out of here soon?"

"Lucky enough. I'm writing up your release paperwork. As soon as that's complete, an attendant will come to help you to your vehicle. However, no driving for the next couple of days. That wound needs a chance to heal."

"Thank you, Doctor, for this—and for my father."

Dr. Martine looked up from her notes, pulled down her glasses, and smiled. "Do me a favor, Mr. Poole. Let's not make a habit of this," she said. Then she turned and walked out the door.

Mari started folding up the blankets that she'd brought for her night's stay and filled a small duffel with other personal items. "I'm going to go down to the cafeteria to get some coffee for us. Do you want anything else?"

"I'm good. Just hurry back. I feel safer when you're around."

Mari shook her head and smiled at Poole as she left the room. A minute later, there was a soft knock on the door, and Father Michael entered.

"You're too late for last rites, Father," Poole said. "The doctor just told me I'm going to live."

"Then my prayers have been answered, John," Father Michael replied as he sat down in the chair next to the bed.

"The doctor just told me that the poison in my system was a toxin commonly found in puffer fish. Since Dunbar inhaled the powder and had it stuck all over him, he was a goner before he even knew it."

"That confirms what the police lab said too. It looks like your Captain Morgan got the last laugh. But that's not why I'm here, John. Your father asked me to keep something safe for you," he said, holding up a sealed manila envelope.

"Why are you giving it to me now?"

"He made me promise to give it to you only when the search for that Madonna's Heart was over. If you had ended up leaving the island before that, I was to destroy it all."

"Do you know what's inside?" Poole asked.

"The only thing he said was that it held some answers for you. He asked that you read the contents alone, but he said that you were free to share them after that if you felt it was appropriate to do so."

"It seems my father is still full of surprises."

"I suppose you're right." Father Michael nodded. "But you shouldn't be surprised that he loved you and wanted the best for you. I hope you understand that now."

"I do, Father It's just that I didn't tell him that when I had the chance."

"Yes you did, John. The fact that you came down here was evidence enough. I'm convinced that he died with contentment in his heart. Perhaps you'll find the same thing someday, either in that envelope or along your life's journey. When that day comes, I hope you'll let me know."

"I will, Father. Thank you."

"I have to go now, John. There's a meeting at Holy Trinity to determine how to deal with that Madonna's Heart, as well as Morgan's burial site. It looks like I will be in charge of the matter for the church."

"They couldn't have chosen a better man. God be with you, Father."

"And with you, my son," Father Michael said as he left the room.

Mari came back with their coffees, followed closely by a hospital attendant with a wheelchair. "It looks like they're going to kick you out of here, John," Mari said.

"The sooner, the better. I wouldn't mind going back to the *Rebecca* and doing absolutely nothing the entire day."

"I can arrange that, Mr. Poole. Doing nothing is one of my specialties," Mari teased. "What's in the envelope?"

"You just missed Father Michael. He dropped this off before a meeting at Holy Trinity. I guess it's some stuff from my father. I'm supposed to read it later."

"You go right ahead. I'm done with mysteries for a while."

"Mari, you took the words right out of my mouth."

FORTY FIVE

August 1688

I t was the morning of the twenty-fifth when Dunn received the news. The great Sir Henry Morgan, pirate, privateer, governor of Jamaica, and leader of the Jamaican Counsel, had died. He had spent the last month of his life at the plantation house, drinking heavily and remembering the days he spent there with Teresa. He rode to the family chapel daily to visit her grave, always leaving a bunch of jasmine flowers for her.

After Teresa's death, Morgan tried to spend time with Angelica. But his visits to the plantation became more sporadic as the rum and his dropsy took their toll. Over the final months, Morgan's visits were hard on her. She asked Dunn to be present on those occasions, and he could see that Angelica had grown distant. She was the image of her mother, now a young woman of sixteen. She didn't recognize the man she called her father; he had turned into a common drunk. Conversely, the sight of Angelica saddened Morgan, reminding him of his loss, which drove him to the rum bottle even more.

Dunn remembered his promise to Morgan, and his preparations were nearly complete. He had built two caskets of the same mahogany with which he built Senora Castillo's seven years earlier. He prepared both as instructed, and ordered the plantation house to be vacated while he completed his task.

He pulled the cart up to the veranda and dragged one casket into the living room. He then carried Morgan from the bed where he died and placed him in the casket with his bedding and pillows. Morgan had told him not to do anything fancy, just to place him in the box and be done with it. Once he had positioned the body,

Dunn placed several bunches of jasmine flowers in with him and nailed the casket lid tight.

Morgan had gained a great deal of weight, and Dunn strained to put the casket on the cart. The other casket was already sealed tight. Without delay, Dunn steered the horses down the path toward the family chapel. The tools he would need were already there, ready to be used.

A half hour later, he pulled up to the small stone structure. Before he started the work, he pulled out the letter that Morgan had instructed him to read. He hesitated for a moment, wondering what last words Morgan had for him. Sadness fell over him as he looked out over the bluff toward Cabarita Island.

He climbed down off the cart and walked through the grassy field toward the ocean. The morning breeze was coming from the north, and it made the page flutter as he pulled it from the envelope. He slowly read the letter and looked toward the horizon when he was done. Then he read the letter again, shaking his head and marveling at how odd the hand of fate could be.

Dunn put the letter in his coat pocket and walked back to the cart. He untied the prying tools, shovel, and broom for cleanup. He'd already known that he had a long morning ahead of him, but now there was much more work to be done.

By the end of the day, he had accomplished his task and completed the favor that his captain had asked of him. Henry Morgan was now buried next to the mother of his child and the love of his life. As promised, he would take the other casket, filled with bags of sand, to Port Royal in the morning. There would be a grand celebration of the life and exploits of Morgan, the pirate. Most would remember him as a leader of men, a wealthy plantation owner, and a ruthless privateer. Some would remember him as a drunken sot who drowned his greatest loss in bottles of rum.

Dunn would remember Morgan as a father, and as the man who taught him to be a man. As the man who spared his life for the love of a woman. As the man who, in return for a few simple favors, had made him wealthy beyond his wildest dreams.

FORTY SIX

Poole sat on the aft deck of the *Rebecca* as Mari fixed some lunch in the galley. It had been over two weeks since Dunbar shot him, and his wound was healing nicely. The doctor said that he could take off the sling he had been forced to wear, and he felt like a free man again.

He had arranged with his office to extend his stay while he recovered. At first, he and Mari spent much of their time dealing with reporters and the authorities in the wake of the Madonna's Heart discovery, but now they were just hanging out on the *Rebecca* and, for the first time since he'd been in Jamaica, he was truly relaxed.

A week ago, he had celebrated his fortieth birthday at the café, and he couldn't think of a better place to do it. Robert and Father Michael opened up their wine cellars for the event, and Robert served a succulent wild boar. Mari was as protective as a mother bear, especially when Abby showed up without her boyfriend, Tommy. Even Ryker Wilson attended, and he earned the loudest round of applause when he gave Poole a bulletproof vest as a birthday gift.

Now it was Mari's birthday, and they were anchored just off Cabarita Island for the afternoon. She brought out a couple of sandwiches and two Red Stripes and sat next to him on the deck. They both propped their feet up on the gunnel and watched the world go by.

"Thank you, Mari," Poole said. "I should have been the one making you lunch. It's your birthday, after all."

"Don't worry about it, John. I've decided that you can milk that gunshot wound for another couple of weeks before the whip starts coming out. Your company is all I need for today," she said.

They touched their bottles and drank the cold beer as they looked up at the bluff above Port Maria, where they could just make out the bulldozing equipment carving a road up the hill. "It's amazing that they're starting construction up there already," he said. "The church didn't waste any time once its claim for the ruby was confirmed."

"Father Michael is beside himself, he's so happy. He's going to have a wonderful church when they get done," Mari said.

Poole laughed. "And the biggest wine cellar on the island!"

"What do you think the church will do with the Madonna's Heart?"

"My guess is they'll keep it at Holy Trinity for a while. But it's so valuable that I'm sure the Vatican will get involved somehow."

"Is it worth as much as Dunbar said?"

"I read it could be worth more. Possibly the most valuable stone in the world."

Mari whistled. "And to think that bad boy was in my backpack."

"Along with enough lethal poison to kill an elephant. I'm just glad we all got out of that mess alive."

"But you could have been one wealthy man, John."

Poole looked over at Mari and smiled. "I *am* wealthy, with you in my life," he said, and meant it. "Besides, between the *Rebecca*, that small insurance policy, and the cash in my father's bank account, I'll be just fine for a while."

"What about the gold coins and jewels in the safe deposit boxes?"

"I should be getting back the valuation on those any time now. I'm hoping it comes in low so the local tax man doesn't take too big of a bite out of my vast inheritance," Poole said, laughing.

"Then what—when the estate is all wrapped up? Back to Seattle?"

"I'm still sorting that through, to be honest. I have a law practice, a home, and friends up there. But there are many things here that would make it hard to leave," he said looking into her eyes.

Mari turned away and grabbed their plates. "Well, you'll figure it out soon enough. Maybe the answer is in there," she said, pointing to the unopened manila envelope that Father Michael gave to him in the hospital.

Poole looked down at the envelope that was propped up against the leg of his deck chair. For some reason, he kept putting off opening it. He wasn't sure if it was because he wasn't prepared for what was inside or because it would be the last communication he would ever have from his father.

"Listen, I'm going to clean up and maybe take a nap. You do your thing out here and come and get me when you're ready to go back to the marina."

Poole stood up and walked over to Mari. He gave her a small kiss on the cheek. "Thank you," he whispered in her ear. "For everything."

Mari disappeared inside the main cabin, and Poole returned to his deck chair. He emptied his Red Stripe and set it down on the deck next to the manila envelope. He hesitated for a moment, then picked up the envelope and opened it.

There were four separate sets of documents and envelopes, each clipped together. Each had a small yellow note with a handwritten number under the clip. It was clear that he was to read the packets sequentially. Poole looked out over the harbor of Port Maria and felt the ocean breeze against his back. He took a deep breath and started reading.

The first section, marked with a one, was a carefully sketched genealogical tree, starting in the present day and working backward. Poole's name was at the top of the tree, above the names of his father and mother. Slowly he followed his father's line through the generations. Poole could tell that the research must have taken the better part of his father's lifetime, so he took his time reading every name. The final page started in the late 1700s and it finally worked its way down to a name that was circled in red. Dunbar was right: John Morgan Poole Sr. had discovered that he wasn't a direct descendant of Sir Henry Morgan.

The last name circled on the page was William Dunn.

"The boy who lived," Poole said to himself, shaking his head. "Looks like I might have to change my middle name." He chuckled at the thought.

He stood up to stretch his legs and grabbed another Red Stripe from the galley. Then he returned to his perch on the aft deck.

He was about to open the second section when his cell phone rang. He looked down to see the familiar number of his Seattle office, and he answered on the third ring.

"Hi, this is John."

"John Boy! This is Tom. Happy belated birthday!" Poole's law partner, Tom Patterson, said.

"Good to hear your voice, Tom. Sorry I couldn't make it up for Angie's party. Doctor's orders."

"No worries. She's postponed it until you get back, but she sure does miss her second husband. I think she thinks I'm too much of a slave driver."

"You?" Poole responded in jest. "You don't work that hard!"

"You know me too well, my friend. But hey, there's a reason why I called. I've been handling all of your files, but you received some personal mail from a law firm in San Diego that I wasn't sure I should open. It came in certified, so it could be important."

"I'm here for a couple more weeks, Tom, so you might as well open it up. Let's just hope I'm not being sued."

"OK, I'm going to put you on speaker." There was a click and Poole could hear the ruffle of papers in the background. "Holy shit!" Patterson nearly yelled.

"Tom? What is it? Read it to me!"

"OK, partner. Here it goes."

> Dear Mr. Poole,
>
> This law firm represents the estate of Charles and Donna Markham. We have been administering a trust established for your benefit since the passing of your mother, Rebecca Poole, five years ago. The terms of the trust dictate that you are to receive the remaining principal and interest of the trust upon your fortieth birthday, which occurred last week on April 15. Herewith we have enclosed a check for the remaining trust balance. We ask that you sign and return the heir receipt

enclosed, which will release the Markham estate and this firm, as trustee, from any liability for the administration of these funds. If you fail to return the heir receipt, we will consider your negotiation of the enclosed check as a complete release as herein described.

"That's it, John."

"Jesus, Tom. I didn't see that coming. I never really knew my mom's parents, and I had no idea that I would be getting anything more than a couple of bucks a month from that trust. How much is the check? Can I pay off my car loan with it?"

"I think it's safe to say you can."

"OK, quit holding out on me. How much is it?"

Patterson paused for a moment. "How does $4,000,276.12 sound?"

Poole sat there in the deck chair and didn't say a word. He was stunned.

"John, are you there?"

Poole awoke from his silence. "Are you serious, Tom?"

"Serious as a heart attack, buddy. You've got to get your ass up here to take care of this, the sooner the better."

"Thank you for the advice, counselor," Poole said sarcastically. "For now, put that letter and check in the company safe. I'll be up as soon as I can to deal with it. Jesus!"

"Jesus, is right, John. What are you going to do with all that dough?"

"I hate to say it, but with what I'm going to get from my father's estate and now that check, I may consider a lifestyle change. You're not interested in buying me out of the practice, are you?" Poole asked.

"How much are you asking?" Patterson said with a laugh.

"One dollar, today only."

"No, how much do you really want? Seriously."

"One dollar. And I'm as serious as your heart attack."

FORTY SEVEN

Robert pulled out all the stops for Mari's birthday party. He set up a long buffet with jerk chicken, barbecued pork ribs, fresh sushi, seared tuna, and a myriad of salads, side dishes, and desserts. The beer, wine, and rum flowed, and guests danced and sang the night away.

Mari was radiant in a short, flowered sundress, and Poole couldn't take his eyes off her. Abby asked him to dance, but he begged off. There was only one woman he wanted to be with that night. Her smile lit the room, and his heart raced when she looked his way, flashing her bright, perfect smile.

The party was winding down, and Mari was with a group of her friends while Poole and Robert exchanged stories. "I'm coming back up here in the morning for leftovers, Robert. This food is too good to go to waste!"

"No leftovers go to waste around here, Mr. John. You just have to take a look at my belly to figure that out!" Robert laughed.

Poole grasped Robert's large hand and held it. "Thank you, Robert. I'm honored to call you my friend."

Robert gave him a big bear hug, but he was careful not to squeeze his shoulder too hard. "Why don't you go see about that little cousin of mine?"

Poole nodded and walked over to Mari's table. "Hey, birthday girl, are you having fun?"

Mari looked up and smiled. "It's about time you came over and paid a little bit of attention to me, John Poole."

"I've been paying attention from afar," he admitted. "There're a couple of things I have to do on the *Rebecca*. When I'm done, I'll come back up."

"Don't be too ong, or else I'm going to track you down."

"Aye, Captain!" Poole said, saluting with a smile.

He walked down to the *Rebecca* and stared briefly at the name on the stern before climbing aboard. The generator was running, and the main cabin lights were aglow. The open manila envelope was lying on the dining table where he left it. He picked it up, moved over to the seating area toward the stern of the cabin, and stretched out.

Poole pulled out the first section and set it aside. There were three sections remaining. The second section, marked with a two, was another genealogical tree, but this time the name Henry Morgan sat at the top of the tree, along with Teresa Montoya Castillo. Under it was the name Angelica Morgan Castillo, and although there was no spouse listed, under Angelica was the name Teresa Morgan.

Again, Poole slowly followed the tree down, reading every name and trying to imagine the lives these people led. Finally, Poole reached the last page of the tree and followed the names until he reached the final name on the list, again circled in red. Poole sat for a minute, somewhat stunned at the revelation. It all made sense, now that he thought about it—his father's conversations with Father Michael about how life can be one great circle, and their conclusion that there must be a higher power that brings people together.

Poole took a long pull on his Red Stripe and reread the last page. He followed it down to the final name.

It was Maria Robeson.

"No wonder my father sought her out," Poole said aloud. "He must have made the connection right before he hired her as his diver. Morgan and Dunn, together again. Who would have thunk it."

Poole shook his head and considered the ramifications. He would not have been born if it wasn't for Mari's distant relative, Teresa Montoya Castillo, and her insistence that his distant relative, William Dunn, be spared. The Lord does work in mysterious ways, he thought.

Then he picked up the next section, marked number three. It was a smaller manila envelope, and the flap on the top was closed with metal prongs. He opened the envelope and pulled out an old, soiled letter encased in plastic. It was dated January 1681.

Dear William,

I am writing this letter to you in the wake of the passing of my lovely Teresa. I know that she was close to your heart as well, and I want you to know that I understand and feel your grief.

I don't know how long I will be on this earth, but I ask that when I finally die, you bury me next to her. I couldn't imagine being anywhere else, and I beg that you do this for me. If I am able, I will give you instructions before my passing, which will allow you time to plan and prepare.

You did a fine job in constructing the family chapel, which now I suppose is our family crypt. I chose that spot specifically and plotted the exact dimensions for its placement. When we bury Teresa, it will be on the right side of the chapel as you enter it, as that is the traditional place for a queen to rest. When I am buried, it will be on the left side.

My burial will be a job for you alone. This is very important and will be for your own good and safety. You will find that as you dig my grave, you will run into some obstacles. These are sacks of mementos from our excursion to Panama City. I will have no use for them when I'm gone. So in return for your lifetime of devotion to me and Teresa, and for doing this last favor for me, I give them to you. Pull them out and put my casket in their place.

You should keep the treasure in a safe place. And I ask that you use it not only for your benefit, but also to provide for Angelica when I am gone. I want you to look after her and make sure that she is safe and cared for during her lifetime. I know that you will not fail me in this regard.

Lastly, William, I want you to know that I will miss you. You have become a fine young man, and I have grown to think of you as the son I never had. I wish for you a full and happy life and hope that, with this final gift, I will help you achieve your dreams.

H. Morgan

Poole finished the letter and put it back in the manila envelope. His whistle cut through the silence. "So our good friend, young Mr. Dunn, was the recipient of the lost Morgan treasure," Poole said to himself. "I guess it's sort of fitting, in a way. That Morgan was an interesting guy—hard on the outside but with a pretty soft center."

Poole wondered what Dunn could have done with the treasure. Yet another mystery, he thought. It occurred to Poole that there were local landmarks with the name of Dunn, like Dunn's River Falls and Dunn's Point. Once again, there are no coincidences when it comes to the Morgan treasure, he thought.

He stared at the last section, another small manila envelope, marked number four. He undid the clasp and pulled out two folded sheets of paper. His name was printed in block letters on the back of the outer sheet in his father's now-familiar hand. "No time like the present, John," he said to himself as he let out a slow breath, started on the first page, and started to read.

Dear John,

I've already said my good-byes to you and hope that you have reconciled the events of the past and are able to move forward with fonder memories of me. If you are reading this letter, then my good friend, Father Michael, felt that you were ready to learn about your heritage and that of Mari. I kept the information about her connection to Morgan a secret for her protection, more than anything else. I knew that there would be others looking for the treasure, and I didn't want her to be hurt in any way.

Although I was initially disappointed that we weren't related to Henry Morgan, I'm comforted by the fact that we can trace our heritage to William Dunn. He became quite successful in his own right and made a name for himself on the island. I suppose that was in no small part due to Morgan's "lost" treasure.

There was never any record that Dunn spent lavishly, other than to acquire some land near Ocho Rios for his own sugar plantation. Of course, there is no way of knowing for sure, but I believe that he hid the Morgan treasure as Morgan instructed him to, and it remains in that place to this day.

The gold key that you found in my safe is a small example of the Morgan treasure. I found that while digging around Morgan's grave, hoping that there would be some straggling pieces. I've tried to follow the remainder of the treasure, but the going has been a bit more difficult. That being said, I've done some research that you may find interesting. If you so choose, the key taped to the inside of this envelope will give you a start.

I wish I could have been there for you, son, and I wish I could share these new adventures with you now. I will miss you with all my heart.

Dad

Poole blinked the moisture from his eyes as he finished reading the letter. He steeled himself and pulled out the small safe deposit box key stamped S-22.

Poole stood and placed the entire packet back on the dining table. He pulled another Red Stripe from the refrigerator and leaned against the table, fingering the key as he took a sip of his beer. He was lost in thought when the main cabin door opened, and Mari walked in with a pout on her face. "John Morgan Poole! A girl can only wait so long!"

Poole smiled. "I'm sorry, Mari, I ended up reading the rest of the contents of that envelope. I guess I lost track of time."

"Well, you owe me," she said, smiling back. Her gaze drifted to the envelope. "So what was in there?"

"Some parting gifts from my father, I suppose. And a few things that I need to share with you."

Mari looked down at the key in his hand. "That's not to another safe deposit box, is it?"

"Looks like it, but I'm still trying to sort out everything. It's been a long day, and there's been a lot to process."

Mari grabbed the vodka from the refrigerator and walked closer to Poole. "It *has* been a long day, John, but it's my birthday, and I'm not done celebrating," she said with a mischievous look.

"But, I think you need—" Mari put her finger to his lips.

"No," she said as she took the key from his hand and placed it on the table. "I think you need to hold that thought until tomorrow. I have other things to discuss."

"What do you have in mind?"

Mari took Poole's hand and led him toward the stairs to her stateroom. "I think *now* is a perfect time to talk about that kiss."

THE END

ACKNOWLEDGMENTS

I would like to thank Donna Morgan Plum, who gave me the inspiration for this book when she once told me that she was a direct descendent of Henry Morgan, the pirate.

Thanks also go to my many friends and family members who suffered through draft manuscripts and gave me valuable feedback. I will forever be grateful for their support through this endeavor. In particular, I want to give special thanks to my longtime friend, Rebecca Pritchett, who forced me to finish chapters so that she would have something to read at night. Her comments and encouragement helped shape this novel.

None of this would be possible without the guidance of my lovely friend, Teri Garcia, an author in her own right, who gave me the courage to start this book and was there every step of the way. Words cannot express my gratitude.

Finally, I want to thank my sons, John and Tommy, who gave up several movie nights and waited patiently for dinner when I lost track of time at the keyboard. I love and appreciate them more than they know.

ABOUT THE AUTHOR

Michael DuBeau obtained his law degree from the University of Washington and is a practicing attorney in the greater Seattle area. He is a native of the Pacific Northwest and spent several years as a commercial fisherman in Alaska while working his way through school.

Michael currently lives in Issaquah, Washington, and is the proud father of two sons. He plays guitar, badly, and is a songwriter of little note. A member of the Pacific Northwest Writers Association, *Poole's Gold* is his first novel.